DEATH AT FAIR HAVENS

Advance Review Copy

Release date: April 26, 2022
Length: 318 pp.
Format: softcover; ebook
ISBNs: trade pbk. 978-1-948559-65-2;
Kindle (MOBI) –66-9; EPUB –68-3; PDF –67-6
List Price: print $17.95, ebook $5.99
Trim: 4.37 x 7"
Audience: mystery, cozy mystery

Wanda Duff is an unconventional New England clergywoman, addicted to chicken wings, high-octane ice cream, and saying yes to anyone in need of a prayer, even the folks her town might think don't deserve one.

When parishioner Niels Pond dies unexpectedly at the Fair Havens assisted living facility, Wanda's duty to minister to his family is beset by her suspicions about the circumstances of his abrupt passing. Wanda finds an unexpected co-detective in high school vice principal Prudence Rye, who fled town on graduation night a decade ago and returned only recently.

Rye puts her job on the line to investigate the mourning Ponds with the surprisingly edgy Wanda. As they expose difficult family truths and uncover a dangerous operation operating out of Fair Havens, Rye and Wanda discover curiosity has an unanticipated cost.

Comfortably gossipy, with a fresh take on the characters and ethos cozy mystery fans will love, Maria Mankin and Maren C. Tirabassi's Death at Fair Havens launches a series that celebrates intergenerational women's friendship and the power of inclusion, curiosity, and love.

DEATH AT FAIR HAVENS

MARIA MANKIN &
MAREN C. TIRABASSI

Published in the United States by Brain Mill Press.

Print ISBN 978-1-948559-65-2
EPUB ISBN 978-1-948559-68-3
MOBI ISBN 978-1-948559-66-9
PDF ISBN 978-1-948559-67-6

Cover design by Ampersand Book Covers.

DEATH AT FAIR HAVENS

1

"HOW MANY CREEPY SINGLE MEN CAN THERE POSSIBLY
be in a twenty-five-mile radius?"

Wanda addressed the spiked heel of the cute but cruel
shoe whose partner she had kicked to the other side of
the room. Partner. There was something she wasn't going
to find anytime soon. As her thick hair grayed and the
wrinkles, of which she was quite fond, deepened, much
of the charm seemed to be stripped from the men who
queued up to take her to dinner.

Age aside, her magnetism for unbalanced singles in
her area had increased exponentially with the addition of
one word to her dating profile—clergy. Wanda guessed
it was a major deterrent to many men who might reach
out, to whom the words "Open and Affirming" meant
little. Her church, with its oversized justice-seeking
heart and passion for combating climate change—even
if it might be one compostable roll of toilet paper at
a time—was her first love. She couldn't romantically
connect with someone who didn't get that the path she
walked took her on Jericho walks to protest deportation
and into prisons to give voice to the angry and forgotten.

"Divorced twice," of course, made her more approachable but also, it seemed, less lovable. Several particularly unpleasant dates had the audacity to compare her to a used car—most likely sound under the hood, but suspect due to past experiences.

Not this one though. John had been earnest, aged, and eager to share about being "born again." He'd shown up with photos of twenty grandchildren (or possibly twenty photos of one) and a long list of complaints about the neighbors he was supposed to love. Wanda wasn't sure which of them had left more disappointed, though she suspected him, what with her foot lodged so well up his righteous…well…

Time for comfort food.

She looked longingly at a leftover container half full of diablo wings and soggy French fries, but at nearly eleven p.m. frozen yogurt would be less likely to invite heartburn as company. Ben and Jerry's Half Baked or Cherry Garcia? Cherry Garcia, she decided. The container felt fuller.

Wanda took the pint to the bedside table to soften up. She shed her cute skirt and the black sweater that wore well for both bad dates and the office for soft flannel pajamas. *Christian Century* or the new N. K. Jemisin? The magazine followed her shoes into the corner, and only then did the Jack Russell raise a sleepy eyelid.

"Some watchdog you are, Wink."

Wink didn't lift his snout from his paws. He could smell the difference between his fifty-three-year-old Beta and a stealthy, fear-sweating burglar. He was only waiting till she finished throwing things-that-were-not-balls and was ready to climb into bed and warm it up. Only then would he deign to join her.

Wanda's cell rang. That was bad news this time of night. Sick, dying, traffic accident, house fire, kid missing. "Hello?"

"Reverend Duff?"

Nice voice. "Yes?"

"This is—"

"Luke? Luke Fairchild."

"You're good."

"I compensate for crap hearing with careful hearing. Makes folks forget my designer hearing aids. And you've got that gorgeous tenor. Unforgettable." Wanda would love Luke Fairchild to call her late at night and ask her to come over. All six feet of dark Italian good looks in a package that announced, "I work out," and that smile…

"Well, thank you. Sadly, this isn't a social call. I have a pickup at the Fair Havens memory loss unit, and I think the family could use some support. The Ponds are on your church rolls?"

Luke was the director of Fairchild Funeral Home, the most entrenched funeral service in the area. His great-grandfather, Francesco Fraticelli, had purchased the home, then reinvented himself as Francis Fairchild and expected his descendants to follow suit in accommodating themselves to fit New England styles and sensibilities of grief.

Luke was respectable by day (and by night when he was on call), but Wanda had stumbled onto his alter ego. Before she had decided online dating screened creeps better than bartenders, she'd tried the music scene for late-night company, driving far enough to avoid encountering parishioners. One night, she'd discovered Luca Fraticelli and his fabulous band. They kept each other's secrets.

"Niels Pond? I was there Sunday doing my rotation for afternoon devotions, and I remember seeing him jogging around the keyhole drive, picking flowers and tossing them in the little fountain. He was actually jogging!"

"It seems to have caught people here by surprise, too," Luke said. "His roommate, Joe, seems very upset. A nurse—I don't know him, so he must be new—was quite forcefully sedating the man so he didn't upset the family. I thought…" His voice drifted off, but Wanda could feel the criticism he was stifling for professional reasons. "I'll wait on getting Niels ready in case you want to say some words with the family over the body."

"You're a sweetie. I'm out the door." And he *was* a sweetie. Most funeral directors wouldn't donate half an hour of their interrupted sleep so a minister could stagger over and pray. Wanda valued the extra bit of care that would never appear on the bill. Heck—she valued the phone call. Even that was rare these days.

Had to love that versatile black sweater. She dragged it back over her head to go now with a gray skirt and flats. She took some care twisting her hair into a bun at the nape of her neck. No pencil stuck through it tonight.

People called her a "laughing pastor," but these nights were what mattered. *In the valley of the shadow of death…*

When she got to Fair Havens, Wanda realized that Luke's kindness and her own sleep sacrifice had been well-meant but unnecessary. They nodded at each other with the decorum that was so much a part of their jobs. Under the harsh overhead light, the normally cheerful yellow room looked gray and disheveled. Niels's roommate, Joe, indeed had been sedated and the curtain drawn around his bed. Niels was gone, too, his body there but vacant, and more still than Wanda had ever seen it. Luke was touching his shoulder. Wanda knew it was Luke's practice to make physical contact when no one else was.

The Pond family was waiting for her, clearly out of politeness and not necessity. They wanted to go home. Niels's wife, Bellona, was stiff in Wanda's hug, and it wasn't just New England reserve. Maybe she was angry. People got angry at Alzheimer's—the way it took their loved ones long before it really took them. That anger usually transferred to God. Bellona's sons, Wil and Ro, had grown since their high school youth group days, though it couldn't have been more than three years. The boys, both athletic young men, one tall and fair and the other dark and more muscular, were quiet.

Zoe Laferriere, also a parishioner, was filling out paperwork for Luke. She had brought cocoa for Ro, Wil, and their sister, Leslie. She had teddy bears on her uniform top tonight, and she sat close to Leslie with obvious familiarity, her pen scratching out information. Wanda remembered that Zoe's daughter, Nicole, and Leslie Pond were friends. Bellona and Niels's youngest, a high school junior now, was the only member of the family in tears. Zoe pulled the girl into a comfortable hug.

"Pastor, you come to say some sweet words for this dear family?" Zoe asked in a maternal voice with the soft edges of Creole from her native Haiti. Wanda thought the accent thickened at will, but she acknowledged being suspicious of Zoe because she was in full-scale conflict with Wanda's musical director, who was also the high school choral coach, over Nicole's considerable talent. Singing was not the kind of practical career that Zoe expected of her children.

Wanda also felt, unreasonably, that Zoe was trying to tell her how to do her job. She took a deep breath and let it go. It was late, and she was bad-date cranky. Zoe was doing her own job—compassionate professional caregiving that didn't evaporate at the moment of death. Then, because Wanda was staring at Zoe, she noticed the other woman's foot move and shut the bottom drawer of the dresser. In fact, all the drawers were open at least a couple inches. Why? Wanda wondered. Who would be searching?

She looked across at Joe's dresser. Drawers closed tightly by CNAs whose jobs were finished, with no second chances, if anyone fell because of a tripping obstacle. Several of those people were waiting for green cards and wanted to stay under the radar in the current political climate. In fact, might Zoe be in that situation? No, Wanda was sure her documents were in order. Zoe and her husband had put all six of their children through the local schools. Nicole was the last.

Why would Zoe be shutting, or opening and shutting, Niels's dresser? Wanda suddenly realized that the nurse was watching her, and it wasn't a warm and cuddly gaze. Wanda snapped back into her professional role.

And, of course, Wanda did have words to say, standing at the head of Luke Fairchild's gurney. She murmured the sweet old shepherd psalm. She laid her hand in blessing on Niels's cool forehead. Still in his fifties. The dementia had stolen both the wisdom of the scientist and the dignity of the man. Now he looked old, but no longer angry, agitated, or aggressive.

Maybe Bellona was grateful. Wanda wouldn't blame her.

Wanda had a sudden fugitive epiphany, realizing that the sacrifice of book, bed, and frozen delight had worked in Wink's favor. She remembered too late the pint of frozen yogurt sitting on her bedside table. By now it was in the belly of the beast. She was tired. She fiercely roped in her attention.

The family filed out, promising vaguely in Luke's direction to stop by to plan the service. Before she could evaluate the wisdom of it, Wanda stepped forward and put her arms around Leslie. Ever the prickly teen, this one, but Wanda could feel her trembling.

And then Leslie let go the tension and allowed Wanda to hold her as a sob escaped. Wanda put a gentle hand on her spiky blond hair and whispered a prayer. Bellona stepped forward to take responsibility for her youngest, and Leslie stiffened up again.

Then they were gone. Waste of time? No. Wanda wished Luke would find other ways to waste her time, but he was busy with the removal. She looked around for staff who might need a moment of comfort and came face-to-face with LNA N. C. Harris. As she'd come in, Wanda had heard him telling Zoe that he'd checked on Niels an hour ago. He was a recent transfer, and not a man Wanda cared to spend too much time getting to know. Between her career and her personal life, she'd had plenty of opportunities to witness deep-seated nastiness, and his mere presence set internal alarms off. She gave Zoe a hug and got one in return from the older woman that, in spite of herself, soaked the stress out of Wanda's shoulders.

But the muscles knotted again as she got into her car. On Sunday, after she finished the hymn-sing and greeted the little congregation she ministered to at Fair Havens after her regular service, Wanda had come out into the spring sunshine. She was parked in this very spot near the door. Niels Pond had been out front with Zoe. It struck her as odd at the time, because she couldn't recall seeing a patient outside of the fenced garden without a family member present before.

Wanda was curious about whether such behavior would raise an insurance issue, but that thought was chased from her mind when a car careened up the drive, picking up speed as it jumped the curb, missing the pair by inches. Niels went over like bowling pins but popped up again with the anger that was his dementia's worst symptom. Wanda jumped out of the car to help, but Zoe waved her back and hustled Niels inside too quickly to see the driver shoot them both the finger and roar away.

As she sat in the dark now, Wanda recalled the forest green beater but not its driver. She'd been late to another appointment, so she hadn't gone in to check on them or to ask about the walkabout policy. She realized, in retrospect, the driver must have been impaired, and she should have at least called the police. As Wanda put the car in reverse and headed home, she remembered how her second husband, Brian, often teased about her twenty-twenty hindsight. She wondered if he was right and that her gut's insistence that Niels Pond was far more likely to have been killed in a freak accident than to have died in bed of natural causes was worth a second look.

2

RYE STRAIGHTENED THE PILE OF FOLDERS ON HER desk. She tapped them into a neat stack, then put them aside and leveled her gaze at the young man sitting across from her. He had a lip ring, and his hair was cut into a short mohawk. She couldn't help noticing how nervous he looked. She glanced down at the disciplinary note he had delivered.

"This is the third time this month you've been caught smoking behind the tech wing when you were supposed to be in gym, Jason," she said. "You know I have to suspend you?"

The teen nodded, eyes fixed on the window behind her. "Whatever."

"Whatever?"

"Yeah. It's fine."

She sighed. "Can I ask you a question?" Rye took his shrug as assent. "You're graduating next year?"

He grunted.

"You want to work at Denny's forever?"

"What's wrong with Denny's?"

"Nothing," she said. "Your boss has only nice things to say about you." He didn't respond, but she noticed the blush that spread across his cheeks. "You get decent grades. You could get out of here. You could do anything."

"Not anything."

"You're right." She cocked her head. "You don't really have the build to be a gymnast."

"I can't pay for college."

"There is such a thing as a need-based scholarship, but putting that aside, I wasn't saying you have to go to school." She shook her head. "I just think you should take these next few days to think about what you want. Maybe try channeling a fraction of the energy you spend on short-order eggs and hunting down dime bags into figuring out what might make you happy ten years from now."

"Can I go?" He was twisting his backpack strap between his fingers, and Rye found herself wishing she could step outside her role as vice principal for a minute to shake some sense into his head.

"You may. But Jason?"

He turned at the door. "Yeah?"

"Think about it. This town? It's not…It doesn't have to be the end of the road for you." She took a deep breath and left it at that. He was his own particular ball of misery and defiance, and he would only get it when and if he decided he was interested. Jason half nodded in her general direction before slouching out of the room.

The door hadn't even swung shut when Principal Mendoza marched in. Rye swallowed a groan. Mendoza was about as good a boss as she'd ever had, but in the last year she'd learned he never stopped by without an unpleasant task to unload. He certainly could handle the school board with aplomb, but when it came to sticky student matters, he preferred to supervise at arm's length.

"Am I interrupting?" Gerard glanced around her office. "I see you have a full house out there today." He jabbed a hand in the direction of her waiting room. Rye knew she had at least six kids left to see before the end of school, half of them cases Anna Beth Mavis, Stoneridge High School's guidance counselor, would have handled were she not out on maternity leave.

"Very busy. Meting out punishment to the wicked will not wait."

Mendoza cleared his throat. "I hope you're not referring to the consequences of misbehavior as 'punishment'?"

She hid a smile. "Not to their faces, no."

"Well, I have a priority case for you."

Rye sighed. "Not another Adderall crackdown?"

"No, no." Mendoza smoothed his mustache with one large thumb. "Leslie Pond." He paused to see if she recognized the name. She didn't. With a thousand-plus students to keep track of, she was only aware of the ones who made regular visits to her office. "Well, anyway," Mendoza pushed ahead. "Her father passed away two nights ago, and she went MIA the morning after he died."

"What do you mean? Are the police involved?"

"She took her cell phone and backpack and disappeared." He shrugged. "She and her mother are not close, as I understand it, and I think her family assumed she needed space to process her father's death."

"No one went looking for her?" Rye's own mother had left when she was eight. She understood maternal alienation all too well.

"I don't know the details," Mendoza said. "But Leslie's here now. She showed up for Spanish today as though nothing had happened."

"So one night away? Did you call her mother?"

"Sophie did." The school administrator had the patience of a saint. She handled all Mendoza's problems that Rye didn't get saddled with. "She apparently can't get away, so Leslie's brothers are coming."

Rye stared up at the big man. "You want me to babysit her?"

"We can't have her disappearing again, not from campus."

"Why can't she stay in class?" Rye asked. "She did come in herself, after all."

Mendoza stared at her. "The girl's father just died. She shouldn't be in class. She should be at home. With people who care about her."

Rye bit down on a comment about the kinds of people who care and yet don't bother to get the police involved to find a missing teenager or have the time to come in and pick her up when she returns. "The brothers? They're over eighteen?"

"Of course." Mendoza looked offended, as though he didn't bobble this kind of detail all the time. "Lovely boys. Wil and Ro Pond. Graduated a few years ago."

"Twins?"

"What? No. Ro's adopted. He's a few months older than Wil. I think the Ponds got pregnant with Wil while they were in the process of adopting."

That was the thing about small towns, Rye thought as Mendoza excused himself to usher in Leslie. Everybody was always head deep in everybody else's business. When she'd moved to Texas, she'd been blissfully anonymous. She'd spent a decade experimenting with roller derby and home brewing. It had been exhilarating to pick up a new hobby and then drop it when she was done. No one questioned her commitment or remarked on how she'd stopped coming to meetings.

Rye had grown up in the fishbowl that was small-town New England, and it had been a relief to escape. When she'd returned to take care of her father, she'd pulled this town on again like an ill-fitting coat. A long-term substitute teaching job had been a few months' commitment that had snowballed into the offer of a two-year contract as vice principal at her old high school.

She still wasn't quite sure how she'd let her dad convince her it was a good idea to stay. Maybe Rye had missed him more than she wanted to admit. Maybe there was something appealing about showing off how well she'd turned out to the people who hadn't expected much from the rebellious girl who'd fled on graduation night. Maybe it was the fact that jobs like this, out of the classroom and in administration, didn't fall into a person's lap every day.

The door opened and shut, and a gangly girl folded herself into the chair across from Rye. Leslie Pond was all limbs and sharp angles, and her blond hair had been chopped short and dyed white-blond at the tips. It was May, already muggy and hot, but she wore striped leggings and a black long-sleeved T-shirt. Rye's mind went to needle marks or self-harm but then dismissed the thought. She would already know this girl if either one were the case. Leslie hugged her bag tightly to her chest. It was clear to Rye that this was a kid who preferred to fly under the radar.

"Am I in trouble?" she asked after a minute.

Rye realized she'd been staring and straightened up. What was she supposed to do with this girl exactly?

Offer counseling? "No, Leslie. You're not in trouble. Did Principal Mendoza tell you that he called your brothers, and they're coming to pick you up?"

She shook her head. "I have a car. I don't need them to come."

"Oh, okay. Well..." Rye didn't have a file for her. She never went into a meeting unprepared, and this was why. Her desk phone rang, and she lunged for it while throwing an apologetic "one minute" finger up at the girl across from her.

"This is Vice Principal Rye."

"Ms. Rye, this is Wanda Duff. I'm the pastor at Trinity Church.

"Oh. Okay?" Rye pulled a pen from the cup on her desk.

"I think we've met before. You go to that Thursday night yoga class at the Y, right?"

Rye nodded. "I do." She glanced at Leslie, who had pulled out her phone. "What can I help you with, Reverend Duff?" Leslie's eyes flashed up, then back down to the screen. Her phone was no longer holding her full attention. Rye sat up a little straighter and watched the girl while listening to the woman on the other end of the phone.

"Please call me Wanda. I was directed to Principal Mendoza by a woman in my congregation. She's involved with a family that's had an unexpected death, and she mentioned that one of the children was a student at Stoneridge and had gone missing."

"I'm handling this case for the principal," Rye said.

"And have you met with Leslie Pond? I just got a call that she's been found."

Rye twirled the pen between her fingers as she tried to decide how to proceed. She decided to take a page from Jason's book and offered a noncommittal grunt.

"I'll take that to mean that Leslie is with you right now."

Perceptive. Rye tried to bring the woman's face to mind, but she tended to keep to herself, even when she ventured out to community spots like the Y. "Yes."

"I was wondering if we could meet for…lunch, maybe? Or a cup of coffee? I have a few things that I'd like to discuss with you if you're going to be the point person for Leslie at school."

There was something about the woman's tone that made Rye agree. She took down the information for a bakery across town. She hung up as the door opened and Sophie ushered in two very different, very handsome young men who apparently belonged to the awkward duckling seated across from her. The blond one swept Leslie up into a fierce hug, while the darker one extended his hand and flashed Rye a modest model's smile.

"Thank you for keeping an eye on our Leslie," he said, his voice soft. "I hope our family drama hasn't been too much of a burden."

"That's her job, Ro," the other young man said, laughing. He looked tired, but that didn't dim his natural charm. Rye felt keenly for this ordinary-looking younger sister, although something in Leslie seemed to light up when her brothers appeared.

The room descended into sudden silence as the three of them tripped into a conversation in ASL, their signs flashing too quickly for Rye to follow. What was this all about? None of them seemed to have hearing loss. Rye had taken a few courses in college, but this was far more advanced than anything she'd ever managed. Or maybe more slang. There was a tension beneath the pleasant smiles that the young men shot Rye as they ushered their sister to the door. The dark one—Ro, she thought—said, "We really appreciate your help. We'll take Leslie home, and she'll be in school tomorrow. Okay?"

"Of course. Make sure you sign out at the desk," she called after them. Then Rye hurried to the door to watch as they did so and made their way into the hallway and down the front steps, their hands in constant motion.

Code, it felt like. Or a secret message, not meant for her.

3

THE BEST OF THE LOCAL JOINTS WAS CALLED JUST THAT, and everyone hit Locals at some point almost every week. Wanda was waiting for her takeaway, her head buried in her Kindle, but she glanced up at the right moment to see the younger woman approach. They were in yoga together, but in class, the younger woman wore her hair—unmistakably the color of rye whiskey—pulled tightly back, changing the shape of her face significantly. And Wanda was always fully occupied trying to avoid embarrassing herself by the lack of balance that came with hearing loss and two left feet.

In a pencil skirt and blue boatneck top, with her hair swinging, Rye was a different woman. Wanda realized she knew her from somewhere else. Oh, dear. Wanda bet on this remarkably young vice principal not remembering her.

"Prudence? Ms. Rye?"

Rye turned and looked curiously at Wanda, who stood and put out her hand. In a town where the vice principal was known by more people than she knew herself, Rye took the offered hand and waited.

"I'm Wanda Duff. We talked earlier today?"

"Oh, yes. The minister for the Pond family. We have an appointment at the bakery, right? After I meet with Leslie's family?"

"Exactly. You know…are you waiting for a table?" Wanda looked at the crowd and guessed there was a wait.

"I was just going to get supper at the bar."

"Well, I'm waiting for takeout, but I would love to buy you a drink and chat for just a minute."

"Sure." Rye didn't sound completely fine with this arrangement, but Wanda was professionally used to reticence.

"I'm sure you're ready to unwind when you finally get away from the high school."

They moved into the more soothing light of the bar and were lucky enough to find a couple stools together. Wanda ordered Rye a beer and got a Diet Coke for herself. Image was everything, and clergy were supposed to drink Diet Coke…or at least abstain from dark ales and fruity cocktails when discussing anything serious.

"I wanted to tell you that I am so impressed with what you've been doing at the high school. The kids in youth group really like you. And vice principal, as disciplinarian, is not exactly a likely-to-be-liked position."

Rye smiled. "Well, I'm also pinch-hitting for the guidance counselor on maternity leave, so they do get a chance to see me in a slightly better light. But thanks."

"I was hoping to encourage you to make a home visit on the Pond family." Wanda raised her hand when it looked like Rye was going to comment. "No, I don't have any real fears about terrible things going on, but I feel like your touching base will open up an outlet for Leslie to share her grief when she's ready."

"That's not exactly in my job description."

"Visiting students who've had a loss? No, I suppose not. But surely a follow-up to cutting school would be acceptable."

"Maybe. I can't say I'll report back to you or anything."

"Of course not. No, I just want someone else to see the family dynamic—maybe show Leslie that folks care about her. That's all." Wanda drained her Coke. Sure, she had her own reasons for getting a second set of eyes in there, but Rye would do better entering Bellona Pond's territory as an innocent. And Wanda knew damn well that some of what she was feeling was here-and-now suspicion, and some of it was the never-again ghost of remembering Marie French.

"I do have a parishioner, Lara Alesci, who is a friend of the family. She's mentioned that Niels Pond's illness has taken a toll on the kids, and I'm sure his death is devastating."

Rye paused before she replied, studying Wanda's face. "You seem so familiar. Do I know you from somewhere besides yoga?"

Wanda didn't manage to completely hide the *oh, shit* from crossing her face, but she didn't let it fly out of her mouth, so that counted as restraint. "Well, Pru—"

The younger woman twitched. "It's just 'Rye.'"

"Rye, then, and please call me 'Wanda.'"

"Sure."

"We have met before. When I first came to town, I used to date your father's old partner, Ryan Phennen."

"Oh?" Clearly she was searching, but she didn't yet remember.

"All those New Year's Eve parties—must have been six or seven of them. Ryan and I were on again, off again, but somehow we were always lonely enough at the holidays to hook up…I mean get together."

Wanda could see wheels turning. Rye must be trying to connect the sober pastor in front of her with the short blond woman dressed in glitter and spiky heels—the one who could dance, drink, and play X-rated charades with the best of them. And use the expression *hook up*.

Rye got it and groaned. "I confided a lot in you, didn't I? Some mess of a relationship every year."

"All completely forgotten."

"There's not enough liquor on the planet to erase some of those stories."

"Desmond Tutu has famously said, 'The God in me greets the God in you.' And I'll say, the blackmailer in me recognizes the blackmailer in you. We may as well holster our weapons."

Those had been some fun conversations—often wrapped up in coats out on the deck under bright stars. Neither one wanted to remember too many details of their confidences, much more open because they were sure that they would only see each other annually.

Thankfully, the waitress arrived with Wanda's food just then, boxed and wrapped, and they could press pause on the stroll down hazy memory lane.

"The bakery. Cancelled, then?"

Wanda decided to go with her instinct. "I'd like to keep the date. I have more I'd like to discuss after your visit to the Pond family."

"I'm going to get it over with in the morning, so that should work out fine."

"It'll be nice to have a conversation with you and actually have a shot at remembering it." She winked and relinquished her stool to a kid with bright pink braids.

He waved his pony at her, and she complimented its sparkly mane before heading out the door.

She glanced back and saw Rye helping the child build a paddock out of forks and looking more relaxed than Wanda had seen the younger woman at yoga, or with a drink in her hand.

RYE STOOD ON THE STOOP AND GAZED UP AT THE house in front of her. She'd grown up nearby. Her father's home was smaller, although the same era, same style. A white clapboard two-story Victorian farmhouse with green shutters and a gravel drive. The porch stretched three-quarters of the way around the house and was cluttered with old chairs and small stacks of ceramic gardening pots. It was a lovely building and clearly well lived in. Rye wondered if this was the place where Ro, Wil, and Leslie had grown up. Judging from the swing set she could see around back, it probably was.

She steeled herself. This was not her specialty. She hadn't done any family visits since she'd arrived back in town, but after a parent's sudden death and an adolescent disappearance, Mendoza, the school board, and Wanda all seemed to think it was necessary. Why it fell to her…well, maternity leave didn't last forever, Anna Beth!

As she approached the door, Rye heard voices raised inside. She knocked, and the conversation stopped abruptly. When the door opened, Ro Pond, his face flushed, stood before her.

"Yes?" he asked.

"Hi." Rye held out her hand. "We met the other day? At Leslie's school? I'm Vice Principal Rye."

It was obvious that he didn't care who she was. And he had been the polite one.

"Yes. Right." He edged past her onto the porch. "My mother's inside. I'm sorry I can't stay. I have an appointment."

Wil pushed past Rye, following his brother out and down the steps. "But why do you have to go see her now? Mom needs you here."

"I'll be back in a few hours."

"We're planning a funeral. Just because you have a new family now—"

"Wil!" Ro cut his brother off sharply. "I don't want to have this fight again. I'll be back later." He turned his back on the taller man and slammed the gate open. He hopped into his car and roared off, the sound of acceleration bringing a woman to the door.

"Mrs. Pond?" Rye asked hopefully.

The woman looked at her with a vague smile. "No." She looked past Rye to Wil, who stood staring after Ro.

"I'm sorry to bother you, Ms.…?"

"Alesci. Lara, though, please."

"Lara Alesci, of course. Wanda mentioned you."

"Reverend Duff sent you?"

"Not exactly." Rye shook her head. "I'm Prudence Rye. Vice principal at Leslie's school. Principal Mendoza, on the recommendation of…er…Reverend Duff suggested that I come by and speak with Mrs. Pond personally about Leslie."

"Oh, of course, of course," Lara said, extending an arm gracefully to allow Rye to step into the house. "I'll just go and find Bellona. Have a seat anywhere." She gestured to the living room to her left and disappeared up the stairs.

Rye picked her way past bookcases and a mishmash of antique furniture, none of it from the same era, though each piece was lovely. She settled gingerly on the edge of a chair by a piano, which seemed to serve more as a repository for photographs than music. She studied the frames on display. Quite a few were of the entire family from years ago. Three children, two light, one dark, and their statuesque parents in front of European cathedral facades, on university campuses, at soccer games. The more recent shots were mostly of the children. Wil and Ro at their high school graduation. Leslie and another girl around the same age in swimsuits at the lake. The picture closest to Rye was the most intriguing, though. It must have been taken in Niels Pond's Fair Havens room. Somewhere institutional. Lara Alesci and Bellona Pond sat together beside him. All three were laughing, and Rye noticed that Bellona held hands with each, her fingers casually intertwined with those of her husband and her best friend.

"Can I help you?"

Rye stood up in surprise and turned to greet the woman in the doorway. Bellona Pond was an imposing woman, though she was only few inches taller than Rye. Her black pants were crisply pressed, her blouse tucked in tidily. There was not a hair out of place. Rye was used to being the most authoritative person in the room, yet this woman gave her pause. She held out her hand anyway and was met with a firm handshake. "I phoned earlier. I'm Leslie's vice principal."

"I know who you are. That was not my question."

"Of course." Rye was out of her element. What had Wanda wanted her to ask about? Her mind was a blank.

"I appreciate your coming, Ms. Rye, but I'm tremendously busy just now."

"I realize that. Principal Mendoza and I wanted to share our condolences for your unexpected loss…"

"Unexpected? He had Alzheimer's for five years. I don't know if you have any frame of reference for such a thing, but my husband was a brilliant, innovative scholar. He was renowned in his field. The loss of his faculties was not just a tragedy, it was a crime." Her face crumpled for just a moment. Rye reached out to pat her hand, but Bellona pulled back sharply. "My husband was…He deserved so much better. So much more time."

"I've heard only the best things about him," Rye replied. "And I really didn't mean to intrude during this terrible time. I just wanted to be sure I touched base with you about Leslie—"

"What about her?"

"We're concerned about her recent disappearance, especially given the difficulty of your circumstances right now. We wanted you to know that we're happy to provide any support your family might need over the next few months." Rye was proud of herself for resisting the urge to raise her voice to this woman. Bellona Pond was obviously in a lot of pain, but it seemed impossible that she wouldn't be more concerned about her teenage daughter's erratic behavior. Did she even know where Leslie had gone?

"I have no idea what you think you could do."

"Well, the school offers grief counseling—"

"I can afford to send my daughter to therapy, should that be what she needs."

"What are you talking about?" Leslie Pond poked her head around the door. Rye wondered just how long she'd been standing there. "I don't need therapy. I'm fine."

"Is that why you caused us so much trouble? Running away like that? Is that what you call 'fine'?" The anger was real but cold. It frightened Rye, and she was far from a seventeen-year-old girl.

"Don't yell at her." Wil slammed the screen door as he stomped back into the room. His face was flushed, and Rye wondered whether he'd been crying or listening all this time, or both.

"Don't raise your voice to me."

"I'm not!" He smacked his hand against a side table and lowered his voice to a stage whisper, every word clearly enunciated and as cold as ice, as cold as Bellona's had been. "I am not raising my voice. I'm asking for a little compassion for my baby sister. We can't all just pick up and move on like you have."

The mother and son were mirror images of each other, frozen in conflict. Rye wished to be anywhere else—detention? A root canal? Dinner with her father's new girlfriend? Honestly, even that would be an improvement. Leslie finally broke the standoff. She hurried to her brother's side and leaned her head against his arm.

"Wil, it's fine," she murmured. She pulled her head back and made an effort at playful. "And who are you calling 'baby'?"

He wrapped his arms around her tightly and glared over her head at his mother. "Well, Ms. Rye, you heard it here first. We're all just *fine*." He slung his arm around Leslie's shoulder and led her out of the room and up the front stairs as Lara descended toward them.

For a moment, Rye tried to imagine what it had been like for the last few years in this house. Three very different children trying to lead normal lives while their father slowly wasted away across town. Was this a mother who was trying her best to hold it together on her own and was falling apart under the strain or someone who was relieved to get her life back?

"Is everything all right, Belle?" Lara asked softly, giving her a gentle squeeze.

"It's…fine," Bellona murmured with a sigh. "Aside from the fact that my children hate me—"

"They don't hate you," Lara said. "They're hurting. You're hurting."

"The most important thing right now is that you're here," Rye found herself saying unexpectedly.

"What?" Bellona looked up at her as though she'd forgotten Rye was in the room and the reminder left an unpleasant taste in her mouth.

Rye flushed. She shouldn't have intruded on this private moment, but since she had, she couldn't very well stop now. "The most important thing you can do for your children right now is to let them know that you're here. They just lost their father. They're old enough to know they could lose you too. So just be…around." She shrugged. "Sometimes, that really is enough. It's what they'll remember."

"Very wise words," Lara said with an appreciative smile. "It can be hard to have the long view."

"I know this is going to be tough," Rye said. "That's why I'm serving as your liaison with the school. I know Wanda—Reverend Duff, rather—is your connection with the church, but we want to offer you our support. It's important to me, especially, that Leslie feels like school is a safe place for her."

"Well," Bellona sniffed, then rubbed her nose with a handkerchief, "I suppose I understand that."

Rye could see that was as close to a "thank you" as she was going to get. "I'll be checking in with you over the next few weeks and a couple times over the summer, and we'll see how it goes." She held her hand out to shake once again and made her escape.

5

WANDA COULD HEAR THE LYRICS TO "HAKUNA MATATA" as she came down the hall. It was Tony Stereo at full volume, and, yes, he was as good as Nathan Lane playing the meerkat Timon. She stuck her head around the corner and cut him off at the Elton John/Tim Rice pass, just in case he was going to do the whole warthog dialogue. "No worries, huh? Maybe you don't have enough work to do?"

The choir director was perched on the admin's desk, and he swiveled with a broad smile. "Good morning to you too, Queen of Mean—or is it Bishop? Guess somebody didn't have a good date night."

"No date night at all, Stereo. Not since last Friday night's Religious Right Rip Van Winkle. I've had more fun at an organ concert."

Wanda was notorious for her preference for piano and intense dislike of the "other" keyboard instrument, but Tony's leer made "organ concert" just off-color enough that Lisa Vaughan, admin extraordinaire, broke into giggles at the pastor's expense. Wanda, ever a football fan, made the classic time-Out sign and rolled her eyes at them.

Tony Stari Tomeo was choir director, instrumentalist, and all things musical at the church—not to mention Wanda's best friend. His mother was from Iceland, and he took more than his middle name from Scandinavia; he had the tall blond thing going on, and his beard came out in red stubble when he didn't shave. Tony gave Wanda a crooked grin and nodded at Lisa with a suggestive look that failed to convince either woman Tony would ever be on deck in their ballpark.

In an exaggerated whisper, he mouthed, "Lisa thought we should sing 'Circle of Life' at the Pond funeral."

"Say what?"

"'Circle of Life,' and that only because I convinced her 'Let It Go' from *Frozen* was not appropriate."

Lisa was a good sport. "I thought 'Circle of Life' would be familiar to the kids."

"The youngest of those kids is a high school junior."

"What can I say? Lily programmed my phone with Disney radio, and that's all we've been listening to on the drive to preschool for the last three months."

Wanda leaned against Lisa's desk. "I'm not seeing this as anything but a very traditional service, and you"— she pointed at Lisa—"need to get out to see an adult movie. I'll tell you what. You go on a date, and I will babysit Lily. It will be a lot more fun than any of the Methuselahs I've been seeing."

Lisa curled a loop of her hair around her finger. "I think I'm happier in my jammies with my sweet Lily after hearing about some of the loser guys the two of you find online. Do you remember the one with the 'dropkick Jesus through the goal posts of life' tattoo?

Or how about Mr. 'I'm-not-really-gay-but-you're-so-*musically*-sexy'?"

"Enough!" Wanda and Tony came in on the same cue.

Lily was three, and Lisa was raising her alone, her deadbeat ex gone long before Lily was even a baby bump of responsibility in the designer-for-discount wardrobe of the petite brunette. Lisa was in no rush to replace him and was oblivious to her own good looks, completely unaware of the uptick in dads dropping off at the church's day care.

Lisa had falsely believed when she was younger that she wasn't a people person and trained to be a vet tech, but job openings had been scarce. She was happy in the church office, fortunately; after all, it involved a lot of petting, comforting, and restraining parishioners, and Lily was on the premises in the day care center. Lisa might be a bit IT challenged, but her friendly phone calls and kind face were a vast improvement over the Tyranno-secretary rex who had preceded her.

"So, I'll bite," Wanda said. "Why 'Let It Go'?"

Tony groaned, and Lisa stuck out her tongue. Tony spent too much time with teens and Lisa with preschoolers.

Lisa explained. "The Ponds were all tied up, you know. Alzheimer's was making Bellona and the three kids tense. They wanted—I mean, they didn't, but they did—want Niels to go, to die and be free. They didn't want to see him so changed. And they said it—that they hoped he would 'go' soon—right in front of him, like he wouldn't understand them sometimes."

Wanda knew people did that because they assumed everything would be forgotten, so it didn't matter. "Lisa, you sound like you knew them."

"Of course I did. Lily and I are at Fair Havens every Saturday and at all the holiday parties seeing Grandma Dottie. The Ponds came on the weekends, too. I mostly let Lily free-range over there, and she brings a smile to all the faces. I kept her away from Niels, though. He was too young and strong, and he could switch from smiling to angry in an instant."

"I didn't know you went there so much. I guess I'm usually only in on weekdays or for Sunday afternoon services."

"We give Dottie a roll around the grounds or bring in Dunkin' Donuts if the weather's bad. You know Joe Jackson? He's a real sweetie. I was sorry they put him in the room with Niels. But, you know, it certainly didn't seem like Niels was going to die anytime soon."

"That's what I thought. I was really surprised, too."

"Too mean to die, the staff said. I know you aren't supposed to say that because personalities change…" She blushed. "But Niels's family blocked his offers a lot. You know, when people won't let the person with dementia choose the conversation and insist on interrupting at every error, which, of course, derails the person speaking. Eventually they give up. The Pond family didn't realize they were being judgmental, but they always went for reality orientation, and that's a recipe for anger. And, honestly, I think he may have been a bit of an angry guy anyway."

The teasing look had dropped off Tony's face. He was obviously no longer thinking about Niels's personality. "Really?"

Wanda looked at her best friend. "Things tough with Nana Tomeo?"

"Yeah. She's desperate to stay at home, but Mom doesn't think it's safe. Now when she leaves Nana's house, Mom takes the knobs off the stove so Nana can't start cooking something and forget it. And everyone is always correcting her—you know, telling her that people are dead over and over again and that she's just forgotten. They make a big production of I-told-you-that-five-times-now."

"I took a great workshop on communicating with people with dementia because Lily and I are all Dottie has for family. Healing Moments, it was called, if you want to check it out. They really stressed going with the flow and not worrying as much about something you say being true as affirming people's happiness. Let me tell you, the Ponds did not get that. It was like they thought they could drag him back to knowing things. And when that didn't work, they treated him like he was already dead and gone." She waved her hand. "I'm sorry. I shouldn't be criticizing them. Not now especially. It was just sad to see."

Tony smiled. "Well, I'll try to take your advice. Sounds like a little creative storytelling might go a long way."

"As long as you're not telling them to me!" Wanda interrupted.

"I never lie to you, boss-lady," he said. "And in case anyone is interested, someone *was* on a date last night. Smooth Latitudes—the menu is to die for. Anyway, I was at the top of my 'creative' best. I told him I was a mutual funds investor and wore a red tie to prove it."

"With the lavender shirt?" Wanda asked.

"Ouch," Tony said. "You are killing me."

Wanda sat on the edge of the long copier table. It took her just an infinitesimal bounce to get there. Tony and Lisa had offered an unexpected wealth of eldercare wisdom, but it was the validation of her own instinct that Niels Pond was nowhere near death that really nagged at her, as well as the suggestion that he was not as perfect as people often became after death, but a man who could have ended up on someone's bad side. "So you saw him, Niels, I mean, every week, Lisa? And you didn't think he was getting frailer?"

"He was the same. But his family seemed like they were getting tired. I've only seen Leslie there for the last month or so."

"Tony, you haven't been to Fair Havens, have you?"

"Nana Tomeo is going out of her house feetfirst. We will not be mentioning a 'place like that.' You'd think it was the ice floe where they send you to die."

"PC, Tony, PC." Lisa wagged a finger.

His conducting hand came up with another finger just slightly higher.

"Children," Wanda said.

"No. I haven't been there, but Nicole—you know, from the choir? Her mother, the mighty dragoness Zoe Laferriere, works there. And wishes Nicole would too, instead of doing frivolous things like singing in high school musicals after school."

"Nicole is the young woman with the beautiful soprano, right?"

"The very one. The very unnecessary-talent-that-will-only-cause-vanity-and-not-lead-to-worthwhile-work most gifted singer I've ever tried to encourage toward a professional career."

Lisa looked up. "Nicole is Leslie's best friend."

Wanda suddenly caught a glimpse of the time. "Tony, please, please, please can I borrow your car? Mine's in the shop. I was going to walk to my meeting, but I am definitely going to be late."

Since she had his keys in her hand already, he didn't have an opportunity to object.

6

WANDA THOUGHT THE BEEMER'S STEERING WHEEL was stylish, but (a) the car made her feel like she should still be in training wheels, and (b) it didn't help her pray. For her, "power train" described what went around her tree at Christmas, and "laps" were Wink's desired resting places. So much for her Formula One, Two, or Three driving.

She preferred to use her 2011 Fiesta's steering wheel as her prayer mandala. It was round. She faced it and touched it a lot. Wanda was not a model of traditional spiritual practices, and she was more likely to want her days off to include movies, malls, or museums than meditation, but when she was in the car she was usually going to or from the hospital, to a family planning a funeral, or away from a chaotic wedding rehearsal. She would put her hands at two and ten and address the undeployed airbag and God with some of the deepest thoughts of her heart.

She was going into this meeting more unpre-prayered, but it still gave her a rush to emerge from the Beemer and enter Harvey's very small-town bakery.

Rye rose, hand outstretched. "We have to stop meeting like this."

"Better here than in downward dog. There's not much need for formality after an hour of staring at another person's derriere."

"You have a great down dog."

"True. Four points on the ground—I love it. I am, however, a complete failure at Vrksasana."

"Uh, Vr-what? Remind me."

Wanda puffed a mild mental expletive. Rule number seventeen of pastoral care—never make a professional educator feel that he or she was not the smartest person in the room. "Tree pose. I cannot, simply cannot, stand on one leg."

Both relaxed in the safety that was yoga and not New Year's. Rye glanced out the window. "You have a great car. It looks exactly like a friend of mine's."

"It probably is if you mean Anthony Tomeo."

"He's wonderful. The kids love him, and all the musical groups sound amazing. And the choices are current, but somehow he keeps the royalties down."

Wanda smiled. "Tony's the choir director at my church. He's the same with older folks—he knows when to challenge them and when to channel the sixties. My car's in the shop, so I stole his. I wasn't sure how long you had before you needed to get back."

"I just do piles of paperwork on these teacher workdays, but let's get down to business. I'm sure Mendoza will have plenty for me to do when I get back from my 'break.'"

"How did you find the Pond family? *Triple-berry scone and a mocha.*" Wanda had server second sight. It was a gift in her line of work.

"Green tea and a sesame bagel toasted with butter, please." Rye paused, waiting for the server to depart. "They were…fine."

"Fine? Dad's dead. Kid ran away. Fine?"

"I'm not really sure what I can share with you…"

"Hey, I've got the same set of oh-so-carefuls in my work. I'm not asking you for critical confidential information. I'm just looking for impressions so that, between us, we can maybe help this family."

"My impressions are based on a very short visit."

"Bellona pushed you out, did she?"

Rye sighed. "Not exactly Ms. Congeniality, is she? But still, it seems…I don't know. And why or who is Lara Alesci? She seemed more important to Bellona than the visiting church friend you led me to believe."

"Niels has been sick for a long time. There's gossip that they're more than friends—though I think *they* think they're completely discreet." Wanda took a sip of her coffee. "Anyway, Lara is a doll. Bellona's, well, more of a cold fish. That's my church experience, not gossip. Wil and Ro were inseparable contentious brothers, you know, hug-and-hitters? I had them in youth group, and they were a handful. And Leslie always just tagged along. They didn't seem to mind, though. Then I heard last year that Ro found his birth mother and everyone got contentious on a seismic level. That's back to gossip though. I haven't seen it."

"And you are sharing this with me why?"

"Because if you're going to help Leslie, you need to know it. She matters to me. She was a lonely child, always on the sidelines. I'm guessing she's a lonely teen. But I don't think I have a prayer if you know what I mean. Teenagers don't really hang around churches."

"Leslie is a junior. She's not going to be hanging around school a lot longer either."

She took a deep breath. "You are a lot closer to Leslie in age than I am. She needs a young role model. Not just brothers. That bond's going to be important after this loss, but it's not going to be enough. I'm worried about her. And a year for an adolescent feels like an eternity."

"There's something more, isn't there?" Rye's focus was almost unnervingly like her father's. Like sheriff, like daughter.

"Yeah, but…"

"Tit for tat. I get it. The visit was brief. Ro was on his way out to meet someone, and Wil was not happy. Could have been the birth mother, I suppose. Wil said something about Ro having a new family."

Wanda restrained herself from asking whether Rye had seen Ro's birth mother. She'd been curious about the woman who had come into the family's life recently. She wanted the whole story from Rye first.

"Lara was nice," Rye continued, "but it felt a little strange that she acted like it was her house." Rye sat back to allow the waitress room to put down her food. "And nobody told me much of anything. Parents usually can't stop talking. Lies, half-truths that they wish were true, incidental random filler. All families want me to let *them* go. The Pond family wanted me to go away, but they didn't play the game to get me out of there. Bellona was straight-up rude and kept telling me to leave."

"Is that common with home visits?" Wanda asked. "When I see people, they're polite, but the ones who want me to go transform into monosyllabic teenagers, whatever their age."

Rye sighed. "Families are not usually unpleasant. The Ponds were, to each other, in my presence. The vice principal comes over or calls them in, and families close ranks. It doesn't matter whether they had claws out five minutes before." She looked enviously at Wanda's scone. "That's why it felt so wrong. They didn't even try to fake being cooperative. Honestly, it made me suspicious, and I hadn't been. I really hadn't thought anything of it. Now, though…"

"I know what you mean," Wanda said. "I'm not trying to be melodramatic, but this whole situation feels off to me."

"You think the family is hiding something, maybe helped him end things? That's a huge accusation."

"I know. And that's not the worst possibility." Wanda shrugged.

The silence hung. Rye looked as though her inner sheriff's daughter was warring with school boundaries. "Grief twists people up."

"I wish there were a way to know if Niels was sicker than we think, or more despairing."

"Look, Wanda, this is out of my depth, but I do feel a responsibility to Leslie. I used to be close with a guy who works at Fair Havens. I'll see if I can reach him and let you know if I get any weird vibes. Okay?"

"That's more than I could ask. Thank you."

Rye wrapped up her bagel and tossed it in her bag. "I'll call you."

Wanda watched her go, glad that Rye's plan had driven the unanswered question from her mind. Was there more? Did the man have enemies? She wondered whether Zoe had reported the jumping-the-curb incident. And that thought logically suggested a joyride before returning Tony's car. It would be sinful not to experience what zero-to-sixty might really mean.

She straightened as she heard a familiar tone. Just a dull ring that told her she had about thirty seconds before the right ear hearing aid went dead. Given that she had put batteries in both of them at the same time, the left ear would not be far behind. Of course, she had batteries in her purse. No one with her relatively youthful hearing impairment didn't carry them, well, religiously.

Wanda smiled. She was going to take that joyride. Cruise a little farmland down Route 119. She would say a prayer for a situation that seemed like it was becoming more difficult by the day. And daydream. Sometimes she thought best when she was unplugged. She would drive for half an hour without her hearing aids, look at the world around her, and listen on the inside.

Sometimes what everyone, everyone, everyone in the world thought of as a disability was her safe harbor, the place she could go to shut the world out and concentrate. She knew that she could, in fact, always pull the hearing aids off and put them in a bag, but she didn't do it very often. That was a dereliction of duty. But when the batteries went, it was just serendipitous. It was a reminder from God and the wizards who designed those damnably miniscule batteries that it was an opportunity to embrace silence.

And she did embrace silence, but it wasn't a joyride. As soon as things were completely quiet, Wanda came heart-to-steering-wheel-mandala with the truth. She needed to before she piled any more of her baggage on top of today's sad but common grief. Niels Pond had died, and just because Wanda was as sure as she could be that two years ago her former parishioner Marie Kennedy, who'd had Alzheimer's, had been "helped along" to a premature death by one or more of her children didn't mean that he had been.

Right to die. Assisted suicide. DNR or AND—Do Not Resuscitate or Allow Natural Death. How about NEA or CMH—No Easy Answer or Clergy Migraine and Heartbreak? People who thought legislation could fix everything were not currently in a situation for which dying ahead of the inevitable was a decision. Many of them were looking back, their perspective warped by relived pain.

Marie Kennedy had been terribly ill but not certain she wanted to die as soon as her family thought she should be "allowed to." Those family members had been variously motivated by love, exhaustion, personal philosophy—and one, at least, by hatred. Wanda could not prove anything. She was at the bedside soon after death because of an anonymous phone call. If the caller had not insisted on being anonymous, she might not have been as suspicious as she was.

Wanda had done nothing. The self-doubt she kept stuffing down now about Niels Pond might be nothing more than an old guilt waking up.

She pulled off the side of the road, put in a new hearing aid battery, and played the soundtrack to *Hamilton* all the way back to church.

7

RYE WAS PACKING UP HER BAG WHEN HER EMAIL chimed. She had a strict policy about not checking work email after six, but according to the clock in her office, she still had five minutes. She sighed and clicked on the icon to bring it up.

> *Dear Vice Principal Rye,*
>
> *I want to apologize for the way Bellona and the children acted when you visited earlier. It's been a very difficult time for us, and we are not at our best. I hope you'll forgive some bad behavior and stop by Fair Havens this evening. I have a few concerns I'd like to share with you. I'll be working on Niels's final paperwork if you have a chance to pop in.*
>
> *Regards, Lara Alesci*

Rye thought longingly of her plans for the evening—a five-mile run followed by a heaping plate of her father's carbonara, shared with him on the couch while he picked apart whatever his current favorite police procedural happened to be. Not exactly a wild night, but perfect for unwinding.

She resigned herself to a quick stop at Fair Havens to speak with Lara and judge for herself Wanda's suspicions. And maybe she would see Andy Soucek. There was a chance. It would beat a cold call.

Mendoza had been on her case about Leslie's erratic behavior in class, in response to which Rye had unwisely pointed out that at least the girl was showing up, a vast improvement on last week. He hadn't found that amusing. Apparently, Leslie had been picking fights with kids in just about every class, and, while her teachers were as sympathetic as they could be, it was maybe a day from escalating to Rye, with one incident close to warranting a week's suspension.

In Rye's opinion, suspension would be the worst possible thing for the girl right now, but the policies of high school were nothing if not antiexception. She needed to nip this in the bud, and if that meant postponing training, it would save her a headache in the long…well, run.

She grabbed her keys and headed out to the faculty lot. Her '02 Toyota Camry looked to be in good company. Her friends Camila and Mike were still here, albeit for different reasons. She waved at Mike, visible on the track where he was watching the girls' softball team run drills, clipboard in hand. Mike Nifterick taught PE, and although he looked like he could have been an enforcer for Captain Hook, the kids adored him, and he coached every season. His motorcycle was parked at the far end of the lot, where he could keep half an eye on it during the day. He'd become a little paranoid since a prank last year during Spirit Week had seen it doused in rainbow glitter. More summer days than not, his leg hair still sparkled purple, green and red in the right light.

Camila Santos carpooled to school with her sister, Ana, who taught AP Spanish. Brazilians by birth, they spoke Portuguese, and Ana could sub in for French, Latin, and Japanese without breaking a sweat. Camila tutored her struggling biology students after school, although by this time of night Rye usually saw the twins racing each other on the track. They ran marathons all over the country together and spent just about every school vacation in Denver visiting their family and training at altitude. There was no sign of either sister, but Ana's Mini, a distinctive shade of plum with a white racing stripe, was still parked beside Rye's Camry.

Rye got in and shoved a few empty coffee cups to the floor to make room for her oversized crossbody purse on the front seat. The car was littered with the debris of her hectic schedule. A gym bag sat on the floor in the front, while six or seven pairs of shoes were scattered in the back seat, jockeying for position with a bag of old clothes she needed to take to Goodwill and the tools she'd borrowed from a friend of her father's and forgotten to return. She put the tools on her mental list for the weekend and made the short drive over to Fair Havens in record time.

She followed signs to the memory loss unit, sneaking in without the code behind a family returning from dinner with a walker-slowed grandmother. When she got to the front desk, though, Fate was against her. Zoe Laferriere was not one of the vice principal's biggest fans. Rye mentally thumped herself for the oversight. She knew Nicole's mother worked here, had talked with her about it during a college counseling session when Nicole brought up questions about financial aid. That same session had brought the elder Laferriere's full anger down upon Rye. Apparently suggesting that her daughter apply to a few schools that might nurture her prodigious musical talent had not been appreciated. Studying the woman's striking face, well-lined and fiercely beautiful, Rye knew she was up against a formidable force.

"Fancy meeting you here!" Rye wasn't sure if she or Zoe was more surprised by this asinine opening.

"At my job?" Zoe was not impressed. Rye couldn't blame her.

She scrambled for something, anything cogent. "I'd have thought you might get a day off to be with Nicole. I know she and Leslie Pond are good friends." Rye hadn't remembered that consciously, but as soon as the words tumbled out, she knew she'd seen them around together. "It must be hard for her to know what to say to Leslie."

"Yes, well, some people are better with words than others." Zoe's first language might not be English, but she hadn't raised six children without learning how to deliver a solid burn.

Rye felt her cheeks flush. Something about this woman made her feel like she was a naughty child. She doubled down on her commitment not to make her students— even the intolerable ones—feel this way when they were sitting across from her. "It's such a shame. I know Leslie is having a tough time."

"Well, of course," Zoe said. "Her father just died. What would you think?"

"I heard it was unexpected." In for a penny. Rye plowed ahead. "Everyone has been telling me how healthy he was, how they expected him to live many more years."

"This disease, it's a funny thing," the older woman shrugged. "It takes and it takes. Never gives back, not an inch. Someone seems healthy, but the rot, it's in the brain."

"You've seen this before, then?" Rye pressed. "A seemingly healthy person dying suddenly?"

Zoe narrowed her eyes. "It happens, yes."

"Often?"

"You ask a lot of questions for someone who didn't even know the man. Who doesn't know anyone in this unit." Zoe let the implication hang in the air.

"I was actually looking for Lara Alesci."

"Zoe, can I get a hand when you're free?" A cheerful voice behind her sent a shiver of recognition down Rye's spine. It had been over a decade, but the sound still filled her with joy.

She turned and studied his face as he took her in. Andy had shaggy black hair and sleeves of tattoos that ran up both arms and disappeared under the short sleeves of his scrubs. His face was plain and covered in a stubble she was certain he didn't have in the twelfth grade. "Seuss?"

"Rye?" His eyes widened. "I knew you were back in town, but—" He seemed to be trying to gather his thoughts. He finally landed on the innocuous, "I wasn't expecting you. And it's just Andy now."

"Oh, of course." Rye shook her head. She still remembered the year he had gotten the nickname. His mother had died of an overdose around the same time her own mother had left. It had been a week or so after Halloween, and Andy had worn his Thing 1 costume every day for months afterward. In second grade, it had seemed weird and terrible and sad in a way most of the other kids couldn't understand. Rye did, though. She knew what it was like to cling to a last good memory any way you could. Andy hadn't seemed to mind the nickname then, and it had followed him until graduation. Clearly, twelve years later, he was trying to put some distance on it.

"Andy. It's good to see you." Rye had those words on the tip of her tongue for every encounter with high school friends since she'd come back to take care of her father last year. For once, she meant it.

"You, too. You're at the high school, right?"

"I'm the vice principal," she said. "Funny, considering all the things we got up to back then." It felt unreal to be having this conversation here, after all this time, surrounded by an infirm audience and the distinct smell of bedpans.

"Seems like it makes you the perfect person to bust kids on their shenanigans," Andy said.

She smiled. "Maybe so."

"So are you here to visit someone?" he asked. "It's not that I don't enjoy this blast from the past, but we're not generally a hotspot for young folks."

Rye wondered if Andy still lived with his grandmother, or if it was just that her speech patterns had long since rubbed off on him. Shenanigans? Young folk? "I am, actually. Lara Alesci said she would be here tonight. She asked me to stop by."

"You just missed her. She got a phone call and had to go. Left me with a load of half-finished paperwork, actually."

"Well, shit," Rye said, then glanced around to see if any of the residents were close enough to have overheard. She got a dirty look from another nurse, a large blond man who was shifting a tiny woman into her wheelchair. Rye ducked her head apologetically.

"Was it important?"

"I don't know. It's about one of my students. Her father was Niels Pond."

"Oh, Leslie," Andy said. The smile dropped from his face. "That poor girl. She was in here a lot. Zoe was actually one of Niels's primary caregivers in the last few months."

"I was actually just asking her if she thought he'd been getting worse recently," Rye said.

Andy shifted from one foot to another. "Zoe, Ms. Lamb needs a bath. Would you mind taking this one for me? I'll take Mr. Harrison off your hands. I know he's been pushing your buttons today."

Zoe reluctantly nodded. "I suppose so. Finish up with this, though." She waved disdainfully in Rye's direction. "We don't get paid to gab."

Andy gently pulled Rye by the elbow into the hallway, away from the large dining room. She could feel Zoe's eyes boring into her back. "I really shouldn't be discussing it, but I'll say this—he had a rapidly worsening case of early-onset Alzheimer's, but healthwise, he was fine. It's one of the reasons Zoe worked with him so much. Physically, she's as strong, or stronger, even, than I am, but she didn't raise his hackles the way male nurses did."

"So he wasn't sick or frail?" Rye thought about what Wanda had said, that his death had seemed unexpected. Odd, even.

"No. I think it made it even harder for his family to see him that way. He'd lost weight, but otherwise he looked normal, you know? Sometimes the kids forgot. They would get him talking about his work—he was a bigshot in the communication sciences and disorders field—and he would almost seem like his old self. He could be abruptly aggressive when he lost the thread. It was intense."

"But he wasn't on death's doorstep?"

Andy leaned in. He smelled like Purell and clean laundry. "I wouldn't say this, except, well, I know you're working with the family. One of the guys here, Harris, he's new. And sort of…off. I heard from Zoe that he came to us because we're so short-staffed we were willing to take on someone with a questionable record."

"What do you mean?" Rye asked. Andy took a step closer, and she fought the unexpected urge to lean in and sniff his neck. A part of her brain was consumed with how long it had been since her latest breakup. Too long. Instead, she took a discreet step back to clear her head.

"He's worked at other facilities that have had deaths like this. Unexpected, you know?"

"Really?"

Andy nodded, then straightened up suddenly. "Hey, Harris." Rye turned to see the blond RN standing behind her in the doorway of one of the private rooms. "Did Mrs. Dominic get settled down?" Andy asked.

The other man just stared at him, then at Rye. "I'm sorry," Andy said. "I haven't introduced you. Rye, this is N. C. Harris. He's a new transfer. Rye's an…old friend." Andy's voice was strained, and Rye wondered if he was afraid the larger man had overheard them.

Harris just stared at her. He managed to make her feel violated and vulnerable without saying a word. "Nice to meet you," she lied before turning back to Andy. "We should get drinks this weekend. I'd love to catch up."

"Sounds great," Andy said. "Do you still have the same number?"

She nodded. Harris hadn't said a word, but he also hadn't dropped his gaze. "I'll give you a call later." Andy leaned in and gave her a quick hug.

Rye booked it to the door. It was only when she got there that she realized she didn't have the code to be let out without the alarm going off. She was about to turn around when she realized Harris had followed her and was already keying it in. She pushed the door open and hurried out to the parking lot. Although it was barely seven, the sky had gone black with an impending storm, and she shivered as she walked to her car.

Rye could hear Harris's steps behind her, but she didn't want to run. A chase provoked some men into action. Rye was no slouch at self-defense, but even she didn't like her odds against him. He probably weighed twice what she did, and although he didn't look like a gym rat, Rye was well aware of the disadvantages of her petite frame.

She had her keys clutched between her fingers, but by the time she reached her car he was barely a step behind her. It would be impossible to get in without giving him an opening, so Rye turned to face him. He stopped, his hand deep in his pocket, clenching and unclenching around something. Her stomach jumped. She had opened her mouth to scream when he pulled a battered pack of cigarettes out of his pocket.

"Smoke?" he asked, his voice soft.

"No. Thank you."

He slid out a cigarette and took his time flicking the lighter to it, his eyes trained on her the whole time. "Are you Andy's girlfriend?"

Rye weighed her options. Some men backed off if they thought a woman was the "property" of another man. Others saw it as a challenge. She didn't know enough about this man to wager a guess which it was. She finally settled on the truth. "No."

"We should get a drink sometime," he said, echoing her words.

"My schedule's pretty packed right now."

He blew a cloud of smoke accidentally-on-purpose into her face, and she sneezed twice. It seemed to break the spell. Harris shrugged. "Maybe I'll see you around." He turned and sauntered away.

Then he stopped and started to turn back. Rye threw herself into the car and peeled out of the parking lot without her seatbelt or headlights on. She was halfway home when she saw blue lights in her rearview mirror.

"Damn it." She pulled over, grabbed her wallet, found her license and registration, and sat back to wait.

When she got home, her father was on the porch in the old rocker he'd built when she was a girl. Hardy Rye, former sheriff, devoted single father, and occasional pain in the ass had never been out of the loop when it came to this town. And he'd always found his way to that chair when she was in trouble. Tonight was apparently no exception. He pushed himself up and grabbed his cane to walk to the stairs. The skies had opened up on the drive, although it had eased off to a light drizzle by the time she'd taken the long gravel road up to her childhood home. Rye's blouse and skirt were soaked as she trudged up the path.

"This rain will be great for the garden," she said, stopping at the bottom of the stairs. The porch light backlit her father, but she could imagine the expression on his face.

"You think in a small town it isn't going to be big news that you got pulled over tonight?" His tone was neutral, but Rye was aware that came from years of interrogations and was no indication of mood.

"Ryan made me walk the line! He knew I hadn't been drinking. He was messing with me. He's a jerk." She rolled her eyes. "Plus, you know he's still bitter about that whole disaster at the county fair. Thanks for that, by the way."

"This is my fault?"

"You know he's held a grudge ever since you beat him in that stupid pie-baking contest. You couldn't just let him have the win? It's not like your self-worth is determined by competitive cooking." Well, not his entire self-worth.

Her father glared at her. It was like looking into a mirror. "He lost fair and square. If he couldn't handle the heat…"

Rye shook her head. "I guess when I'm paying my fines, I'll take comfort in the fact that you puked all night after you devoured your glorious victory. Punishment to fit the crime—isn't that what you always tell me?"

"He gave you a ticket?"

"Two, in fact," Rye said. "To be fair, I had forgotten to put on my lights."

"That's not like you."

"I know. It was stupid."

Hardy accepted that with a nod, then turned back to the front door. "Dinner's on."

"I need to get changed. Maybe take a shower."

"Well, you know where the microwave is," he said as he stumped back inside.

Rye watched the kitchen light flicker on, then the blue light of the TV in the living room before she headed to her apartment in the old barn beside the house. She was thankful her father loved to cook and that he was good at it, but there was no way she was going to sit next to those disappointed sighs for the rest of the evening.

Unless he'd made chicken parm, of course. Then all bets were off.

8

WANDA GOT STOOD UP TO HER SENIOR PROM. SHE hadn't been wildly enamored of the boy, but she also wasn't the kind of girl who'd had dates lined up, so she'd decided to enjoy the required high school experience. And her parents had encouraged her. It was the thing to do, so she'd done it. Or tried to, at any rate.

Her first whiff of trouble had been when Tom didn't ask about corsage colors or mention when he would pick her up. Nevertheless, she'd sat there on the sofa dressed up in a hand-me-down prom dress until it was perfectly clear no pumpkin was going to roll up to her door.

It would have been worse, but fortune smiled. One phone call, and Wanda was out with a college freshman at a local production of *Pippin*. She had shed that sea-green silk confection in the middle of the living room and wiggled into a tight little black skirt with a low-cut teal blouse (she knew her colors) and had a wonderful time.

Her mother, worried that she would be scarred for life, had cleaned up the dress and ignored the massive curfew violation. Wanda didn't date Sam very long, but for the rest of her life she'd credited him with the preservation of her self-confidence.

No, it hadn't scarred her. Not at all. Unscathed by teen angst, that was Wanda. Nevertheless, she had no idea why Prudence Rye wanted to spend her life overseeing people in the midst of God's one evolutionary failure—adolescence.

Of course, any fears she might have about rejection had nothing to do with Wanda's (disastrous) choice of husbands. Spouse number one, Lenny, had used her hustling hard work as a travel agent to put him through law school, then cheerfully divorced her for a tall, willowy redhead. Spouse number two, Brian, was the world's best housemate ever, ever, ever until he came out of the closet and tearfully divorced her for a tall, muscular redhead.

As a matter of principle now, Wanda avoided auburn singles and was covertly sensitive about being stood up. Tony knew this, and yet here she was with a bison burger and beer in front of her and no Tony to dish with. His last-minute cancellation to see his redheaded wonder date from last week, who had an unexpected free night, stung more than a little.

It wouldn't be so awkward if she weren't already here, having said "party of two" and ordered a Sam Adams Porch Rocker. She pulled out the latest Deborah Crombie and thought briefly of ecclesiastical revenge—like maybe asking him without warning to sing a solo of "Children Will Listen" from *Into the Woods* at the next baptism. Yes, delicious…

Her plotting had started to go seriously off the rails when Luke Fairchild slipped into the booth across from her. His hair was soaked and starting to curl, and she couldn't quite stop herself from imagining him on the cover of the romance novel she had covertly downloaded to her Kindle the other day.

"May I join you?"

Wicked anatomical responses flitted through her head, but she went with honesty. "Tony just stood me up for brew and burger, having been offered a more buff alternative, and I was just trying to decide whether to eat here or slink off licking my Friday-night-slights. I'd love the company."

"Well, I'm starved. I just had an empty run back from a cemetery in Western Massachusetts more obscure than a small asteroid in the belt between Mars and Jupiter and almost as distant. Thank goodness I can always tuck the hearse in the back of the parking lot here without Griff getting upset that I'm ruining business." He flagged down the waitress and ordered enough for two before turning his attention back to her.

Wanda laughed at the realization that some restaurant owners would see a hearse in the parking lot as anti-advertising. She pointedly took in Luke's casual attire.

"No family attended. Just me and the folks who opened and closed the grave."

They were quiet. Wanda sipped her beer and waited. The view across the table was doing a lot to soothe her wounds.

"I always say a little something anyway. I know it's not the official ritual that you do, and I don't toss in any dirt—that would be presumptuous. But saying a few words seems like the right thing to do."

"I think that's lovely. God made that body—loved that body. Your saying even a short sacred good-bye means something, especially if there aren't any family or friends left. It's not like we clergy have some magic formula!"

He looked down at the book in her hands. "So you're a mystery fan? What do you think about Ace Atkins keeping the Spencer franchise going after Robert Parker's demise?"

He had her where she lived. "I wouldn't read them at first. Then I went with the half-finished Christmas book. Then I decided I was too purist, and I caved. He's got the Boston setting down perfectly. The plots are okay, though I think they're getting better each time. He doesn't write Hawk very well, but I like the new kid—Zebulon Sixkill—and Mattie was really sweet…"

Luke laughed. "I guess I shouldn't ask if I don't want the fan breakdown."

"You haven't read them, have you?" She could feel herself blushing, and it annoyed her. She was allowed to be enthusiastic, damn it! But that adolescent response—to cling to bland, safe topics in front of a crush—somehow it was that and not the ability to eat cheese fries without bloating that had followed her into middle age.

"Nope," he admitted. "My sister's a big fan, though. Maybe I'll give them a try, too—with your endorsement, of course."

"Audiobooks. Lots of time in the car." She took a deep breath. "Speaking of mysteries—"

They paused as his food arrived. She finally dug into her burger and fries as he made room for an ahi on Caesar and a plate of fried pickles. The rare tuna looked delicious, but a brew joint was a brew joint, and Wanda felt safer playing to their strength.

They ate in comfortable silence for a few minutes. In stressful and very public jobs, it was nice just to relax.

Wanda dipped a fry in the ketchup and started again. "The Pond funeral?"

His eyebrows rose, but he didn't say anything.

She silently wished he would give her a little help here. "We…I think that it…it was surprising. His death."

Luke frowned. "What do you mean?"

"Well, he wasn't exactly a frail old man. In fact, he was strong enough that people were actually a little afraid of him. He was restive and seemed unhappy because he was still at the point where he knew he was cognitively impaired."

"So?"

"I guess I'm curious what was listed as cause of death. I'll get the clergy record, I know. I was just wondering."

"It was Alzheimer's or heart failure."

"Well, which one?"

"Which one?"

"If it was heart failure, do you think it's possible it might have been brought on artificially? Maybe pill hoarding? A suicide attempt? A mistake?"

"Why would you think that? Is there evidence? I wasn't asked to wait on an autopsy." Luke seemed irritated at the possibility. "He's been embalmed, Wanda. This was an open-and-shut case."

She held up her hands in surrender. "Okay. I hear you."

"And if it's not—" He rubbed his hand through his hair. "If it's not, this could be a big problem for me. Do you understand that? If this was a suicide, or worse…If someone fed him pills, I could be in serious trouble for destroying evidence."

"But like you said, the police didn't ask for an autopsy. You were just doing your job. The death took place in a medical facility." Wanda could see how distressed he was, so she did her best to hide her own disappointment that physical evidence from Niels Pond's blood was gone. Sure, the organs were there, but they were going into the ground or to the crematorium unless there was real evidence of malfeasance…because "fed him pills"— Luke's words—was really frightening. Marie Kennedy's ghost appeared before her, and Wanda gulped the practically full glass of beer just as exorcism.

Luke fortunately was staring down at his plate and missed her failure in temperance, but it was clear to Wanda that his thoughts were elsewhere. Probably thinking back to the body, to whether or not he should have seen some sign, though she couldn't begin to imagine what kind.

"I'm sorry I brought it up, Luke. I'm sure it's nothing. It was just nagging at me, and I thought if anyone would know…"

"Sure."

"I really am sorry." She really, really was sorry.

He stood up and grabbed his coat. "Listen, I need to get going." He pulled out a twenty and dropped it on the table. "Just need to look through a few things—" Luke waved good-bye over his shoulder as he headed out the side door to his hearse.

"You and the hearse you rode in on…" It was her graveyard funny for him. And since he usually gave her a ride to the cemetery, he would reply, "Don't look a gift hearse in the mouth."

This investigation that she and Rye were doing had the potential danger of damaging good friendships and unsettling people who should be able to deal with their loss in peace. And it really was the suspicion of murder that was bothering her. Wanda's faith did not condemn death by suicide. In fact, she never used the word "commit," as if self-termination were a crime. She would happily let it go because the family pain would just be greater if they thought Niels had ended his own life. But murder was different.

Wanda reached for Luke's virtuous ginger ale and drank some. Who were the suspects? Niels's wife? Her lover? Not the children. Not possible. Staff? Intentional euthanasia by terminal sedation or dehydration was certainly a real thing, though not as newsworthy as drug diversion by medical staff with addictions. But surely the staff person pitied a frail elder and thought the person would be better off dead. Niels was anything but frail. He was almost a danger to other patients and visitors. Maybe someone was angry with him. Maybe there was someone from his past, but she had no way of investigating that.

Had someone wanted to scare him? That car's near miss had come within inches of Zoe and Niels. It had seemed like a random reckless driver at the time, but now Wanda wondered.

Wanda stared at the plates of half-eaten food across from her and sighed. She flagged down the waitress for the check. There was no way she was sitting in front of all this food. Call it adolescent image crisis, but she could not bring herself to finish this meal alone.

Wink, at least, would be happy for the leftovers.

9

RYE LOOKED UP FROM HER COMPUTER AS GERARD Mendoza knocked, then entered without waiting for an acknowledgement—a common occurrence, but not one she hoped for this late in the day. She pasted a smile on her face.

"Gerard! What can I do you for?"

He sighed and settled into the chair across from her, an uncomfortable fit, as that chair usually accommodated the bony bottoms of young wannabe delinquents, not the far more adequate backside of the school's boisterous head.

"Rye. Rye, Rye, Rye." He shook his head, one hand swiping his face in a feint of exhaustion. "You know I think your work is exemplary." She nodded, her stomach in knots. "We're lucky to have stolen you away from that fancy prep school, and I appreciate how you've taken on a lot of extra work since Anna Beth went on maternity leave. It's not easy, and you've done well."

"Thank you." She sensed a *but* coming.

"But," he said, "I got a call last night. From the sheriff's office."

"Well, that was just a misunderstanding."

"You were pulled over under suspicion of driving under the influence."

"But I wasn't. The officer acknowledged that I had no alcohol in my system."

"Yet you were driving erratically. The officer gave you a ticket and a warning."

"I know," she said. "And I apologize. I was driving a little faster than I should have been. I'd had an…unsettling encounter. You see, after I visited the Ponds—"

"Oh, yes." Mendoza's frown deepened. "I asked you to be a liaison between that poor family and the school. Now I've gotten an angry call from Bellona Pond about it."

"You did?" Rye's face heated up. She hadn't thought their meeting the other day had gone so badly as to warrant a follow-up with her boss. She'd behaved appropriately. The family, on the other hand… "I'm sorry. I had no idea she was unhappy. I planned to schedule another meeting with them on Monday to follow up on how we might better help Leslie."

"I know. And I'm going to give you one more chance with them, because, quite frankly, I don't have anyone else I can put on it right now. No guidance counselor, and as much as I would love to do it—" He paused, and Rye got the distinct impression that he would not so much love to deal with Bellona Pond again as pretend she didn't exist. "—it's really not within my purview to handle these sorts of cases."

"Of course," Rye said.

"But you're on thin ice. I was all set to extend your contract, but if you continue to have problems with this family, and if the school board decides to pursue action after your…unfortunate incident last night…" He shrugged. "My hands will be tied."

"The school board?" Rye asked. "I didn't do anything wrong."

"Well, you've said yourself that wasn't entirely true."

"I wasn't drinking. Do you know how many funerals I've had to attend of students who were victims of drunk driving accidents?" Rye felt herself getting flushed, but she couldn't stop. "Six! Six children have died since I started teaching a decade ago. I would never, ever put my life or the lives of others in danger that way. I didn't have my lights on! That's all—it was twilight, and I did not have my headlights on."

He held up his hands in a placating gesture, then slowly levered himself out of the seat. "I'm not accusing you of anything," he said. Rye didn't agree, but she kept her lips tightly shut against any unpleasant retorts she could make to the contrary. "I'm simply letting you know where you stand."

"Sure. I understand." The politics of the school system infuriated her, but she understood them just fine. As if this job weren't thankless enough.

"I want to support you here, I really do, but you've got to show me that you're taking this seriously."

"Have I given you some indication that I'm not?"

He gave her a stern look. "You're putting me in a difficult position. I'm trying to give you a second chance, but you need to show me that you want it. You need to step up."

Rye mentally tallied how many times she'd heard him use that exact expression with students. *You need to step up.* It irritated her to hear him use it on the teenagers she had gradually connected with, but to be patronized by it herself? Deep breaths. "Sure."

As soon as he left, she pulled out her phone and texted Mike and Camila. *Is it too early to start drinking?*

She finished the last of her emails and closed her computer before she got two responses, almost timed to the ringing of the final bell.

Nope.

Absolutely not. Meet at my place in thirty?

Rye texted Mike an affirmative and finished packing up her bag. If she was going to be accused of drinking, she might as well enjoy it.

By the time she reached Mike's apartment, six-pack in hand, the rain had started up again, and she had to make a mad dash up the stairs of his building. Ana's Mini was already parked out front. She banged on the door until Mike roused himself to let her in, then carefully chained it behind her. It didn't matter that he looked like he followed *Beauty and the Beast* villain Gaston's diet of a dozen eggs a day. Mike was a nut about security, and even knowing she was coming by didn't prevent him from keeping all his deadbolts in place.

"Jesus!" He stepped back as she shook herself like a retriever coming out of a pond. "Give a guy some notice, why don't ya?"

"Sorry." She held out the beer, and he accepted it in the apologetic spirit it was given. She shrugged out of her coat and boots and left them drying by the radiator. Camila had already changed into workout clothes and was using Mike's pull-up bar as she watched a soccer match on TV. Her sister was lounging on the couch, a bowl of chips and salsa nestled safely out of reach of Camila's swinging limbs.

"What took you so long?" Ana asked.

"Surprisingly long line at the liquor store. Seems like everyone in town likes overpriced craft beer now." She gestured to the kitchen, where Mike was pouring three bottles into pint glasses, with a seltzer on ice ready for Ana.

"What'd you get?" Camila asked, dropping to the floor, graceful as a gymnast. She wasn't even sweating. Rye envied her that. Camila's figure was one part genetics, one part extremely hard work, but Rye never got over how beautiful her movements were.

She shrugged. "Something from the fridge you showed me last time." If it had been up to her, she would have grabbed a case of whatever-is-on-sale, but Rye knew her friends preferred small-batch brews. She blamed her own lack of interest on an ill-advised stint with home brewing; her taste buds were still recovering from an attempt to make a cilantro ale.

Rye collapsed on the couch and pulled at her blouse until it came untucked. She wished she'd thought to leave her bag of gym clothes in her car, but she'd finally broken down and taken it in to wash or possibly toss last night, and now she had nothing dry to put on. "So I got pulled over by Officer Douchebag last night."

"Ryan?" Ana smiled. "I know. He texted me."

"How are you friends with that guy?" Rye took a beer from Mike and moved over to make room for him on the couch. He muted the game, though his eyes still tracked the action.

Camila grinned. "Have you seen Ryan's baby brother, Tyler? He works out down on Lincoln, and Ana's been getting up at five thirty a.m. for months now to do that boot camp class he runs. I've gone with her a few times. I can stay on Ryan's good side if it means my sister has a better shot." She dropped down from the bar and grabbed her phone to show Rye and Mike a picture. "He's gorgeous, right?"

"But Ryan called Mendoza! And accused me of drunk driving even though he didn't want to give me the breathalyzer! I had to twist his arm to do it so I could prove him wrong."

"Really?" Mike's eyebrows arched. "Guy's got balls, I'll give him that."

"There's nothing brave about falsely accusing someone of something they didn't do just to get back at that person's father for beating him in a stupid contest five years ago!" *And not promoting him,* Rye added silently.

"I bet he called your dad, too," Camila said.

"Of course he did."

"Well, Hardy's a reasonable guy," Mike said. He had a soft spot for her father. They reffed police-sponsored Little League games together.

"About some things, yes," Rye said. "When it comes to anything involving me and trouble in this suffocating town? He gets a little prickly."

"Hey!" Camila protested. "Some of us are pretty happy living in a place where we don't get hassled by the police about our documents all the time."

Ana looked up. "It feels like every time we travel to a race out of state these days, some officer makes a comment." Her cheeks were burning. "The police here are a cut above, trust me."

Rye felt ashamed. "Of course. You're absolutely right." She couldn't help but see this place through adolescent eyes, even all these years later, but she knew for others it was a haven. Her father had spent his career building a police force that reflected the community values he aspired to.

"And let's be fair, Rye. You stayed here. You could have left after your dad was on the mend, but you didn't," Mike pointed out.

"This is not exactly the venting I was looking for." Her friends were right, but it didn't ease the anxious ache in her chest.

"Sorry," Mike said. "But it's true. You didn't have to take the job. Mendoza didn't force you. And it seems like now you're just angry that something might force you to leave again."

"It's almost like you don't want to leave this 'suffocating' town," Camila added, smiling wickedly. "Almost like it's growing on you…"

"Like a fungus—specifically that pink kind you're not even supposed to breathe in or it'll kill you." Rye took a swig of her IPA and made a face. So bitter. "I still think it's overkill to get into so much trouble for going a few miles over the speed limit without my headlights on."

"I bet Mendoza threatened you with the school board, didn't he?" Mike asked.

"How'd you know?"

"It's his go-to move. He hates handling the messy stuff."

Camila laughed. "God forbid he make the decision to fire you. He's like the head of the mob. Never gets his hands dirty."

Rye stared at the television. The New England Revolution missed a goal. "He can't fire me for this."

Ana patted her arm. "Sure. You'd have to really blow it. Everything else is going well, right? I mean, he loved you a week ago."

Rye took another sip of her beer. Way too hoppy for her taste. "Yeah. A week ago, everything was just great."

10

RYE ROLLED OVER AND STARED UP AT THE CEILING A foot and a half above her head. After she'd moved back to take care of her dad, she'd taken to wandering out to the barn behind the house to get a little space while he was resting. Her father had cleaned it out years ago, and all the junk they used to store there had been given to Goodwill or sent to the town dump. It was a clean, sunny building that still smelled faintly of the horse they'd kept when she was small.

It wasn't perfect, of course. It had needed insulation and new windows and doors to make it livable—not to mention the seemingly endless permit process—and after she'd finished with that, she'd also put down new flooring over the concrete. When the renovations were complete, Rye had moved in. She never meant for it to be permanent. She just needed her own space while she was here. And, of course, he could rent it out when she moved on or list it on Airbnb for some extra cash.

After living halfway across the country for nearly a decade, she had found the readjustment of her relationship to her father more difficult than she'd expected. It was hard to admit because they'd been so close. After her mother left, Hardy took over the hair braiding and discussions about leg shaving and menstruation with as much aplomb as any man could. He had even managed to keep his shotgun threats to a humor-minimum when she'd dipped her toes into the dating pool.

The real test, in Rye's mind, had been in college, when she'd brought home her first serious girlfriend for Thanksgiving. The relationship hadn't lasted, but her father's courteous acceptance of her desire to expand her romantic perspective to include both men and women had been the bedrock of her transition to adulthood. Hardy Rye would not understand the word "binary" if it bit him, but his daughter avoided a lot of drama because he simply looked at her happiness rather than the package it came in.

In all the years she'd been studying and teaching, they had talked on the phone every week. Coming home to help him had been a difficult decision, but to her it was the only choice. Her father was the absolute in her life, her rock, and if he needed her, she would be there. Unfortunately, none of that translated into an easy transition to life under one roof. Over the years, they had both established their own routines, and rather than complement each other, they seemed to butt heads more often than not. When Rye finally moved into the barn, it was with a sigh of relief on both sides.

Rye was especially glad for a little privacy on mornings like this when all she wanted was to nurse her hangover in peace. Camila had discovered an old bottle of rum in Mike's cupboard, and she and Rye had made some very poor choices with it before Rye had managed to call an Uber home. At the time, it had seemed like the perfect remedy to all her problems. At this moment, not so much.

She rolled over and looked down into her living room and kitchen. Normally, Rye loved sleeping in her loft. The skylight above allowed her to wake naturally with the sun. Right now, though, she felt like tipping off and falling directly onto the couch below—anything to avoid the maneuvering necessary to get downstairs and into the bathroom. Eight feet, however, was a long way to fall, and if she wanted to make it to breakfast with her father—a longstanding Saturday morning tradition— she needed to suck it up and slide down to the ground floor like a civilized adult. A civilized adult whose bed was at the top of a ladder.

"Rise and shine," Hardy said, his knock and entrance overlapping. He glanced around before looking up and spotting Rye still buried in her nest. "Are you kidding? It's ten o'clock!"

"Mmm."

"Did you forget that Sharon was coming over this morning?" Sharon was Hardy's new girlfriend, and although Rye had nothing against her, she also didn't appreciate the intrusion of Sharon into this family tradition, especially since having guests on Saturday morning never failed to put her father on edge— regardless of whether they were Rye's or his own.

"…maybe."

"I didn't see your car out front." The statement was mild, but years of policing had perfected his ability to turn any topic into a subtle interrogation.

"I left it at Mike's last night."

"One ticket this week was enough?"

"Well, that, and I decided that being accused of driving under the influence was a lot less serious than actually doing it." Her head really hurt, and if her father was planning to stand between her and a hot shower with an extra-large cup of coffee, she wasn't going to swap niceties.

"It's not a joke. I saw Gerard Mendoza at the Stop and Shop last night, and he said the school board could vote to have you removed from your position for that kind of infraction."

"I'm glad my boss is so comfortable sharing private professional matters with you," she said, climbing down the ladder. "It speaks highly of his understanding of words like 'discretion,' 'confidentiality,' and 'unjust termination.'"

"He's concerned. And it sounds like he has good reason to be."

"No, he really doesn't." She hopped down the final rung and turned to face her father. "And even if he did, it's none of your business. I'm handling it. Everything is under control."

"Which is why you drank so much last night that you couldn't drive home. Sure sounds like you have everything under control to me."

"You know what?" Rye's phone interrupted her, which was probably for the best. She swallowed the righteous indignation that was building into a conversation she didn't need to have this morning and answered it.

"Hey, Mike." She turned away from her father.

"Hey, Peanut." His voice sounded far too chipper. Rye's head ached with admiration at his ability to handle a devastating combination of whisky and beer without appearing to miss a beat. It sounded like he was jogging on his treadmill, in fact. Ugh. Her friends were just the worst.

"I'm going to pick my car up this afternoon, if that's what you're calling about."

"Nope." She listened to the whirr of the belt. Yup. He was definitely running. No hitch in his breath to betray it either, damn him. "I was thinking about your problem with the Ponds, actually."

"Oh, yeah?"

"Yeah. I pulled up my old team photos to jog my memory. They played soccer together, but they weren't standout players. Always good sports, though."

"Okay. So?"

"Grouchy much? Sounds like somebody's a little hungover this morning."

"And I have breakfast with my dad," she said, her tone even.

He caught her drift. "Ah, the esteemed Hardy Rye is in the building, I presume."

"Yup."

"Okay, I'll cut to the chase then."

"I'd appreciate it," Rye said, glancing back at her father. He was checking his watch with a significant look.

"The long and short of it is that this time of year, all the teams have alumni reunion parties."

"That's a thing?"

"A very popular thing, in fact," Mike said. "And you're in luck, because the Pond boys will be at a party tomorrow night at Local's."

"For sure?"

"For sure. I talked to a couple of the seniors who are organizing it, and they got a 'yes' from both." Mike paused. "I think it's your best bet to try to smooth things over, maybe even get a few answers out of them."

"Won't it look a little odd for me to show up to a dinner for soccer players?"

"Not if I'm with you. I may have scored us an invite."

"How is it possible for you to be this well-liked?"

"It's a gift, Rye. I'm blessed with both good looks and a personality that defies description."

"Well, you got that last part right, at least," she said. "Pick me up at seven?"

"Will do."

She hung up and turned around to grab her clothes before heading into the bathroom. "See? Under control."

Rye slammed the door before her father could say anything more.

11

WANDA SLAM-DUNKED THE LINT REMOVER INTO THE trash can. It belonged there. She had pieces of the tacky tear-off paper all over her fingers, and the evidence that Wink had curled up and made a nest in her good gray plan-the-funeral-with-the-family skirt while she was in the shower did not seem appreciably lessened. If the lint remover couldn't handle dog fur, what was the use? How much actual lint was there in the atmosphere?

It was strike two. Last week she had been wearing her calf-length black skirt when she went to see one of the church's oldest members, a woman with three orange tabbies. The following day, even after vigorous "rolling," she still sported enough orange fur on the black wool to advertise Halloween.

Wanda's professional palette was limited. The length varied with the purpose—long skirt for nursing home and hospital, shorter for committee meetings, slacks for large denominational events—but it was all black, gray, navy, and charcoal.

She stomped over to the basket and retrieved the roller. After trying one more time, she decided that terrier white on gray would just have to be acceptable. She gathered Bible, notepad, and prayer book and headed out, hoping to arrive the perfectly courteous five minutes late.

Today, however, there was absolutely no traffic, no school buses or sanitation workers to follow. She arrived obnoxiously on time, but with all the large front-facing windows, Wanda didn't dare sit in her car for a few discreet extra minutes.

She need not have worried. When Ro met her and showed her into the living room, it was obvious that the family was ready and waiting. There was no sign anywhere that death had made a disturbance. Everything was clean and cool and elegant. There probably wasn't even lint.

Wanda seemed to remember Rye saying the house was a shambles. Someone had retrenched, and seriously. Was it Bellona? Certainly not a post-runaway teenager and her back-at-home college-aged brothers. Wanda wondered if she would have a chance to ask whether Wil and Ro were in school or working. Suddenly she was glad she had dragged Rye in—two sets of eyes could spot some of the changes in this situation. She remembered all those New Year's Eve stories, probably more than Rye did. What Wanda remembered best was that even when she was madly in lust, Rye could read people, and she could do it well. Like a messy house after a messy death.

Bellona rose, rearranging what looked like a tableau. She and Wil had been on the sofa, obviously just waiting. Wanda could not remember the woman ever waiting quietly for anything. She always spoke with her hands moving, the perfectly cut shoulder-length hair swinging.

Ro perched on the edge of a wing chair, his sister cross-legged and leaning against him, and Lara Alesci was deep in a Boston rocker. Wanda paused for a moment to consider how "out" the pharmacist really was. Lara's warm smile raised the temperature in the room to at least thirty-four degrees, though, and Wanda offered a quick prayer of thanks for her presence here today.

She took Bellona's cool hand. Wanda wanted to hug her, remembering having done so casually on guest story reader days in the elementary school library. This, though, was a shadow of the extroverted, if somewhat brittle, woman Wanda had been expecting to see, and it threw her off balance. When confused, keep it simple. Direct.

"How are you doing?" She glanced around the room.

"We're fine. Thank you for coming over."

The children looked at their mother simultaneously, as if someone had pulled their marionette strings. It was the same expression of concern and denial on all three faces.

Ro finally spoke up, his gaze studiously averted from his mother's. "We're not really fine."

"No," Wanda said gently. "I wouldn't expect you to be."

He seemed to gain courage from that. "Everything happened so fast, and now we're just waiting to set a date for the memorial. Dad's family is deciding how many can travel. Uncle Pieter will certainly come, but we don't know who else can make the trip."

The brother, Wanda thought. The deaf-from-birth baby brother who had set Niels on his vocational path would be coming. That seemed like a very good thing. She guessed their parents were no longer alive.

Bellona interrupted her thoughts before Wanda had a chance to ask a question. "Why don't we talk about the service?" She glanced at her children.

Wil was looking at his phone. Bellona frowned at him, but Wanda felt relieved rather than annoyed. It was such a natural thing to do at his age, and so far, this family had been anything but natural.

Lara eased out of the rocker. "Want to sit, Wanda? I'm going to make a pot of coffee."

Wanda perched on the piano bench. "I'm good. Thanks, Lara."

She took a deep breath, looked around. "I would love to help you shape a memorial service for Niels. There are several things we can decide. Let me lay them all out for you, and then you can pick where you'd like to start.

"First, are there readings you might want, from the Bible or poetry? Second, music. Do you want songs or hymns by the congregation, or a soloist? Third, are there people who will plan to speak, or do you prefer a broader invitation for anyone to speak extemporaneously? Fourth, are there any unique customs from Niels's Dutch heritage that you wish to include?" Wanda took a deep breath. "Most importantly, I would love to know more about Niels—memories, stories, anything that you would like to have included in my remarks."

There was a pause. Wanda willed herself open, friendly, available—a gray-with-white-dog-hair shoulder to cry on. She let it stay quiet. Not her go-to skill, but she had learned. And suddenly it was like a thin layer of ice that had been coating each one of them cracked, and they became people rather than statues. Leslie slouched, Ro smiled, Wil suddenly seemed to have gum in his mouth.

Bellona launched.

"Simple. We want it simple. Straightforward. *De een zijn dood is de ander zijn brood.* 'One man's death is another man's money' is the Dutch expression."

Here was the Bellona Pond who Wanda remembered. Authoritative, direct, crossing and uncrossing her legs as if something had been released, a spring depressed too long. But her Dutch proverb was passive-aggressive. It must mean people made money out of death, which was not true for the church, pastor, or musicians.

"We will print out his professional honors," Bellona said. "Traditional scriptures—you can pick what you want. Hymns—'For the Beauty of the Earth,' 'Amazing Grace.' Leslie, can Nicole sing 'Precious Lord'? Leslie…Leslie? Are you listening? Can you write a poem? The boys will both speak, of course."

Her voiced spiked, and Wanda jumped. Well, those were a lot of answers. She hoped she could remember them long enough to write them down in the car. What else? "Are you inviting contributions to a particular charity? Alzheimer's Research, maybe?"

"Everything's going to NAD."

Lara came back in with a tray and cups, the coffeepot, cream and sugar, and Mexican wedding cookies. Wanda was fond of them but didn't think that her skirt could handle the powdered sugar. Lara set the tray on the coffee table and went over to put a hand on Bellona's shoulder.

Lara glanced over at Wanda. "The National Association for the Deaf. The NAD is the nation's premier civil rights organization of, by, and for deaf and hard of hearing individuals in the United States. One hundred and thirty-five years old. Very important to Niels."

Bellona looked up and met Lara's eyes, and Wanda caught a flash of…what? It looked like a fierce tenderness. Lara squeezed Bellona's shoulder once and bent over to pour coffee. Wanda took a cup gratefully and doctored it while watching Lara hand out cups to each of the kids, making sugar, Splenda, and cream decisions with as deft a touch as…

…a mother.

Wanda knew about the National Association for the Deaf. She took a surreptitious look around the room. Right. She was the only one wearing hearing aids. She'd gotten her first one when she was thirty-three.

Wanda absentmindedly took a big sip and almost spit. Clergy got diabetes enough from job stress without drinking joe-flavored sugarcane. She filled her cup to the rim with more milk in the hope of diluting it.

When her gaze traveled around the circle and found Wil, he was staring at her. She didn't look away. His coffee was black.

He had a suggestion. "I want to read 'Do not stand at my grave and weep. I am not there. I do not sleep.' Do you know it?"

Of course she did. "'I am a thousand winds that blow. I am the diamond glint on snow. I am the sunlight on ripened grain. I am the gentle autumn rain…'"

"Yeah, that one. I like that one."

Bellona broke in, "Wil, you'll want to say something about Dad, not just read a poem."

"Ro can do it. He's so much better at that sort of thing than I am."

"That's not true," Ro said quietly. "You just think it will be easier for me." There was a rawness there that made Wanda feel the sharp edges of heartsick in the room.

"You're *both* going to do it. That's final. You can find a few words to say about your father. He loved you very much."

"No!" The quiver in Wil's voice belied his casual posture. "You know I love him. But he…wanted things perfect, and I am not a speaker. I just can't…in front of…you know, people. Let Ro. Please, Mom…Lara, tell her."

"What about me?" Leslie's eyes were bright with unshed tears.

"You'll write a poem. Like the one you did for his birthday a few years ago," Bellona said.

"I don't want to. That was dumb. It rhymed, and he hated it. I want to be the interpreter."

Bellona started. "No, Leslie. I'm sorry, but no."

"But why? I'm better than all of you. And he would like it. I know he would." Leslie's voice cracked, and the tears she was clearly trying to hold back came bursting out in a strangled sob.

Lara reached a hand out, and Leslie reached up to grab it tightly, just for a moment. Bellona's own face went slack, as though she'd been holding a mask in place by sheer force of will, and her energy and had shifted just enough to let it slip.

"Leslie, you're being ridiculous—" she began, but her daughter interrupted.

"Why?" Leslie asked. "Reverend Duff asked what we wanted, and this is what I want. Dad didn't just leave you, you know."

Bellona looked as though she'd been slapped. Lara held Leslie's hands until suddenly she pulled away.

"Why did he have to leave us? Tell me that. We weren't ready. We are…were…why did he do it to us?"

She started crying even harder, so hard that she got the hiccups.

Wil wrapped a long arm around her and nodded to Ro, who shoved Leslie over and sat down on her other side. The brothers made a tight sandwich of their sister, and slowly her sobs subsided. Lara went and stood behind Bellona and massaged her neck and shoulders.

Wanda needed to remind them that she was still there before this got any worse. Or, not really worse, just more real. She didn't think this family wanted anyone else to see them real right now. "We've done a lot today. I think we could all use a break, and you can think about the rest of the details. Call or email me anytime, and we can figure the rest out. I'll check with Nicole about the song."

Bellona had pulled herself together. "You asked about Dutch customs. Really, there's not much that's different from American customs except this—Dutch people send invitations to funerals, just like at weddings. I wish we could only invite the people we want, but I suppose we can't really do that."

Wanda tried to be noncommittal. This meeting was spiraling, and she needed to stop the spin. Give everyone time to cool off. "It would be very different. Often, the graveside is private."

"No graveside. The ashes will go with Pieter so Niels can be with his parents."

"Oh, of course." Wanda nodded and set her mostly unfinished coffee down. "Will any of your own family be at the service, Bellona?"

"My sister's in Nashua. She and her family will come."

"Wonderful," Wanda said. "I look forward to meeting them."

"And Sonja will be there," Leslie said suddenly. "Won't she, Ro?"

Wanda looked between them. "Sonja?"

Ro shot a look at Leslie that Wanda couldn't decipher, but it was Wil who answered for him. "Ro's other mother." He stood, looking for all the world like a cat who'd just had its tail yanked. "Fathers are a real scarcity around here these days, Reverend Duff, but mothers— we've got more than enough to go around."

She was glad that Rye had forewarned her about this situation. Rye was a smart one. Sure, she had sad stories to cry into a wine glass, but Wanda had been entangled in and escaped from two bad marriages by the time she was Rye's age. And she was a sucker for people in pain, like these people. Rye would stand a short distance away, in a place with perspective. They needed to talk. Wanda knew what this family needed to hear—what every family did, whether it was true or not.

"I'm grateful that you're letting me be a part of this time. Please be in touch with any questions." She stood to go. "What I can see is that you have more than enough love to go around."

12

THE SOX WERE ON THE FLAT-SCREEN HUNG OVER THE menu board for Wing-Time. The pitcher was scratching himself. Nothing else was happening. Ah, baseball, a perfect metaphor for life.

Devin looked up, smiled, and said, "A wing?…"

"…and a prayer." Wanda gave her familiar response. Comfort food. Home away from home.

"What would you like today?"

"Twelve—six diablo and six teriyaki ginger. Hold the celery."

"Wow. Rough morning, huh?"

"That doesn't even begin. An Orangina for waiting."

"Six diablos? You'll need a second one."

"Charge me for two now." She paid and moved to a seat that wasn't facing the screen. She didn't want to steal a base from a patron who wanted to see the game roll on and on. Not that it was busy at two p.m. She pulled her tablet out of her bag and looked at her menu of books. Tony had warned her never to Kindle-shop after nine, when financial inhibitions were weakest. She had a wide selection of unread books due to her blatant ignoring of this particular dictum. She hovered over the latest Scalzi.

She couldn't stop thinking about her visit with the Ponds. Lara and Bellona's relationship was obviously more public than Wanda had realized. Lara certainly seemed comfortable with the kids—in fact, she'd been more in sync with them than Bellona. Of course, their mother was swinging between the numb and manic of grief.

Lara was a member of Wanda's congregation, but she was mostly there for holidays and mission activities. She would bag groceries and make Church World Service school kits. She was always good for charity walks, chaperoning youth trips, and homeless suppers, but no committees, no study groups, no social events, no Sundays.

Since Wanda had arrived, Lara had not gotten married, been in the hospital, or been a primary griever. As a result, Wanda didn't know her well, and for the hundredth time this week (and every week) Wanda wished she were the perfect pastor who had the time to visit people at home when there was nothing significant happening. Then she would be ready for the crises.

Devin brought the wings to the table—the speed of Hermes with a message of deliciousness. The small, addictive morsels smelled amazing. Wanda inhaled and relaxed, and then looked up to see Lara coming through the door.

"Hey, Dev."

"Hey, Lara. What brings you here this time of day?

"Day off. Best wings in thirty miles."

"A hundred."

"Almost that. I'd like six chili-chipotles, and I'll take Wanda's celery. Diet Coke. May I join you, Wanda?"

"Absolutely." The sigh was only mental. "How did you know I wasn't eating my celery?"

Lara chuckled and sat down. "I'm your pharmacist. I know your blood pressure. You probably avoid salt." She looked at Wanda's plate. "Wow. That's a lot of hot."

"It's dunch. Linner? I won't have another chance to eat, what with an assisted living facility visit, a wedding couple, and a prudential committee meeting at six thirty."

"Well, don't let me stop you. Dig in. And thanks for coming by to plan the service and being okay with our drama."

Our drama.

"You probably wonder how I fit into the Pond family," Lara said.

"I don't need…"

"No, you don't need to know, but I'm guessing you're not surprised." She looked up, and Wanda nodded, then shrugged.

"I would like to tell you, though, and Belle is fine with sharing. You're very good at tactful, but you had question marks practically flying off your face. Belle and I have been together—more than dating—for the last three years."

Wanda put down the diablo wing that had been headed for her mouth and picked up a teriyaki ginger instead. Play it safe. She was relieved that Lara thought her questioning looks had to do with their relationship and not Niels's death. Lara was obviously waiting for her to say something. "Well, you two keep a good secret in a small town. I hadn't heard anything more than that you're very close friends."

"I know you're fine with my being a lesbian."

"Of course I am. Our whole church is Open and Affirming."

"Anyway, I want you to know that Belle always loved Niels, even when it was difficult. She still loves him. She was never really untrue to him. Even when he stopped being the man that she loved and married, she did, and later when he got sick, she took care of him. But he hasn't been that man for a long time, and Belle needed someone who could support her while she was taking care of him and her children." Lara studied Wanda's face. "Do you blame us?"

"No, Lara." Wanda didn't blame her. Bellona was not the first lonely spouse of an Alzheimer's patient who'd found comfort in another relationship before the end. Wanda did not think that the mind was the soul, or that a person was already dead when their cognitive abilities were significantly diminished, but it could feel like a widowhood, even so—like the worst solitude of widowhood, in fact, without the sympathy of friends or the socially acceptable possibilities to develop new relationships.

Lara looked at her, silently asking to be understood, even forgiven. Wanda did both easily. Still, she felt a little chilly in spite of the spicy goodness cooling on her plate. The reason she was not turning up her pastoral thermostat had nothing to do with Belle and Lara's sexual orientation, and it wasn't the starting-again-while-spouse-is-still-alive situation either. She had seen that before, too.

It was suspicion. Given what she and Rye were considering, Bellona and Lara's affair played to motive. What if the two lovers had wanted to be free to fully and publicly pursue their relationship and had convinced themselves that Niels himself wanted to be done with his life? Plenty of families were so desperately weary from a memory-loss illness that they believed a person wanted an exit just because they imagined they would, or because they did.

Would Lara and Bellona have helped Niels escape an existence they thought would feel as intolerable to him as it was to them? Would they have "helped" him? Lara was a pharmacist.

Lara was a pharmacist.

And there was something else. Niels wasn't that loving bridegroom before he got sick. That seemed to be what Lara had said. And Lara was implying that her relationship with Bellona preceded the diagnosis, and perhaps that Niels was a troubled man. They had been waiting, maybe longer than anyone knew. Wanda put it away to think about later, and to share with Rye. She was very grateful she had Rye to bounce these thoughts off of, because it was not where her happy-compass wanted to go.

Wanda reached for diablo goodness. "Look, Lara, Bellona needs a lot of support right now. Especially, and I mean especially, because on some level she had to be hoping that Niels would die sooner rather than later and avoid going through all the losses and indignities that come with the illness. Now it's happened, and earlier than just about anyone expected. It's bound to fill her with relief and guilt. You just be there for her. Obviously the kids respect and love you."

"They're the best kids ever. I know they didn't come across that way today, but they are."

"They understand the situation and aren't jealous on their father's behalf. Lara, that's a credit to how the two of you handle your relationship."

Another wing. (And another prayer, to be honest.) She hoped she wasn't laying it on too thick, but she guessed that maybe there was no too-thick in this situation. "So you keep giving them the support they need, and your relationship will grow stronger and stronger. You don't live there, do you?"

"Not yet."

"I think you should probably avoid big changes right now. You can help them balance as a family. But they may need some space. They will always love you for helping them through this time."

What she didn't say as she polished off the last devilish bite and closed the box on the more discreet samurai wings to take home was that a lot of times these bridge relationships didn't last and flourish. They became so identified as part of a stressful time that they were shed when it was over, when someone like Bellona Pond might need to leave behind *everything* that reminded her of her husband's ill years and any difficult years that preceded them, even the lover who brought her joy.

Wanda didn't want to tell Lara that. And maybe it wouldn't happen. She cleared her throat. Lara looked so grateful, so relieved, that Wanda decided to push her luck.

"Lara, did you think…?"

"No. I didn't."

There was silence. Really awkward, because Wanda was pretty sure that Lara didn't know what she had been about to say.

Then again, maybe she did. Lara looked a bit defiant. "I did not think Niels was ready to die if that's what you were going to ask. He was in vigorous physical health, even though his mind was impaired. I was a little grateful that the three kids didn't need to experience the worst aspects of Alzheimer's. But I was surprised. Weren't you?"

"I was. I didn't see it coming at all. No pneumonia. No heart history, right?"

"Right."

"Is Bellona wondering at all?"

"She assumes that sudden death is a part of the illness." Lara dropped a bone, stripped clean, onto her plate. "And that non-wondering?" Lara looked at Wanda sharply. "I hope you will help it stay that way." She cleared her throat. "I expect you will help it stay that way. She doesn't need more questions."

She could not have been plainer. More questions. Who was asking?

Wanda smiled as if it were assent. Fingers crossed.

13

HER FINGERS WOULD HAVE CRAMPED IF SHE KEPT
them crossed all the way to Fair Havens. Instead, she
kept her hands at two and ten on the steering wheel and
prayed for forgiveness. She fully intended to repay Lara's
confidence by asking a few more questions about Niels's
death. She really hoped they would lay her concerns, and
the concerns she had obviously instilled in Prudence
Rye, to rest.

She was not sleuthing.

Wanda's plan was to visit Jenny, a parishioner with
Parkinson's who needed the level of physical care
available in the memory loss unit but who retained
significantly more cognition than her neighbors.
Jenny never complained about being surrounded
by people who might cry and shout all night long,
steal her shoes (and every other pair on the hallway),
weep disconsolately or giggle for hours, cradle dolls,
or otherwise exhibit behaviors that made their family
members uncomfortable. Those families, like the Ponds,
felt the loss of a bright, inquisitive attorney, bridge player,
accountant, or teacher who was replaced by a vulnerable,

sometimes querulous, sometimes angry, sometimes silent person they hardly knew.

Jenny didn't care. She was a lovely antidote to the solicitousness of the staff and the bewilderment and embarrassment of the families. She just liked people as they were, and, in fact, her presence was a stabilizing force on the unit.

"After all," she'd once said to Wanda, "it's the first time in my entire life anyone ever called me the brightest bulb on the Christmas tree. I might as well enjoy it."

Jenny had no nearby close family and only a few visitors from her former employment as a clerk at Macy's. Wanda made it a point to fit stopovers in between other parish calls and committee meetings. Jenny never failed to brighten her day, and holding her shaking hands was a small price to pay for her sweet heart.

Her visit would not be suspicious, and she could pump sharp-eyed Jenny about Niels. Maybe then she could just happen by Joe's room. Perhaps he had a clue as to what happened to his roommate. He certainly had been present, presumably asleep when Niels died, and he might know something. Sleuthing with Alzheimer's patients? It might take patience.

As it happened, Jenny was in the adjoining senior apartment complex playing Pokeno at Tuesday morning games, and Joe came charging toward Wanda as she entered the coded door. A sign!

His thick-as-a-hedge eyebrows went up and drew together. There was still black mixed with the gray, and they were his signature tell. Dementia or not, he used them with a dramatic flair that gave James Earl Jones a run for his money. "Aha!" he announced.

"Aha?" she countered.

"Do you see this? Do you know what it is?" He put his thick hand on a large laundry cart standing in the hallway outside of his room.

Carpenter. Wanda thought she remembered Joe saying something about being a carpenter in his working life.

Wanda ventured a guess. "A cart?"

"Almost. You almost have it. A cart-el. A drug cartel. Shh. Don't tell anyone, but this is a drug cartel. Come into my room, and I will tell you more." The eyebrows rose two or three times in excited exclamation. Wanda remembered with a hidden smile that Lisa's little Lily called them Joe's caterpillars.

Maybe "drug cartel" was a clue, although she guessed that he was comparing the laundry cart with a similar wheeled device used to dispense pills at the hospital. He'd had a recent hospitalization.

Joe gestured to the recliner grandly as she came into his room. She noticed that Niels's side was still vacant. The administrator had rushed the Pond family to get his belongings removed, hinting there would be a charge for every day until they cleared the room. It looked like there wasn't a waiting list after all.

Wanda moved the afghan (her rule—never trust cloth, sit on washable plastic and check it first) and sat down opposite Joe.

"Can I help you?" The voice came from behind her.

Wanda jumped, feeling unreasonably guilty. N. C. Harris stood in the door. A gray man with a gray voice and lanky blond hair, he ought to have blended into the scenery, but she felt oversensitive to his presence. Wanda scolded herself for being unfair. Perfectly lovely man, she imagined, but he made her uncomfortable.

"Nope. Fine. Visiting Joe." Just the facts.

"Joe…?"

What?! Was he really going to ask Joe if she was bothering him? The gall. Wanda was hot with irritation. Harris stood immovable in the hallway.

"We're fine here," Wanda said. "Just going to have a short visit while I wait for my friend Jenny."

"I didn't know Joe was a part of your flock."

Her flock, indeed! Where were they, the eighteenth century? "Since I do the second Sunday of the month services, I consider everyone my friend here. Joe wants to tell me something."

"Don't believe everything a person with dementia tells you."

How tactless! No wonder this guy had a serial employment record. She'd heard that he was in every nursing home and assisted living facility in the state and never stayed long.

"A conversation is more than an exchange of facts."

He still hovered in the door. "Joe's had a bee in his bonnet all day. You know how they get. This week it's drugs. Next week, it'll be a conspiracy about soup."

She glanced at Joe, who looked deflated and anxious. The caterpillars were drawn into a frown. Poor guy. "Well, I'm starting to know exactly how he feels." She tried to keep the steely edge out of her voice.

Harris shifted and was gone. For a nondescript presence, he had really made her feel…well, trapped. There was a sensation of blessed expansion when he left.

Joe looked at her, and she looked at Joe. She smiled conspiratorially and tiptoed over to the door and looked around the edge. In her best spy voice, she whispered, "The coast is clear."

He laughed delightedly.

Drug cartels or Niels? Niels. "I'm so sorry about Niels's death, Joe. You must miss him."

"Miss him?"

"Niels, your roommate? Blond hair…"

A sudden look of recognition. "Niels is a great finger talker. I love his finger stories. They are the best."

Sign language? "Niels used his hands to talk…to you?"

"His kids, his pretty wife, me. Yes. The angry man? That—oh, that high and mighty lady! No. No. Nurses—no. No finger talking with them. They made Niels angry."

"I'm sorry that Niels is gone."

"Niels is gone? Is he coming back soon?"

Oh, dear.

"Joe, Niels is dead. He's…" Wanda searched in her not-very-perfect memory for any information about Joe's religious background. Baptist. She thought he was Baptist. "Niels is…with the Lord."

"Did I tell you about the drug lords?"

She wasn't getting anything here. What did she expect? She wondered whether Jenny would be back soon. "Did you see drug lords on a TV show, Joe?"

"Right here. Right here. At night they come and get the drugs and take them to South America."

"Oh, I think drugs come *from* South America, Joe. They're sold here. Maybe you saw a show on television?"

"No, no, no. The drugs go away." Joe was waving his hands around and beginning to get upset.

Harris would be back any minute and would blame her for getting Joe worked up. She walked over and tried to take his hand to calm him, but he threw them up at the same moment, and his big knuckles clipped her hard under the left eye. She spun and dropped gracelessly, but at least was caught by the big recliner. Falling fully to the floor would have been more embarrassing.

"Reverend Duff! Let me look at that. Joe Jackson, you sit down right over there." Zoe Laferriere was big as life, a force of nature. She had a way of making Wanda feel like a child. Wanda suspected that was due to her own sense of insecurity next to this nurse, who took charge of everything and who had so many children. Wanda regretted that neither of her own marriages had resulted in a child, and Zoe embodied that failure.

"I'm fine."

"N. C. told me you were riling Mr. Joe up, getting him all excited. Now look where we are."

This was not fair. And 'now look where we are,' in Wanda's mind, was a phrase reserved for children. "I'm fine. I'm sorry, but I was not exciting Joe. I was just having a friendly visit."

"Telling this poor man to remember his friend? Makes him sad, and mad. And letting him tell his no-count tales about drugs and bad people—"

"Were you listening to our conversation?"

"Don't want my folks all excited. Makes them have a whole bad day. We want the good days. We want the sunny days. Not trouble days. Don't bring your trouble here."

"Joe?"

Joe Jackson was looking very repentant, very sad—a bit like a dog who knew he had made a mess. Wanda ignored Zoe because she couldn't trust herself to talk to her. She leaned forward to take his hand. "Joe, don't you worry. I'm not really hurt, and I know you didn't mean anything. I'm glad we got to talk. I'd like to stop in and visit you again when I come to see my friend Jenny."

She turned to the nurse. "Is Jenny around yet?"

"Jenny went out to lunch on the van with her friends after their game. Chinese food, I think. Maybe you can go now."

"Could I chat with you for a minute, Zoe?"

"Lunch carts are coming any minute. I don't have very much time." Subtext—you have already wasted an unnecessary amount of my time.

"Well, I'd like to talk with you about a few things in regard to Niels Pond's death, so I'll stop by tomorrow."

"No shift tomorrow."

"Thursday then? Will you be here Thursday?"

"I will." Zoe narrowed her eyes. "Every day is a busy day."

"Thursday it is, then."

Wanda threw her most brilliant meet-the-Match. com-date smile at Joe, whose caterpillars wiggled wickedly. Well, she wasn't ruining his day. Might have been more excitement than he'd had in a while. And she didn't think getting his heart rate up was a bad thing.

N. C. Harris and Zoe Laferriere, on the other hand, were doing their level best to interfere with what Wanda mentally tagged "the Rye-and-My investigation," but at least she had the satisfaction of knowing that she was upsetting them. Was it because they wanted to forget Niels's death and she was bringing it up? No staff wanted to linger on death, but in a facility like this, it was common. A person in the medical field who could not handle the constant presence of death should not work geriatrics.

Maybe this death was not common, though, and Zoe and Harris knew it and wanted whatever was uncommon about it to be smoothed over as quickly as possible. But how would they know that was what Wanda had been talking about? Was there some kind of baby monitor in the room so they could listen in? She had never heard of such a thing.

And who was the lady Joe had mentioned—the one Niels didn't finger-talk with? Lara? Ro Pond's mysterious mother? Who was the angry man? Wanda thought she spent enough time in the unit that she ought to have recognized someone Joe would describe that way. Things were becoming more rather than less complicated.

Wanda slid into her trusty Fiesta, put on her sunglasses, and pulled down the visor. She might not have any answers, but with this bruise blossoming, at least she was starting to look like a detective.

14

RYE PULLED HER HAIR BACK INTO A PONYTAIL, STARED at herself in the mirror, made a face, and then let it down again. Being raised by a single father, she had spent many years in the rugby shirts and Lee jeans he had brought home for her from Sears. It wasn't until she'd gone off to college that she'd been introduced to a world that included mascara and dry-clean-only fabrics. Over the years, friends had taken pity on her and shared their tips until she'd finally emerged with a style she was comfortable calling her own.

Tonight, she had chosen her signature going-out uniform, at least as it had been adapted to her role as vice principal in a town where too many people knew her name. She brushed some lint off her dark jeans, admiring how well they sat as she twisted and turned. Far from having a model's physique, Rye had made her look suit her petite frame. Everything she bought was tailored until it hung properly.

With her auburn hair—too many dates used the American rye whiskey simile—she leaned heavily on greens to get her through situations like this. She straightened her top, a scoop-necked short-sleeve blouse in mint that made her feel put together enough to crash a twenties-something reunion.

Or so she'd thought when she left the house. Now she was hiding in the bathroom, trying to decide when, exactly, she'd gotten old. Rye stared at her reflection. The lines around her eyes and mouth had deepened in the last few years. She'd recently purchased a new bra that promised better lift, although the only difference Rye had noticed was that it subtly constricted all day until she was dying to get home to pull it off.

She shook her head. Surrounded by bright young things all day every day at work, Rye had thought herself immune to these judgements, but apparently her self-esteem was not unshakable.

"Rye?" Mike knocked on the door. "Are you alright? That kid is here, you know. The blond one? Wil?"

"I know," she called, her face flushing. A side effect of having freckled skin was that each emotion seemed to spread pink across her face and neck. She blotted herself once more with a cold, damp paper towel, then opened the door.

"What's wrong with you?" Mike asked, clearly amused.

"Nothing." She pushed past him. "I just got a little flustered when I realized I'd turned into Rip Van Winkle."

Mike laughed. "Maybe get a drink and a grip. You look like a freshman trying to ask out a junior." He threw her another glance. "Well, maybe it's the other way around."

"Great, thanks."

"You don't want the kids calling you 'cougar' on Monday," he said with a wink.

"That is not even remotely funny," Rye muttered.

"It kind of is. From where I'm standing."

"Are you going to introduce me or what?"

Mike shrugged. "I thought you already met?"

"We have, but I need this to look, you know, accidental. Natural." She grabbed his beer. "Give me that."

"Don't you dare finish it. It's nine bucks here for a domestic."

Rye rolled her eyes. "I'm not going to. I just need a prop."

"You're wound so tight!" He wrapped his arm around her shoulder in a half hug. "If you don't start dating again soon, I'm going to sign you up for my summer kickball league. You need an outlet."

She gave him a shove back toward the party. "Let's just get this over with already."

Mike sauntered out in front of her, and she watched as he casually inserted himself into a couple of conversations with old students, joking around with them before moving along. She was towed along silently in his wake, trying to act like a date, although she was pretty sure that vice principals and teachers were not actually supposed to fraternize. What was the misconduct guideline du jour? She prayed she didn't look as awkward as she felt.

By the time he made his way around to Wil Pond, she had to keep her arms tucked tightly to her sides. She could feel sweat beading on her back and could only pray it wasn't staining the flimsy material. Silently, she cursed herself for forgetting the cardinal rule of fashion strategy—wear layers.

Taking a deep breath, she wiped her hand on her jeans and turned on a bright smile as she heard Mike cue her.

"Hey! Wil!" he said, clapping the younger man on the shoulder. "Long time, man!"

"Wil?" Rye turned around, her face schooled into the picture of innocence. "Pond?"

"Oh, hey," Wil said, his grin wavering as he made eye contact with her. "Coach Nifterick! How have you been?"

"Oh, same old. Coaching on the girls' side right now, softball season."

"I heard they're doing great," Wil said, nodding enthusiastically. He was sipping a nine-dollar beer as well, and Rye had to remind herself that even though he looked like he was all of seventeen, he wouldn't be drinking at a school-sponsored event if it wasn't legal.

"They are. I'm proud of how hard they've pulled together. Got a lot of freshman and sophomores this year, but we've really come together as a team."

Rye nodded and hmmed as the two of them compared the current school teams with those in Wil's day for a few minutes until Mike finally excused himself to grab another beer. He glared at her, having noticed that her fake sips had become real ones the longer they stood around chatting. Rye guiltily held it out to him, but he shook his head.

"So, Wil," Rye glanced around. The bulk of the party had moved into the old arcade at the back of the diner, where teens and twenty-year-olds alike were lining up to challenge each other in air hockey and *Hoop Dreams*. "How are you...uh...doing?" She blushed. "I'm sorry. I'm sure this is a really hard time for you. I hope my visit the other day didn't make things worse."

She was starting to babble, but Wil held his hand up and smiled, genuinely, for the first time. "No, it's okay. Thanks for asking. We were a little tense the other day. You were just doing your job, and I'm glad you're concerned about Leslie. Not every school administrator bothers to make a home visit. Guess you got more than you bargained for."

He swirled his beer around for a moment before continuing. "You see, it's been…a lot. My dad, I mean, I know he's been sick for a long time, but I really thought— I mean, we all thought he had more time."

Rye wracked her brain for the information she'd discovered in Leslie's file and on her own Google searches about the family. "He worked with the deaf community, right?"

"Yeah." Wil signed something to her, but she could only shake her head ruefully. "All of us sign. My uncle's deaf, and my dad was sort of a big deal in the ASL community. He wasn't against technology, surgery, or speaking, but he believed in the deaf community having a language. On the other hand, he was a proponent of integrated deaf and hearing education. He was appalled with how little people seemed to know or care about what it's like for people with hearing loss to function in a hearing society."

"I guess I'd never thought too much about it," Rye admitted.

"Most people don't unless they personally know somebody who's hearing impaired," Wil said. "Dad was trying to change that. If he'd had more time…" He shrugged. "Who knows what he could have accomplished?"

"It sounds like you were really proud of the work he was doing."

"I was. I am."

"Do you think you might follow in his footsteps? Maybe try to finish what he started?" Rye could feel the part of her that relished the short-term guidance job starting to emerge, and she tried to rein it in, keep it casual.

Wil shook his head. "I don't know. When I was young, Ro and I talked about maybe working together."

"You two must be close," Rye said.

She saw the cloud as it passed across his face, but Wil kept his tone light. "Yeah. Things have changed a little, you know, recently, but yeah. We are."

"You mean because of your dad?"

"Him, my mom and Lara. Ro's mom."

There it was. Rye zeroed in on the source of Wil's bitterness. "I'm sorry— Ro's mom?"

"You must have noticed that Ro doesn't exactly look like he sprung from the Dutch blondes who produced Leslie and me?"

Rye thought quickly. She didn't think she needed to betray that she'd checked the file, at least not in this achieved-with-difficulty casual setting, although if he was going to tag her for administrative chops, he should know she would. Where did she learn about the birth mother? The records…no, it was Wanda. Play dumb.

"Of course, yes. I met him so briefly at school, and then he was leaving as I came over. I didn't even think about it."

"Yeah, well, thanks, I guess," Wil said.

"For what?"

"That's pretty much the first thing most people notice about us as a family. I guess it's nice to meet someone a little more…oblivious."

Rye tried not to take offense. She pushed through her embarrassment, trying to balance how-she-knew-what and a beer. "You were saying something about his mom?"

"Oh. Yeah. Sonja showed up about a year ago. She had Ro when she was, like, fifteen. Gave him up so she could go to Brown and get her master's in social work. I guess she wanted to try to keep other girls from getting into the same situation she did."

"Sounds like she handled it pretty well," Rye said, half to herself.

"Well, yeah. She gave him up, though, so what the hell does she need from him now?" His voice rose enough that heads were turning. "His family needs him, and she just shows up and…" He bit off whatever he was going to say and drank the rest of his beer. He took a deep breath. "I gotta get going."

"Yeah, of course," Rye said, bobbing her head. "I'm really sorry. I didn't mean to upset you." Or make a scene.

"It's fine." He waved his hand. "'S not you." He turned and headed back to the arcade, patting Mike on the shoulder as he passed him.

Mike sauntered back over a minute later, offering Rye a plate of nachos. "So, how'd it go?"

Rye watched Wil for a moment longer. "It was…fine. That family's got a lot going on right now, though."

"More than the dad dying?"

"Yeah." Rye wondered what to say and settled for, "A lot more."

15

RYE WAVED GOOD-BYE TO MIKE AND WALKED DOWN
the block to a little dive bar called Ed's. Andy had texted
her about meeting up for a drink, and since she'd already
gone to the trouble of dressing up on a Sunday night, it
seemed like a shame to waste it all on twenty-year-olds
who looked more like jailbait with every birthday.

Of course, she hadn't expected to sweat through her
new shirt, but she swung by her car on her way over and
grabbed a cardigan from the back seat. It didn't exactly
scream "date night," but this might not even be a date.
Her instinct on this sort of thing was rusty at best. Was
it a date if he didn't even bother to call? As far as she
could tell, her students never used their phones to place
actual calls, but she was from the ambiguous generation
that floated somewhere between answering machines
and emoticons. After all, she still saw the benefit of
dialing if a two-minute conversation could replace ten
minutes with no affect and tired thumbs.

Nevertheless, here she was, text-date or no. She
pushed the door, wiping her fingers discreetly after they
touched its tacky surface. She remembered why she went

to Locals now that she was at least pretending middle age. She saw Andy at a tall table in the back with a beer, so she waved and grabbed herself a drink before heading over. Was it a date if he didn't buy her a drink? Would he think it was less a date if she came to his table with her drink already in hand? She thought not, but she couldn't quite convince her sweat glands.

"Hey," she said, pulling out the second chair and sliding in next to an old video poker game. It whirred at her, the colors a constant blur of low-grade graphics that she tried to ignore.

"Hey! Glad you could make it!" Andy leaned over and pecked her cheek.

Rye blushed. She'd forgotten how comfortable Andy had always been with things like casual kisses and hugs. She preferred to reserve that sort of thing for her nearest and dearest; he had always been more of an open book. "Sure. I was right down the street anyway."

"Oh, yeah? Big plans tonight? Did I pull you away from something fun?" he asked, his eyebrows wiggling suggestively at her.

Rye laughed. "Nothing like that, no. My friend Mike and I were just having a drink, and I ran into one of the Pond kids."

"Oh." Andy's expression instantly morphed into what she thought of as his caretaker face.

"Yeah, Wil was at some alumni soccer reunion or something. Mike makes an appearance at those things when he can. I said hello and managed to just about ruin his night." Her phone buzzed in her pocket, and she pulled it out. *Bitch.* She didn't recognize the number, but this was the fourth lewd message she'd gotten tonight. Texting was also the strategy du jour of the bully.

"How did you manage that?"

"I don't know. My usual flare for conversation, I guess," Rye said ruefully. "I somehow stumbled into some family drama I hadn't even known existed, and he got a little worked up."

"Oh, you mean about Bellona and Lara being together?" Andy asked.

Rye's phone buzzed again, but she ignored it. Also, she really didn't want to play games with Andy, and he knew she had come to see Lara at Fair Havens, but she was trying to get more information. "They're friends, right? I thought…"

"She and Niels? I had a front-row seat for that whole show. The three of them were always close. When Niels first came to stay with us, he was in much better shape. They were all inseparable back then." Andy shrugged. "I actually wondered if maybe they were all…I don't know. In an alternative arrangement."

"Like a threesome?" Rye tried to reconcile the frigid but frenetic Mrs. Pond with that lifestyle and fell far short. "Seriously?!"

"That was a very early thought. You understand I'm not really supposed to speculate about that sort of thing with residents. You and your colleagues must be equally circumspect with students, I'm guessing."

"Oh, no. We speculate all the time. Half our staff meetings are just rampant speculation about what some of those kids are up to."

"Really?" Andy's eyebrows shot up.

"High school is all about the drama. It's impossible to ignore, trust me. Getting older does not make any of us immune to the trickling of the rumor mill. Not the serious stuff—we have procedure for that." Rye replied with a smile. "But I know what you mean. Just because we hear about these little soap operas doesn't mean we want to touch the situation with a ten-foot pole unless something looks like a 'child at risk.'"

"Exactly," he agreed. "And in most cases, with the people I work with, the drama is kept to a minimum. Or it's centered around a patient's children—their histories and tensions with each other. It's rare to see real romance unfold over the course of years. Now, residents imagining that they are married to each other? That's the course that never does run smooth."

"I believe it."

"Well, anyway, it turns out Niels, Bellona, and Lara never were a threesome. It was always just a balancing act for Mrs. Pond between her husband and her best friend."

"And now that her husband's gone?"

"They must be more than friends." He shrugged. "I could be wrong, but Lara has been handling most of the details with us, and she was certainly there for that family every step of the way. The kids adore her. She's their rock."

"Wow." Rye took a long sip of her beer. She'd forgotten just how public private life was in a small town. And the dad's death must be making it much worse. No wonder the kids seemed stressed. They'd gone from having one mother to three practically overnight.

"Yeah." Andy smiled and returned to his digging operation. "But if the mama drama didn't come up, what did happen tonight?"

Rye took a moment to study the tattoos that covered both his arms. He'd been the first person she'd ever known to get a tattoo, and clearly the sleeves suited him. The ink stood out even with the dark hair on his arms.

He caught her looking and grinned. She could feel the heat spread across her cheeks as her phone went off again. "Your phone must have buzzed twelve times since we sat down," he said. "Everything okay?"

"You can hear it?" Rye asked, pulling it out and checking the texts. The first few seemed tame compared to the ones that had come in most recently.

"I think you're leaning against the table or something," Andy said. "I can feel the vibration in my leg."

"Sorry about that." She shoved her phone back in her pocket.

"Is it important?"

"No," Rye shook her head. "I think some kid probably got my personal number and decided to send some inappropriate messages." She drained the rest of her beer. "Pretty stupid, really, since it shouldn't be that hard for me to trace the number back."

"Does that happen a lot?" Andy looked concerned.

Rye had forgotten that—despite all the ink and a haircut that could only be achieved by taking mid-nineties photos of Keanu Reeves to a barber—he was a tender soul. "Not really, no. But honestly, it's not a big deal. Some kids have a lot of frustration, and the only way they know how to release it is by spewing as many four-letter words as they can at a world they can't control. Or the nearest representative of authority—which is all too often yours truly."

"I'm sorry you have to deal with that."

"Me, too," Rye said. "But hopefully I'll get it straightened out tomorrow."

Andy nodded. "Speaking of which, I know you have an early day tomorrow, but I have a couple of tickets to go see an encore showing of *Fight Club* at the Oliander at nine. Any chance you want to join me?"

Rye thought about how early her alarm was going to go off and then shrugged with a grin. "Far be it from me to turn down vintage Norton and Pitt. I mean, I'm old, not dead."

16

"NOT 'IN THE BULB THERE IS A FLOWER' IN THE LATE spring." Wanda shook her head at Tony, an amazing musician who, every once in a while, did not read the lyrics.

They were planning the Sunday worship bulletin. Wanda was truly glad she had a musician who cared about the liturgical seasons of Lent, Advent, Epiphany—not to mention the minister's sermon theme. Most musicians didn't care about anything except music (mostly the choir's music or the praise band's).

Tony loved to have a seamless worship experience, even when that meant dipping his toes into deep theological waters, although he never stopped laughing at the whole concept of a season of "Ordinary Time" from roughly June to December, with a dollop of January and February thrown in. "And what does that *mean* exactly? Ordinary like the Fourth of July? Ordinary like Halloween?"

Trying for stern, she interrupted, "'In the Bulb' is a winter song, Tony. We all need to remind ourselves that there are some crocuses that are going to emerge from the gloom of snow and ice and human sadness."

"So, we can use it for the funeral?"

"Perfect for the funeral. And honestly, maybe the tenderness will melt that frozen family." Wanda was relieved. "For Sunday, how about 'All Things Bright and Beautiful'?"

"Childish."

"'God of the Sparrow'?"

"Hard to sing."

Wanda took a deep breath. "So what do you have?"

"'This Is My Father's World'?"

"Gender-exclusive language."

"'Joyful, Joyful, We Adore You'?"

"Used in too many movies—not to speak of anime—and it's the anthem of the European Union."

"How do you know this stuff?"

"Trivia in bars."

"'All Creatures of Our God and King.'"

"Gender-exclusive, long, and boooring."

They both were laughing as Lisa knocked on the door. "Someone to see you, Reverend Duff."

So not a parishioner, who would have been told to walk right in.

"I'm going." Tony unfolded himself from the most comfortable chair in the office. "'For the Beauty of the Earth'?"

"Sold. And that's what you wanted in the first place."

Tony shrugged, an expression of ultimate innocence on his face as he headed out the door.

Wanda stood to greet a small woman in her forties with black box braids and a conservative but hip blazer and jeans. She looked vaguely familiar, but that was true of so many people Wanda met in her line of work.

"Reverend Duff? I'm Sonja Mari."

"Hello, Ms. Mari." Wanda was not enlightened, but she was used to pretending she knew people long enough for the context to give them away.

"You don't know who I am? Well, I guess that's a kind of relief."

Hmm. perceptive. Sonja Mari helped herself to the comfortable chair without an invitation.

"I meet a lot of people, and I am…I'm getting older." Wanda smiled, her most planned genuine smile. "Some people can't remember faces, and some people can't remember names. I am doubly blessed."

"We haven't met. I'm Rocco Pond's biological mother."

"Oh, of course! He looks like you—that's what I must be trying to connect. I like Ro a lot. You should be—"

"Proud? No. Bellona and Niels should be proud. I gave him life and a genetic stew, but I do not deceive myself. The incredible young man I've discovered over the last year owes his mature behavior, energy, interests, and kindness to the family in which he was raised. I am purely a beneficiary, a very humble one. Trust me, I understand that."

Wanda could tell that her visitor had come with a speech to deliver, so she limited herself to a go-ahead nod.

"I want to be clear that Ro came looking for me, not the other way around. I gave up my rights to him when I decided I wanted to finish high school."

"You hoped he would have a better life than you could provide."

"I told myself that. And people like me—social workers—told me that as well. I myself am very hesitant to give that platitude out as ultimate truth for everyone. But in our case, Ro was a winner. Great folks, great sibs, and a comfortable financial situation."

"And how can I help you, Ms. Mari?"

"Call me Sonja. I'm not sure that you can help me, but I wanted to introduce myself anyway. Being in Ro's life has been wonderful for me, and he tells me it's been good for him, too. I think, however, that I'm complicating things at a very bad time. Maybe you can help. Maybe not. I figured I wanted you to meet me rather than hear about me."

Too late for that.

"What makes you think you're complicating things?"

"Wil is feeling threatened. The boys were so close, born the same year, always in school together. Like twins but better. Now they've both lost a parent, but Wil feels like Ro has gained one. He's not really jealous, just hurting."

"So, it's causing them to fight?"

"Oh, no. Or, yes, a little. But Wil just wants me to go away—back to Boston, or at least out from underfoot. He wishes I had never appeared. He's a nice guy. Like I said, the Ponds raised good kids. It doesn't matter, though. My priority in this 'case' is my son, my biological son. And as long as Ro wants me to stay, I will."

"What about your work? You live in Boston?"

"Being here sets up a long commute, but I don't mind. I work four long days and have three off."

"What about Leslie? Have you gotten to know her at all?"

"Leslie reminds me of who I used to be. I made a lot of mistakes. There was no one there to help me avoid them, and I would love to help her. It's not my place, though. She has a mother—two, it seems—but I like her. We're friendly. At least when Wil's not around."

Wanda took a moment to consider whether that was how she felt about Rye. Someone who was like she had been—a little wild on purpose, but also overly responsible. Talk about two not-a-fun-girl jobs—minister and vice principal. Was Rye someone she could influence for good? And, in Rye's case, as someone who didn't have a mother, much less two? Surely the age range was wider. Wanda was nineteen years older than Rye, but if Sonja had Rocco when she was a high school sophomore, Leslie would be…She put away the reflection for another time. It bothered her.

Sonja was here and now, and quite enigmatic enough. Wanda should try to get some answers. "So how does Bellona feel about you if you don't mind my asking?'

Sonja uncrossed her legs and stood up, ready to go. She was nothing if not a woman with her own agenda. Wanda wondered whether that had been true when she was sixteen or if that was what the lonely years had taught her. "It's hard to admit this, but I honestly have no clue." She gathered her purse. "Niels was not an easy man, you know. That anger wasn't just dementia-related. I know that people want to rewrite the past and make everything wonderful. It wasn't. He was a perfectionist and sharp-tongued with anyone who disagreed. Fortunately, he thought his kids were perfect. But nobody else. I tried to reach out once about ten years ago, and he scared me off. And I don't scare easily."

"I imagine you don't. Do you mean that Niels had enemies?"

"Maybe…yes. Not at work. Maybe here in town. But he was a very good father. And don't ask about anything else because I don't know."

"Thanks, because I would have to ask."

"Both of us. Mandated reporters." She smiled and slung her bag over her shoulder. "Good father." Sonja stood and headed for the door. She turned. "Have you ever seen Lara crying? Distant? Rattled, maybe?" She searched Wanda's face, but all she was going to find there was surprise. Sonja shrugged and let herself out.

Wanda opened her desk drawer and pulled out her bagged lunch, snagging an apple to munch while she gave their conversation a little thought. The social worker had clearly completed her agenda—though Wanda still wasn't a hundred percent certain what that had been—while Wanda's own questions had gone not just unanswered but unasked. A force of nature, that woman. Not unlike Bellona Pond.

Yes, she was complicating the family dynamics. And yes, three mothers might be one or two too many—at least as far as these nearly grown kids were concerned. Wanda could buy that. She had the answer to whether Niels had known about this woman's interest in having a relationship with his son. Had she ever visited Fair Havens? Was she the 'mean woman' Joe had described?

Why had Sonja Mari come here? To the church, to Wanda? Any way she turned it, that was where she stuck. Was this a preliminary to coming to the memorial service, to finding out whether Wanda would have objections? Sonja hadn't asked about that, though, and she did seem direct.

Subtle, no. So, she just wanted to see Wanda.

Well, knight to the queen's bishop. Wanda needed to find out a little more about Sonja. And she needed some shampoo.

17

IT WAS "GOOD EXERCISE" TO WALK TO THE DRUGSTORE
where Lara Alesci worked. Wanda wished her Fitbit
knew she was walking, but she'd left it sitting on her
bureau at home. She wondered whether feeling guilty
when looking at an inanimate object was completely
normal. The Fitbit would not judge her. It was merely
a symbol of broken resolutions (January), slowed-
down fasting (Lent) and warm weather clothes-rack
repentance (now). Still, thinking about this symbol of
self-control might keep her mind off the season opening
of the local dairy bar.

Shampoo and a new lipstick were grabbed quickly,
without the usual perusal and inner debate. Two quick
birthday cards and a sympathy card. Her basket looked
normal, and now…pharmacy advice. She grabbed a
gummy vitamin version of fish oil.

Wanda leaned over the pharmacy counter. Nandi
Patel was counting pills into bottles. Some things must
be presorted. He smiled but looked over his shoulder
to where Lara was reading tags on the mesh basket of
prescriptions yet to be picked up.

Lara came over. Wanda wondered whether Lara was hesitant or whether that was only her own conscience's early warning system.

"Hi, Lara. Imagine seeing you a couple times in as many days."

"Can I help you?" Yes, she was definitely a little stiff.

"I'm having trouble with fish oil. I'm supposed to take one daily, but it just sits all fishy in my stomach and I burp a nasty taste. On Sunday mornings, I am a marine hazard to my congregation. I was wondering whether these gummy versions would solve the problem?

Lara looked her up and down doubtfully. "You don't strike me as a gummy vitamin kind of person."

"I've never taken any before. In fact, until I was here this morning, I had no idea how many vitamin options came as…candy."

"Oh, yes. It's a millennial favorite. It's not really a good idea to use for everything, and there are some dangers with children in the house. But if you are not completely gumdropping it on other vitamins, it might stop your fishy burp."

Wanda nodded at what was only confirmation—gummy fish had been solving her fish oil problem for the last several months, and now she could segue over to her real objective.

"Say, Lara, the strangest thing just happened." Stick with close to the truth.

"Yes?"

"I had a visit form Sonja Mari at the church. She came in to introduce herself to me, I suppose? I'm actually not really sure why she came."

"Ah, the uninvited guest. Our Sonja."

Our Sonja, indeed.

Use honesty. "Well, it is such a sensitive family dynamic, and her visit was so uncommunicative and awkward that, well, I was here already. I thought I would ask you what you thought about her."

Lara was quiet.

Wanda took a breath and continued. "You shared so much the other day, and I'm grateful, but it seems random that Ro's biological mother would come to talk to me out of the blue. I'm leading her biological son's adoptive father's memorial service. But she didn't ask my permission to attend or anything."

Lara turned to her assistant. "I'm going to take a quick break. Two Smart waters to my tab." She turned to Wanda. "Let's go out to the bench."

"Sure. Oh, maybe I'd better buy this stuff. Can I do it at the pharmacy?"

"Sure. Every register goes to the great St. Peter Rite Aid in the sky. Do you have a loyalty card?"

Lara rang it up, looking curiously at the lipstick. Wanda flashed her key ring tag quickly, paid with a credit card, accepted the water. Just outside the door in the parking lot was a bench in a nice patch of sun with a raised flower bed and a lonely tree. A place for old people and preteens to wait for rides.

"Reverend Duff, we all appreciate your interest in the family, but it feels to Belle like you're a little too curious."

Wanda choked on her water. She was being too curious?! Sonja Mari had come to her. As had Lara.

Lara held up a hand. "She really doesn't understand that pastoral care after a death is normal, so it feels nosy. She's a very private person, as I'm sure you know. I've told her that this is just what you do for anyone, what any minister would do, but she finds it invasive. So, for all of our sakes, could you just hold back a bit?"

It wasn't fair. Except it really was fair, and Wanda knew it. She did want to know more, but she certainly was not going to share her suspicions, vague as they were.

Still, it simply wasn't fair.

"I'm sorry," Wanda said. The feeling was genuine, even if she was hurt by Lara's implications. Clergy grew tough hides or they found a new profession. "But Sonja came to me. I didn't seek her out."

"Sonja." Lara sighed and took a deep drink. "Sonja is nosy. She gets on Belle's nerves. I think she regrets giving Ro up for adoption. She's extremely complimentary of his upbringing, but it still feels strange." Lara sighed again. "But what can we do? He's an adult. Twenty-three-year-olds get to choose who they spend their time with, even if their mothers don't like it, right?"

Wanda nodded. "I'm sure my own mother would agree."

"She has been more present rather than less since Niels's death. That's been hard, though Ro is making the best progress adjusting. Maybe she's a helpful distraction for him, but it's hard on Wil and Leslie, and on Bellona, though she wouldn't like me to say it." Wanda nodded at this noncommittally. "I won't tell Belle that she visited you, and please don't tell her yourself. Between her and that nosy vice principal from the high school, we feel hounded."

Lara's expression was earnest, but Wanda's annoyance was growing. She knew for a fact that Rye's number-one concern was Leslie and ensuring the girl was getting appropriate grief counseling. Sure, she was as curious as Wanda about the circumstances around Niels Pond's death, but her commitment to her students was unimpeachable.

Lara patted her hand. Wanda mustered every bit of pastoral prowess she had not to pull away. "Then to hear that you're asking questions," Lara continued. "That nice RN with the French name called to tell us. It's a bit much."

Well, that was invasive and uncalled for, but it explained the change in Lara's attitude. With her halo fairly glowing, Wanda resisted saying, 'So excuse me for living.' Instead, she decided that since her subtle interest was only causing problems, she might as well try for something she really wanted to know.

"I understand. This is a difficult time, and I do know Bellona enough to know she needs her space. Lara, I do have one more question, and I hope you'll humor me." She took a deep breath. "What medications was Niels taking at the time of his death?"

"What?"

"What medi—"

"I heard you, I just can't imagine why you would want to know."

Wanda had planned for this. Now she had to pull it off. "I know it's an unusual question, but you're a pharmacist, and I've become concerned about Fair Havens's overuse of tranquilizing medications for people on the cognitive spectrum. Since Niels is gone, it seems easier to ask about him than someone who's still living there. I worry that some of the more difficult patients are being kept in a twilight world to reduce problems for the staff. I promise you that I would not use your information, if anything comes to a complaint, without telling you."

Lara suddenly looked relieved. And relief was not an emotion this speech should have provoked. Still, she did. "I don't know," she said. "But if you promise me that

Niels's name will not be used, I could look up his record. No one else, though."

"Thanks so much."

"I'll call."

"I'd really appreciate it." Wanda wondered why, suddenly, Lara was so compliant. If she were playing hide and seek, Wanda imagined she had been warm...warmer.... hot, and now cold. Belle wanted no personal questions about her family, but a challenge to the very facility in which she had placed a loved one was just fine.

Wow. Wanda needed to see Rye.

"Wanda!" Lara's voice was sharp, agitated, and it brought her back to the here-and-now bench and smart water.

"What?"

"There's a man taking pictures of us from his car. Do you see him?"

Wanda looked up and turned slightly. She'd seen that car somewhere. Where? And, yes, there was a man in a ball cap, sunglasses, with the sun visor down, taking photos of her.

Or Lara. Blackmail about being a lesbian? Surely not.

Wanda was on her feet moving toward the car. Maybe it was stupid, but she was angry.

It roared to life, as much as a Hyundai Accent could roar. Mass plate 37...and it was gone. Wanda looked at Lara, but she looked as baffled as Wanda felt.

18

WANDA JOGGED BACK TO THE CHURCH. HER FITBIT would be glowing. She wondered whether there were demerits for jogging in order to get a car. No. Jogging was jogging. She stopped at the church office for the tzatziki and broccoli slaw wrap she'd left in the church refrigerator.

"Lisa?"

"No calls, no crises. Tony went to the high school. I need something for the email blast and to make the website look more summer-y."

"Hymn sing and make your own sundae?"

"Meh."

"Praise song…? No. I thought not. Do they still have Christian clowns?"

"Oh, creepy. But there are some Christian magicians."

"Better than clowns. Can you do *your* magic?"

"You mean pick a date, book a magician, and write up a little article?"

"That would be perfect, thanks. I'm heading to the hospital to check in on John Caroti after his surgery, then I'm going to Fair Havens. Jenny was out last time I swung by, so I stopped to chat with Joe Jackson. It was the strangest thing—the staff seemed to want to prevent me from talking with him."

"Really? They love it when Lily and I spend time with him, or any of the other people who don't get regular visitors."

"Well, they treated me so badly, it made me suspicious. I wonder what Joe knows about Niels Pond's death."

"What do you mean?"

"There's something not quite right, and, honestly, there was a concerted effort to keep me from asking even vague questions. I mean really vague...passing the time till Jenny got back."

"You think there's something wrong with Niels's death?"

"Of course not. It's just—he was fine, and then he was gone. No heart history. He was depressed and angry about his situation. So, I asked a couple questions."

"That makes me so sad. A little scared, too. What if it isn't safe there? A memory loss unit should be the safest of all safe places to live. I don't want my aunt in a residence where people die suddenly, except in the winter with the norovirus. Maybe I can stop by and chat with Joe. I don't think anyone will bother us."

Lisa was eating a bowl of ramen noodles. Wanda could feel the sodium crossing the room to make her own fingers swell. "Thanks. If you have a chance, that would be great. Don't do anything that makes you uncomfortable though, okay?"

"In other words, be tactful. I've got a great model in you."

Wanda wasn't sure whether Lisa was making fun of her or not, but the admin's eyes were drifting toward her computer screen, so Wanda polished off the unsatisfying wrap and got ready to head out for her visits. If Lisa remembered to talk to Joe on Saturday, she was probably Wanda's best chance of getting new information.

Wanda grabbed a small notebook and a smaller paperback psalms—John's eyesight was good. She ran a brush through her hair and picked up the Rite Aid bag to pull out the new lipstick. *Glamnation Lethal Lipstick Violet Night.* No wonder Lara had stared at it. No, not really Wanda's style. It betrayed the fact that she had just been grabbing random items. She dropped it on Lisa's desk.

"I got, uh, the wrong thing at the drugstore. Would you use this color?"

"Awesome. Love purple and the whole Tish and Snooky's Manic Panic brand. I wear 'Coffin Dust' when I go out."

The phone rang. "Trinity Church." She listened and then began to giggle hysterically.

"Oh, I'm sorry. I'll get her. It's … I'm so sorry. Something here in the office." She put the phone on hold and looked up at Wanda, eyes damp. "It's Luke Fairchild, and I was just talking about coffin dust. Get it?"

Wanda's stomach clenched. She went back into her office to take the call. Her last contact with Luke had been borderline mortifying.

Deep breath. "Luke?"

"Hi, Wanda." His voice was a little chilly, but at least he didn't call her Reverend Duff.

"Look, I want to apologize again for the other night. I didn't mean anything by it, really."

"It's okay, Wanda. It just bothered me that it hadn't even crossed my mind to question the death. And I was wired. And tired." He paused. Her stomach flip-flopped again, and she silently cursed all that broccoli in the wrap. "But really, you shouldn't throw comments around like that. It's upsetting to people, and my life is made a lot easier when the grief-stricken are kept calm."

"I understand. I don't want anything to hurt our relationship—our professional relationship—"

"I'm fine. However, you've obviously been asking questions of other people too." He paused. "As a friend, Wanda, I have to tell you it's not a good idea."

"But I haven't…"

"Wanda, you have. You must have. And unfortunately I have the unpleasant job of telling you that the family doesn't want you to officiate at the funeral."

"What?" His words felt like a physical blow.

"I'm sorry, Wanda. I know it's inappropriate and awkward. Bellona Pond called and said she would like to have the service at the church with another minister, but that she would take the service to the funeral home if you tried to block it."

"Who…does she have in mind? Is there a relative who is clergy?" This happened—this would not be a complete insult. She could be good with this. Generous. She could open and close the service.

"No. Either the Methodist pastor, Lana Grenier, or Rolf Andersen from the Lutheran Church, or…"

"Basically, anyone but me?"

"Yes."

Wanda felt hollow inside. She had been secretly judgmental of clergy colleagues who were upset by some parishioner's request for a former pastor to celebrate a family wedding or officiate at a funeral. She had always thought that clinging to that kind of prerogative was narrow-minded. She had never experienced how devastatingly hurtful it was to be set aside in one's own sanctuary as if she were the wrong color of flowers.

But Luke was still talking. "You understand that I…remonstrated…with her."

He meant that he'd stuck his neck out. His dad would be furious.

"Luke, thank you, really, but it is their loss. I can be a grown-up about it."

He chuckled. "After you kick the wastebasket and use a few nonministerial expressions?"

That sounded like the Luke she knew. In the midst of being very upset, it was a ray of light. He was defending her.

"Did I mention it was their loss?"

He laughed out loud. "God, I mean, gosh, I'm glad you're taking it so well. I've had to have this conversation with other clergy, and they're generally furious."

"I bet they are. It's not a nice feeling, but on the one hand, people come a little unhinged in grief, and, on the other…" She trailed off. *On the other hand, it sucked,* she thought.

"I had an idea. Ed Macklin…?"

"Ed. Yes, Ed would be so sweet. Let's ask Ed to take the service." Ed Macklin was a retired pastor who attended Trinity regularly, and who was gentle, friendly, and definitely not threatening. She could help Ed put things together. At least he belonged to Trinity.

"Um, Wanda. I think the best way to get Ed to agree would be to suggest that you have to go away for the weekend. Some family emergency. I can ask him."

She was quiet. He waited.

"Wanda…"

"They don't want me there at all, do they? It's not just leading the service. They don't even want me to sit in the pew?"

"Uh, no. But, really…it's probably…best. If you were there but not taking the service, there would be a lot more gossiping…from other parishioners, you know?"

"Was that you trying to save my reputation, Luke?"

He was quiet. She waited.

"No. Not you," she said as she realized it. "*They* want to throw me out of my own church." Her fingernails dug into her palms. She blinked back tears and cleared her throat. "I wonder what imaginary relative I can dream up."

"Wanda, I really am sorry. Let's have dinner and talk."

"You just bought me dinner." His walking out still hurt. She needed to brood over this. And, yes, kicking the wastebasket might feel really good.

"Wanda?"

He wasn't off the line yet.

"I'll have Tony talk to Ed about the music, and Lisa will do the bulletin."

"Oh, good. No, I was just going to ask you one thing."

"Yeah?"

"You said that, on the one hand, people can be thoughtless when they're grieving, and don't I know it firsthand? I was just wondering what the 'other hand' was?"

She paused, unsure about whether she wanted to share her suspicions. What did she have to lose at this point? And this was Luke. She trusted him. "On the other hand, this kind of reaction to a few gentle questions leads me to wonder whether I'm very much on target. Something's wrong here, Luke."

19

Something's wrong here. She had said it to Luke, out loud. Nearly as much to Lisa. And she had talked to Lara and to Sonja this morning. All of that was too recent to have played into Bellona Pond's decision.

Lara could have called Bellona while Wanda was eating lunch, but she'd seemed to be honest in her "warning." Anything that she had said before that time had been roundabout and vague. Not confrontational at all. Where had this come from—this accusation that Wanda was nosy, that she was asking too many questions? Zoe's call, obviously, but the family response seemed way out of proportion unless it came from a guilty conscience. How much did Bellona Pond want to be free of her slowly disintegrating and inconvenient husband? Enough to act? Enough to convince herself that Niels wanted a way out? Why else would she be so sensitive?

But, of course, Wanda had shared her suspicions with Rye. Was that where this came from? Maybe Rye had also said something about Wanda's concerns. It was a small town. If so, Rye had gotten Wanda kicked out of both her pulpit and the insider view of the family in one blow.

Wanda took the turn onto the long Fair Havens drive. She had clearly started touching nerves in the facility; the call placed to Bellona proved that. But there must be something else—some reason for the aggression that seemed to be hindering her at every turn.

She had to shake it off. Wanda had the right to be here. She was making pastoral visits. It was what she did.

Earlier, she'd said a prayer with John and his sweet partner, Geoff, in a sunshiny room in the hospital already brightened by several bouquets from happy dog owners who had been training, boarding, and grooming with them for years. The bouquets had paw prints on the tags and came from canine names that had confused the volunteer who carried them upstairs. Wanda felt better just for being with John and Geoff, even in a hospital room. They had the kind of trainer personality that made even humans want to wag a tail.

Wanda was glad to bring a bit of that here.

She clicked her locks, then froze when she saw a blue-gray Hyundai Accent with Massachusetts plate. It was in the parking row behind hers. She was sure it had been the car outside the drugstore. She wondered how she could find out whose car it was. She had no reason to walk past it, but certainly she could make one up. She started to stroll casually in that direction when the door behind her opened. She could hear voices. Instinct sent her scurrying behind a bush. She definitely did not want to be found leaning on a car, snooping for identifying marks in the front seat.

That was when she recognized Lara Alesci's voice. Wanda became even thinner behind the bush—so much for the pantyhose, and please let it only be people with dementia staring out the facility's windows. She couldn't tell what Lara was saying, but she was pretty sure she was talking to Bellona Pond. What business would they have here now? She risked a peek. They were walking past the Hyundai. Good. They went on to a black Subaru Forester and got in.

That was enough of a brush with discovery, or bush with discovery. Wanda headed straight for the door, not in her role as detective but as a completely transparent clergyperson. She turned right into the memory loss unit and walked down the long hall past Joe's door without even glancing in.

Jackie from housekeeping was rolling her cart of linens and gave a cheerful grin. "Jenny's got a new joke!"

"I could use a laugh," Wanda responded, and realized it was true.

She found Jenny sitting in a circle of chairs. They were doing a bouncing ball exercise. Some residents were paying attention, while others were dozing. Jenny was a favorite of all the staff, and she seemed to be getting the ball frequently. She saw Wanda and sent what passed in this context as a "dunk" to Bill Evans, unfolded her walker, and left the game circle with a cheery, "I'll be back."

"Wanda!" They hugged and headed with long familiarity to the pink parlor. Once Jenny settled into her favorite maroon, straight-backed, firm chair ("so I can get out of it"), she beamed at her visitor. "I've got a new joke."

"Norwegian?"

"What other kind is there? Okay, here goes. A customer asked the bartender if he wanted to hear a Norwegian joke. The bartender pointed to a six-foot-tall, red-bearded blond at the end of the bar and said, 'He's Norwegian.' Then the bartender pointed to a burly 'Politiførsteinspectør'—that's 'police sergeant' to you—near the door and said, 'She's Norwegian.' The bartender hoisted a case of Hansa onto the back shelf and leaned her considerable forearms on the wet bar. 'Now think about whether you want to tell that joke because I'm Norwegian, too.' The customer replied, 'I guess I won't tell it after all. I'd have to explain it three times.'"

Wanda groaned. "So what's Hansa to me?"

Jenny laughed and curled her fingers around an imaginary brew and chugged it. "Beer!"

It was a wonderful thing to see Jenny laugh. It was like the sun came out. Wanda wondered if she was related to John Caroti. No. Opposite ends of the European continent. They were related as people who looked at the world and instinctively saw the joy in it. They were friend-makers.

Jenny Fjelstad had the prettiest white hair ever, thick and flyaway and long enough to pull back at the nape of her neck. She loved gifts of fancy hair clasps and had them from countries all over the world in wood and metal and bamboo and leather. She didn't wear any other adornments. It was her thing. Well, there was the holiday jewelry—wreaths, hearts, shamrocks, bunnies, flags, and pumpkins—that she won at bingo. There had never been a wedding ring. Jenny laughed and called her back view her best, and that was why she always had her hair done. Wanda thought her smile was the best view, but she also knew that the purple birthmark from Jenny's left eyebrow to her neck had undoubtedly been a source of unhappiness when she was younger. Parkinson's disease quivered in hand and leg and voice but did not yet impair her cognitive abilities. In fact, she was sharper than the average chainsaw.

Wanda struggled to think of a new joke for her. There had been too much upset today.

"So what's wrong?" was Jenny's opening gambit.

"Noth— Well, yep. Not my number-one day."

"Tell Auntie Jenny. Unless it has something to do with your love life. Not an expert on romance, though you could give it a try. Lifetime in a department store gives me a broad background in peculiar human behaviors."

"I actually came here to pump you for information. But it has to be confidential."

"Like anyone I talk to would remember?"

"Yeah. Well."

"Not a word to anyone, I promise," Jenny said. "Actually, having a secret is pretty rare in a place where you can't even take your own bath."

Wanda could hear an edge in Jenny today, and it made her think that she might need to spend some more time finding out what was bothering her. But this was the window for her mission.

"I've found myself wondering about Niels Pond's death. A friend and I have asked a few questions about it, and the response was…dramatic. Then, I was here a couple days ago chatting with Joe about drug cartels—if you'll believe it—and the staff practically tossed me out. Today, I got a call from the funeral director telling me that the Ponds didn't want me to do the service because I was being too 'nosy.' It seems really strange."

Jenny was quiet. "What staff? Not Andy?"

"No, not Andy. Zoe and Harris actually."

"Ah. You know Joe's memory is not as far gone as he pretends it is."

"What?"

"His dementia and his recognition of reality come and go, and he notices more than many other residents."

"Not as much as you."

"No one, if I may say so myself, is as cognitively clever as I am…but I don't fool myself that it's something I've done. I'm lucky, that's all. And someday I won't be so lucky. This disease isn't always going to be tremors or having trouble blinking. I will be as gaga as anyone here." She studied Wanda's face for a moment before continuing. "No, what I mean is…drugs. There is something happening with drugs here that isn't quite right, and Joe senses it. Do you know Joe's former profession?"

"Carpenter, right? I think I saw it on his resident's form. He has the hands for it."

"You did see it, but it's not true. He was a psychiatrist. But he was embarrassed to be a psychiatrist with dementia, so he filled out his own forms with 'carpenter.' It was his hobby, but you would not want him to frame your house. Stick with a garden bench."

"Oh."

"Does a profession change how you see people?"

"No. Yes. It changes how he might perceive things when he was perceiving something about psychiatric drugs." Wanda tried to think back, but she hadn't really been paying attention to what Joe was saying aside from as an opening to her questions about Niels Pond. "So, what is happening?"

"I don't know. And I don't think Joe does either. I do know that some of the staff are sloppy with what they say in front of residents. They talk about their love lives, criticism of administration, you know." She nodded thoughtfully. "But when I'm around, conversations are dropped like a hot potato. The one thing I can say is that when people die, medications are supposed to be disposed of—as in thrown away—but I'm fairly sure they 'disappear.'"

"Like to a criminal syndicate?"

"No. More like going to a...a poor country."

Wanda paused and thought about the staff. "Ah. I can think of a poor country."

"Let's not talk about this."

"Okay. But Niels. What do you think about him?"

"People die. People who live here that I don't expect to die do, and people I expect to die any moment linger for years. We all take death as a given. Nobody says anything to us, but there is a white rose on the nurses' station, and someone is gone at breakfast. One of my friends had a farewell party when she knew she was going to move to a Medicaid facility because she didn't want folks to assume that she'd died." Jenny laughed, but it was a sad sound. "There are a few things I know. People who give up die sooner. People who laugh live longer. Niels didn't laugh, but...well, I don't know. He was too angry to give up."

"You don't think anyone would have helped him?"

"Murdered him?"

There it was. Out. Leave it to Jenny.

"I'm sorry, Jenny. It was wrong to ask you." And it was. Once it was out in the air, Wanda knew it. This woman, this friend of hers with tremors and frailty. Now she would be frightened of the place where she lived. Stupid, stupid, stupid.

On the contrary, Jenny's eyes were sparkling. Oh, no.

"Like a mystery? Like *Murder She Wrote*? Who do you suspect? The wife? Bit cold, that one. The lover? The sons? A distant relative looking for an inheritance? Ooooh, this is exciting."

"It is not exciting! It's not exciting at all! I am so sorry I ever mentioned it. Don't you do or say anything at all."

"Oh, come on. I can be your eyes on the ground. That's wrong, but I don't have boots. Your assistant detective. Your...Watson. You have no idea how boring life is here. I can..." The older woman looked like a cat with a bowl of Nova Scotia lox left on the coffee table. Forget cream!

"No, Jenny, no, no, no. You didn't hear this. I really didn't mean it. Absolutely do not do anything...*at all*!"

Jenny looked calmer, more quiet. "I guess you really do suspect something, don't you? Otherwise you wouldn't be so worried about me."

Caught. Too astute, this one, and a good actress. "I guess I do, and I would not forgive myself if anything happened to you."

"I know, dear. And I am too tippy and trembly for any sort of stealth, so don't worry about my being inquisitive. But if I hear something—"

"Yes?"

She pulled a cell phone out of the bag on the front of her walker. "I'll text you. It will be the wiggle-finger text where absolutely nothing makes sense."

Wanda laughed, and they chatted, and then Jenny went back to her room to get ready for dinner. Wanda sat a little longer and wondered whether she should try to see Joe. The drug thing was completely different. If she were a real detective, she would follow up on it. As it was, she was already in too deep. It was getting dark in the pink parlor as rain clouds started to make the May sky overcast.

Wanda had plenty to think about as she retraced her steps—waving to Andy (genuinely) and to Zoe (with her clergy game face on). She plugged in the code for visitors and made her way across the parking lot. The

Hyundai was still there. Staff member? Waiting for her to leave, to follow her?

The seat was nicely warm, and she sighed, put on her seat belt, and thought about her audiobook—a J. D. Robb thriller. Maybe not.

She reached over the back of the passenger seat for the CD cases of music she kept there. Her hands touched an unexpected piece of paper. She brought it out and took a look.

Take your own advice. The font would have made her laugh if she hadn't been so scared. Who used Comic Sans to threaten somebody?

There was someone there beside the car. "Are you all right, Reverend Duff?"

The door was opened. It was N. C. Harris. Rescuing her? Or had he just put something in her car? Still, she was so shaken, she couldn't keep her mouth shut. "Somebody. Somebody was in my car."

He seemed to take her seriously. "Shall I call the police?"

She turned the paper over so he couldn't see it and said slowly, "No. I'm fine. Thanks anyway. It was nothing."

"Are you sure?"

"I think so." He didn't move. Harris had a way of blocking out the light. It didn't instill comfort. "I am. Thank you."

He stared down at her. "Curiosity killed the cat, right?"

Wanda looked at him. She wondered if her internal shaking was visible. She made a huge effort to lighten up—her face, her voice.

"I've been hearing that a lot lately."

20

Rye unrolled her mat with a snap, pulling it as far into the corner as she could. If she angled it just right, she could avoid seeing herself reflected in any awkward yoga poses. While most traditional yoga studios would not have mirrors, the multipurpose room at the gym—shared by all manner of aerobic enthusiasts—was almost completely reflective. Only if she came early enough could she claim the single spot of invisibility.

She was halfheartedly stretching into downward dog when another well-worn mat unrolled beside her. She glanced over to see Wanda dropping her bag of props by the wall before settling in.

"Hey," she murmured. Although class hadn't started yet, the room was always eerily quiet beforehand. She had been coming here for almost a year now, and she still didn't know anyone's name. She really didn't need to know that she was taking yoga with a student's parent. Mostly mothers. Wanda herself had been a stranger until Niels Pond's death had led to reconnecting the New Year's Eve party dots.

Wanda grasped an elbow in each hand as she stretched into forward fold. "How's it going?"

Rye tried to sink into her heels and open her heart to the floor, as their instructor was always reminding them to do. She gritted her teeth against the pull in her hamstrings and bent her knees deeper to get some relief. "Oh, I think I'm down the rabbit hole."

"Really?" Wanda looked intrigued.

"Oh, yeah. Did you know Ro Pond's adopted?"

"I'd heard that, yes."

"Well"—Rye shifted forward and pushed herself from high plank into cobra to stretch her lower back—"apparently, his birth mother came back into the picture a year ago."

"Is that a good thing?" Wanda asked.

"For Ro, yes. Wil seemed…distraught when it came up. Angry, even. Apparently, he thinks this is just about the worst time for his brother to have…how did he put it? Another life? Or family? Something dramatic like that."

Wanda came up slowly, reaching her arms toward the ceiling. "Any idea how the rest of the family feels about it?"

"Well, Bellona has her own drama to deal with because of the whole Lara thing. Which is not so secret. My friend Andy—the one who works at Fair Havens? He told me that their involvement was completely out in the open."

Benita, the slim British woman who led all three yoga classes at the gym, chose that moment to turn up the music and begin class.

"So, she's not concerned about appearances." Wanda did an impersonation of a ventriloquist without a dummy. The man in front of her turned around and shot her a dirty look, but she just smiled innocently at him.

"No evidence to speak of that she and Niels weren't happily married, though, either."

"Except for his untimely death."

"Well, yes," Rye conceded. "Except for that."

"Ladies," Benita admonished in her soft voice, "less chatting, more asana please."

Rye grimaced and forced herself to take a few deep breaths, settling her tailbone into the floor. She couldn't help but picture the Ponds and Lara engaging in the threesome Andy had mentioned, and a snort escaped her. Imagining Bellona in anything but crisp slacks seemed impossible. She opened her eyes in time to catch the warning glare from her teacher and the questioning glance from Wanda.

Bellona Pond probably wasn't the most frigid woman Rye had ever encountered, but she definitely made the top five. Trying to imagine her with a single hair out of place or her lipstick smeared after a passionate kiss was an impossibility. It was like trying to imagine a robot in the throes of passion. If the children were a standard to judge by, Niels hadn't been much different. The whole family, aside from Lara, seemed to hold themselves rigidly together. Even the blue streak in Leslie's limp blond hair seemed less 'rocker chick' and more 'clip-on Barbie.'

As Benita gently guided them from the floor into their first sets of sun salutations, Wanda, timing her comment with the loudest thuds of feet against the floor, hissed at Rye, "I've dug up some stuff." She paused as Benita came through correcting form, tilting a pelvis up here and a bum down there. "And you know N. C. Harris?

The nurse?" Rye nodded. "I've had some weird run-ins with him, too."

"I think"—Rye paused to catch her breath as she swung her foot forward into a lunge—"I think he's the one sending me obscene texts."

"What?!" Wanda's response was louder than intended, and the two women were shot several dirty looks.

"Ladies!" Benita scolded. "Focus! This is not happy hour."

"Ooh," Rye murmured under her breath. "That sounds good."

"Locals tomorrow? Five o'clock?"

"Sounds good," Rye grunted, clenching her glutes and abs as instructed as she pulled up into a half moon lunge. "Wings are half-price till six."

"Oh, I know," Wanda murmured. Benita came to stand directly between them.

Rye was reminded of her days as a classroom teacher. She had employed this exact technique many a time to squelch chatterboxes who wouldn't take a hint. The urge to giggle threatened to overwhelm her again, and she instead focused on breathing deeply through her nose. She forced herself to look away every time Wanda tried to catch her eye. The woman was becoming a menace to her concentration.

After a few minutes, she managed to distract herself with the well-toned legs displayed in the row ahead of her. It was probably the exact same thing her own students did after she blissfully assumed they'd taken her scolding to heart and buckled down to focus on evaluating *Macbeth*.

If she and Wanda kept up this sleuthing, Rye had a feeling she was going to have to reevaluate the techniques she'd thought were working with kids. Nothing like bending a few rules to make her feel sixteen again.

21

WHEN RYE PULLED UP IN FRONT OF THE SOUCEK HOUSE after yoga, it was just as she remembered it. Andy's grandmother kept the garden in full bloom from May to October, barring unexpected freezes, and sure enough, even though the woman must be in her nineties by now, the front yard was awash in color. The old porch swing Andy had built with his Scout friends still swung in the breeze. She could hear it creak from where she sat in the car, windows down.

There was a girl, maybe ten years old, sitting under a tree staring at Rye. She'd been in Andy's old tree house when Rye arrived but had climbed down and taken up her post as soon as Rye sent a text to let Andy know she had arrived.

Come on in. His text. *My grandma wants to say hello.*

Of course she did. Rye sighed. Andy's grandmother appeared as sweet as the pies she cooked every year for the county fair, but underneath the white apron she was a tough cookie. Rye had actually always liked that about her until senior year, when Mrs. Soucek caught them sneaking beer into the tree house.

Looking back, Rye completely understood what had at the time seemed like a disproportionate response to the minor offense of sampling cans of Miller Lite pilfered from a friend's fridge. Andy's mother had committed suicide when Andy was only six. She'd died of a pill overdose, and her young son had been the one to find her unresponsive and sprawled out in the tub. His grandmother had immediately invited Andy and his father to move in with her, a decision that had saved Andy further upheaval when his father died a few years later of prostate cancer.

The woman might outwardly seem like time-lapsed poster wife straight out of *Leave It to Beaver*, but she was iron through and through. She had unflinchingly dealt with the hardships life had chosen to throw at her without making Andy feel like unwanted trouble. As much as Rye respected that and hoped one day to be even half as tough, she'd never gotten over the look of disappointment she'd seen on Mrs. Soucek's face when she'd caught them. It was as though Rye had taken a sacred trust and defiled it. She and Andy had only seen each other at school for the rest of that year, and then Rye had fled this town without looking back.

She hadn't seen the family since she came back to town. Slowly, she unbuckled and forced herself out of the car. She straightened her blouse and brushed a few pieces of lint off her jeans before heading up to the front door. The girl stared at Rye as she walked by, and Rye returned the look without a word. When she reached the porch, she took a steadying breath before knocking firmly on the wooden screen door.

"Come in," Andy said, startling her as he appeared out of the gloom.

She pulled open the door and followed him down the hall into the side porch off the living room. Mrs. Soucek wore a floral dress and gardening gloves and had her arms deep into a potted plant. She seemed to be resettling it into a larger container, if the bags of dirt all around her were any indication. She finished her project before looking up, then accepted her grandson's arm as she slowly got to her feet.

"Prudence," she said with a stately nod appropriate for a dowager.

"Mrs. Soucek," Rye said. "It's a pleasure to see you again." The older woman just stared at her. There was no doubt in Rye's mind that this woman was absorbing every detail of a decade. "The garden looks beautiful."

"The credit is Andrew's," Mrs. Soucek said with a wave of her hand. "My knees aren't good enough for big projects like that now, and he has a better eye for color than I ever did."

"He had a great teacher."

Mrs. Soucek gave her another penetrating look and sniffed. She turned her back and made her way out the door and into the kitchen. Clearly, Rye was dismissed.

Andy smiled. "Isn't she in great shape? I can't believe we're going to be throwing her ninety-fifth birthday party this summer."

"She certainly is," Rye said, her voice carefully neutral. That woman had a mind like a steel trap, and Rye had absolutely no doubt that, frail as she might look, she remembered that the last time Prudence Rye had been inside her house was with a police escort. The sheriff also had not been amused. "You ready to go?"

"I'll just let Rachel know I'm leaving," Andy said, leading the way back out to the porch. He waved to the dark-haired girl, and she came running up to him, her expression still sharp when she looked over at Rye. Definitely a Soucek. "I'm going out for an hour or two with my friend. When I get home, we'll finish watching *The Empire Strikes Back*, okay?"

"Yeah, I guess," she muttered. She couldn't keep the pout in place, though, when Andy grabbed her in a bear hug and swung her around until she could barely stand straight.

"Don't forget to finish those math problems either. Otherwise, we won't have time," he warned as he dropped a kiss on her head and extended a hand to usher Rye off the porch.

"Make good choices," the girl called, her voice eerily like that of the old woman inside. What kind of kid even said that—*Make good choices?*

Andy smiled. "I thought we could walk down to Minchin's and get an ice cream. They just opened for the season last week."

"My dad and I went opening night. Used to be our start-of-summer tradition." Rye put a hand up to shade her eyes from the sun as she watched a car pass. "Oh, no."

"What's up?"

Rye did her best to hide her face, but the kid across the street saw her first and fled. "I know him. He's one of the regulars I inherited when I became an unexpected guidance counselor. I didn't realize he lived in this neighborhood."

Andy watched him, his eyes narrowed. "He doesn't, but I've seen him around before." He gestured to the park they were passing. "He—well, he and a lot of your students, I expect—comes here to pick up weed and God knows what else."

"Are the same guys we used to see still selling around here? They seemed ancient when we were seventeen."

Andy's face was grim. "No, this is a new crew. Rachel's dad actually got caught up with them a while ago." His tone had taken on a note Rye couldn't recall ever hearing from him. "In fact, I see him now." He pointed to a beat-up green Corolla that was cruising down the street. The driver must have seen him, because he revved his engine and sped off. "He knows he's not supposed to be anywhere near her, but he'll do anything to move product."

"So Rachel's not your daughter, then?"

"What?" Andy stopped to stare at her. "No."

Rye was a fast walker, but with Andy's longer stride he caught up with her easily as they turned the corner to head down to the covered bridge, a place they'd spent many hours exploring in the past. "Okay."

"That's it? No follow-up questions?" he asked, as they took the riverview sidewalk. "I bet you just spent the last ten minutes trying to figure out whether I was married, divorced, widowed, and with whom."

"Oh, I have a few thoughts, but you don't seem like you're in the most receptive mood anymore."

"She's my niece."

Rye shook her head. "You don't have any siblings." She slid her hand over the railing of the bridge. The water below flowed low over the rocks. It didn't seem so long ago that they'd played down there, barefoot and silly.

"It's easier to call her that than 'second cousin once removed.' She's family. Her parents were going through a nasty split, and she was starting to act out. Bad grades, detention. Nana and I talked about it, and we decided to offer a little assistance while the worst of her parents' situation gets worked out."

"That was decent of you. I know that taking on a troubled kid—even a family member—is a lot. How long has she been staying with you?"

"Almost a year now. She'll hang out through the summer, but after that…who knows? Maybe her mom will come get her." He didn't sound hopeful. "Obviously her dad shouldn't have anything to do with her, but he loves to complicate custody without wanting to spend any time with her." Andy sighed. "She's done better here. And she was a huge help with the garden. Despite what my grandmother says, it's really only been the last year or two that she's struggled with serious joint issues. I tried to do it all myself last spring, and it was too much. I don't know how she did it all those years. Having Rachel made such a difference in how much we were able to plant."

"You really are a good guy," Rye said.

"And yet you manage to make that sound insulting."

"Oh, it's a compliment. I just— I think I forgot how, I don't know, pure you are."

"Pure? Really?" Andy laughed, but it was forced.

"Well, yeah. You must know you aren't exactly like most thirty-year-old guys."

"I don't think that's true," Andy said.

"Really? So you know a lot of other men who garden, bake, and help a ten-year-old 'niece' with homework while holding down a full-time job and caring for an elderly relative?"

"Don't forget that I'm an RN, a profession that by some accounts is only done properly by a woman." His tone was mild, but Rye suspected this wasn't the first time someone had accused him of being too effeminate for his own good.

"I didn't mean it as a bad thing," Rye said. "It's just…different. Refreshing."

"You can't make me feel bad about being a nurturing person. Spoiler alert, Rye. This is what I'm good at, and I like who I am. It doesn't bother me to help older people, who, by the way, may feel a lot of shame at having lost the ability to do things for themselves, like getting in and out of the tub. I change their diapers. I wipe food off their faces and organize craft projects simple enough for them to participate in. I also love getting dirty in the garden. I enjoy making cookies and sending them in with Rachel to sell at her school bake sale. It doesn't make me less of a man."

"I didn't say it does," Rye said. "You're a good guy."

"It has nothing to do with being good!" He rubbed his arms in frustration. "Your friend Mike is a good guy, right? I met him a couple of months ago, and all he talked about was the stats of the high school soccer teams. He drank too much and then called a Lyft and went home with some girl he'd just met. Still a good guy though, right?"

"The best," Rye said.

"Well, then, maybe you can stop putting me on a pedestal or whatever it is you're doing. I'm not fragile just because I happily live with my grandmother."

"Andy, I live with my dad! I'm in no position to judge anyone else's life choices."

"And yet you do."

It was a slap in the face, well-aimed, and, she knew, well-deserved. She was judgmental—of him, of this town, of people who could be satisfied by simple things. It still hurt to hear him say it, though.

"If your dad hadn't been in such tough shape last winter, you'd still be in Austin," he said. "I would just be some guy you left behind when this town didn't fit you anymore, so forgive me if your opinions about my life don't hold much water."

Rye was silent. He was right. "It was never part of my plan to come back and get caught up in this place again."

"But you did. So at least do those of us who stayed a favor and see us for the people we've become—not the ones you left."

Her phone buzzed. It seemed to never stop these days. She didn't even bother to pull it out, but Andy paused. "Don't you want to check that? It could be important."

She was beginning to realize that in his life, a text might be a little more life-or-death than it was for her. "It's not."

"What if it's your dad?"

"My dad doesn't know how to text."

"My grandmother knows how to text."

"Well, your grandmother has always been a more forward thinker than my father." It buzzed again, and Andy folded his arms across his chest and frowned at her until she pulled it out. Sure enough, it was another text she would try not to think about as she was falling asleep at night. "Not important," she said, turning off the screen before he could catch a glimpse.

"Are you still getting those messages?" His posture tightened, heavy eyebrows drawn down in anger. She didn't even see his hand snake out to grab the phone—he was that fast. Rye had forgotten he was also into martial arts. He looked angry as he read what she'd already seen.

"It's nothing. I think I'm just going to change my number. I mean, the text is from a burner phone, so there isn't really anything else I can do."

"And you still think this is a kid?"

"Well, actually, I am starting to think it's from that guy you work with, what's his name? The blond mountain?"

"Harris?"

"I think he got my number and decided to harass me because I wouldn't go out with him. It's happened before. I mean, not to this degree, but guys get it in their heads that if they want you, they should have you. This is a pretty common reaction to rejection, in my experience."

"He would never do that."

"Really? Because he's threatened my friend Wanda twice now. And me once—that first day I saw you at Fair Havens, he followed me to the parking lot."

"I know he comes across as awkward, but he's just not great with people."

Rye's fists clenched around the rail. "Andy, he threatens women. That's pretty much my definition of a bad guy."

"How would he even have gotten your number?" Andy asked.

"I don't know. Maybe you left your phone out on the front desk or something?"

"So this is my fault?" He held her phone out with two fingers. She took it just as gingerly.

"No! I'm just saying, he's sneaky. He's aggressive, and if he'd wanted to get my information, he might have had the opportunity."

"From me." Andy's face was bright red. It reminded Rye of how he'd looked in elementary school when he'd been bullied, a little like a teakettle about to boil over.

"I don't know! I don't even really care! I just want them to stop."

"I get that, I really do, and I don't want someone sending you lewd messages. If I had some hand in that happening…"

He looked so distressed that Rye wanted to take back her accusation. All the signs pointed to a person with more planning and ready cash than any of her students. With Harris harassing Wanda, who seemed a bit old for this kind of lechery, the Niels Pond investigation seemed like a possible reason to try to intimidate her.

"Maybe it wasn't him, but he's the only person in the last few weeks I've had an ugly encounter with. From where I'm standing, that's suggestive."

Andy sighed. "You know, Rye, I really missed you. I realized that when I saw you at Fair Havens. But I think I remembered our friendship without all the drama that came with it." He leaned back against the wooden bridge rails and dug his hands deep into his pockets.

"Drama? What drama? I didn't do anything!"

"I'm not eighteen. I can't go off on wild goose chases with you. I know you're, well, you're you. You can't help yourself sometimes, but I'm not sure I can afford to get drawn into this. I have two people at home who are counting on me, and if I start accusing the people I work with of being stalkers—"

"I'm not asking you to do that."

"I know, but it's easy to get sucked into your schemes."

"My schemes? Really?"

"Yes! Schemes! You can't just…live. You constantly have to be on some quest, some adventure." Andy shrugged. "That's not me. I'm more of a ship in the harbor." He turned and started to head away from ice cream, from the not-a-date date she'd been stupid enough to want.

"Where are you going?" Rye was annoyed to hear the slight break in her voice.

"Home. I'm going to watch *Star Wars* and eat gummy worms. Tomorrow, I'm going to get up and go to work and try not to throw a wrench into my career." He shook his head. "I'll see you, Rye."

She lifted her hand up and gave a limp wave, but he didn't turn around. It was stupid to be upset. Rye had never planned to get involved with him again. Even when she'd taken a job that meant she'd be around town for a while, she hadn't thought it through. Not this. She'd spent too many years in anonymous cities ignoring and being ignored by her neighbors. She'd forgotten the worst part of living in small towns—the past was beautiful and angry and waiting for her on every corner.

22

RYE STOOD ON HER TIPTOES BY THE HOSTESS STAND, wondering whether she needed to wait behind the ridiculous line of students who had decided Locals' happy hour wings were a necessity. Maybe Wanda had arrived early enough to score them a table. After a minute, a gray-clad arm shot up and started waving frantically, and Rye followed it to a two-seater high-top pushed into the corner by the restrooms.

"Scoped out a pretty sweet spot here," Rye said with a grin as the door to the men's room swung open behind her.

"You joke, but this was the last table." Wanda glanced over at the door, where the crowd had basically overtaken the entryway. "And judging by the hordes, we would be waiting until well past happy hour if I'd gotten here a minute later."

Rye grabbed a menu and gave it a quick glance so she would be ready when the harried waitstaff made it over to them. "I haven't been here on a Thursday in ages. I didn't realize it was such a hot spot."

"Two baskets of wings for the price of one. Pretty compelling offer."

"Apparently so. You want to share? We could get two sauces?"

"Only if I get the drumettes," Wanda said. "I only eat the drumettes."

"We're a match made in heaven, then," Rye said, "because I prefer the flats. Well, the thighettes. You know what I mean."

"I do."

"Spicy?"

"Please." Wanda glanced up as the waitress stopped at their table. "One basket of hot, and one of..." She glanced at Rye.

"Parmesan garlic?"

"Sounds great."

"Can I also get a Blue Moon?" Rye closed her menu and handed it over.

"The liter is only four bucks till six," the young woman told her.

"Sounds like it was meant to be, then, doesn't it?" Rye said with a wink. The waitress blushed and nodded, making a note on her pad.

"Could we get both ranch and blue cheese with that?" Wanda added. "It's been a tough week, and we have some heavy dipping to do."

"That's an understatement," Rye muttered, idly watching the waitress hurry to the next table. "If I get into the classroom again, I can teach a semester on inserting foot in mouth." She sighed, glancing longingly at a tray of beers that passed. "That, of course, is if I manage not to get fired before the end of the year."

"That bad?" Wanda asked.

"Mendoza's on the warpath. Apparently, Bellona Pond has quite a few friends on the school board, and I have not been helping my own case by poking around about her husband." Rye gratefully accepted the water the busboy brought. "I don't even know how she hears about these things. I mean, sure, I've asked a few questions, but it's not like I'm leading a one—well, two—woman parade around town demanding answers."

"Yeah, that's apparently my job," Wanda said. "Except that, in my case, I wouldn't be surprised of some of my parishioners got in their heads to bring back public humiliation in the stocks."

"Better than being burned as a witch, I guess."

"We're not far enough from Salem for that to be funny," Wanda growled. "I swear some of the folks in my pews every Sunday are old enough to have been there for a few bonfires. And miss it."

"Do you think if they decide to throw you into a pond you should pretend you can't swim?"

"Well, I can hold my breath for nearly four minutes, so if you cause a ruckus, I might be able to make a clean getaway."

"So we just out Bellona and Lara and see if any of your parishioners' heads explode?" Rye said.

"What's Plan B?" Wanda asked. "Because I'll give them one thing—my congregation would start planning a shower if they heard about a wedding."

"Really?" Rye looked at her curiously. "There are churches that do that? Welcome LGBT couples? Like, in our town?"

"Of course."

"Hmm. Well that's good to know. If I ever get an itch to start wasting my Sundays in a pew, at least I'll know where to go."

She scooted back a bit as a young man deposited food in front of them. The peaceful silence that descended lasted long enough for Rye to remember that she hadn't taken Wanda to task yet about withholding information from her. "I can't believe you didn't tell me about Sonja Mari coming to visit you."

"I'm sorry," Wanda said, studying the wing in front of her as though planning a forward attack. "It seemed unrelated somehow."

"You're new to this whole detective thing, huh?"

"Like you aren't?"

"Do you remember high school? I work in one. I swear three-quarters of my time is spent unraveling a mystery," Rye said.

"Usually there's not a dead body involved," Wanda pointed out.

"Usually, no." Rye put her wing down and wiped her fingers clean. "But sometimes yes."

Wanda glanced up. Something about Rye's tone made her sound older, more tired than her years. "Suicides?" She'd had more than her fair share of funerals for teens, and she could practically scent that kind of sadness coming off the other woman.

Rye nodded. "Rampant back at Westview. Boarding students especially, but even the local kids. They'd go out at night, sneak onto the train tracks. No note. Nothing." She sighed. "Drug deaths, too, of course. Drunk driving. But those seem less mysterious to me, you know? They're poor coping mechanisms but not necessarily death sentences."

"I know," Wanda said.

"I think that's part of the reason I can't let go of this thing with the Ponds. I mean, I know the police aren't really looking into it, just like they never looked into those kids' suicides. Because why would you? It's straightforward."

"Except when it's not."

"Yeah."

They ate in silence for a few minutes, swirling ranch and blue cheese to mute the spicier sauces. When they got down to the carrots and celery, Wanda finally spoke. "I don't know if anything will come of this. Of us doing whatever it is we're doing."

"Besides possibly losing our jobs."

"Yup." Wanda tore open a wet wipe packet. "Are we sure it's worth it?"

"Honestly?" Rye asked. "I'm not sure of anything right now. Andy is pissed at me because I sort of accused him of letting my number slip to that creepy nurse. My dad's gone off because, well, apparently I'm still seventeen, and he has his finger on the pulse of every damn thing that goes wrong for me in this town. Plus, I don't really like his new girlfriend."

"You didn't tell him that, did you?"

"No! Of course not!" Rye swirled the remnants of her beer around the bottom of the glass. "But you may have figured out I'm not great at the whole subtlety thing."

"Well, if it makes you feel any better, I've managed to get on the bad side of not just my entire congregation but also the one guy I actually like who doesn't think it's weird when I make funeral jokes."

"Yeah," Rye said. "In your line of work, dates must be kind of…"

"Awkward? Obnoxious? Few and far between?"

"I was going to say uncomfortable, but yeah. Those things."

"It's worse. You think you're under a microscope? I can't rent an R-rated movie without worrying somebody will check my Netflix queue and judge me. When my friend got divorced and wanted to sneak pints of ice cream into *Magic Mike*, we had to drive forty-five minutes away to avoid even the possibility of my seeing a parishioner."

"You do not strike me as a Channing Tatum fan."

"I'm a minister, not blind. You could spread a tablecloth over that man's abs and eat a four-course meal there. I'm not saying I need his poster hanging over my bed or anything, but it is nice to be able to look every now and then." Wanda said this with a sniff.

"Hallelujah to that." Rye smiled. "So, this guy…"

"Not Channing. Luke."

"You told him about…this? Us?"

"Not exactly."

"What does not exactly mean?"

Wanda sighed. "He's the funeral director, okay? And, like you, I occasionally lack the subtlety to pull off a conversation about a suspicious dead body—a dead body he had already embalmed, therefore making an autopsy impossible…"

"So, no evidence."

"Not from Niels Pond's remains, no. If there were drugs in his system—anything that wasn't supposed to be there—it's gone now."

"Well, that sucks."

"That's basically what I said. And now he hates me."

"He doesn't hate you," Rye said. Wanda's tone reminded her that everyone was an inch away from their younger, more hormone-fueled selves.

Wanda shrugged. "Well, it's not a good place to be in when it feels like everyone else does. You know my friend Tony? He's the organist? We've been friends for years, and even *he* got pissed at me when I said I was going to come to the memorial service."

"Aren't you performing it? Is that what you call it?" Rye asked.

"Officiating. And no, not anymore."

"Really?"

"Yeah. Now I can't even go. Apparently, it's extremely immature of me to even consider showing up."

Rye studied Wanda's face. Even though the woman's tone was cavalier, Rye could tell it was bothering her. She knew exactly how it felt. To be shut out of a professional gig like that—it hurt. And it was the kind of humiliation everyone witnessed. No flying under the radar in a situation like that.

"I'm sorry," she finally said. "That really does suck."

"Thanks."

"I know it doesn't change anything, but if you think it might help our cause, I'll go tomorrow. I can keep an eye on the family and see if anyone's acting weird."

"It's a funeral," Wanda said dully. "Everyone will be acting weird."

Rye flagged down their waitress as she headed to another table. "Excuse me? I think we're going to need one of those brownie sundaes over here just as soon as you get a minute. Extra hot fudge, please, oh, and peppermint ice cream—not vanilla." The young woman smiled and made a little note on her pad before hurrying away.

"I'm full," Wanda protested weakly.

"Don't worry," Rye said. "It's been a crappy week. There's a special extra stomach that emerges for situations like these." She ignored the buzzing in her pocket that signaled what was probably the tenth lewd text she'd gotten since she'd sat down. "Besides, I have a few things to show you, and we're going to need our strength to get through this."

23

THE NEXT AFTERNOON WAS HUMID AND HOT—DOG days in May—and Rye was regretting her outfit choice. Everything chafed. The only funeral-hued clothing she owned was a blouse and skirt combo that now seemed far too revealing for the circumstances. The skirt kept riding up as she walked, so after the service had concluded she'd wedged herself into a corner by the food where she could overhear the family without readjusting her hem every minute or two.

She arranged and rearranged a plate of tiny sandwiches and cookies, trying to look busy. Bellona Pond had spared no expense for this reception, and the food was fabulous. Rye had been to weddings with less impressive fare, and she wasn't about to miss out just because she was technically a gate-crasher.

So far, though, aside from the food, it didn't seem like Wanda was missing much. Family members and friends had probably gotten a lot out of the beautiful tributes in the church—most notably an anthem sung and signed by a deaf choir. Rye had never seen such a thing before, but it had a balletic grace that even she, with her tin eyes, could appreciate. Both of Niels's sons had spoken, and Leslie had signed for them, although another woman had stood up and taken over during the homily and prayers so that Leslie could sit with her family.

Rye had watched the Ponds, and Lara Alesci, who sat shoulder-to-shoulder with Bellona, though she found she wasn't surprised by the family's stone-faced front after her experiences with them over last few weeks. Only Ro betrayed a hint of emotion when he stood in front of the congregation, his voice catching as he described his first trip to the Netherlands ten years ago to meet his father's family.

Rye had no doubt this family loved and missed Niels very much, and she felt a kinship with people who preferred to grieve in private. Not everything had to be a gnashing-of-teeth spectacle. Even at the luncheon, the Ponds remained aloof and polite to their guests, listening quietly as Niels's friends and colleagues reminisced.

Nicole Laferriere wandered over to the refreshment table and filled a plate with an abandon that Rye found refreshing. At sixteen, this young woman emanated a confidence she must have inherited from her mother, in stark contrast to the friend she had come to support. Like Zoe, Nicole had strong features she would continue to grow into, and that some teenage girls might have been daunted by—but in Rye's experience very little overwhelmed Nicole. She was an accomplished performer, and although she was willing to acquiesce to her parents' desire for her to receive a practical education, Rye had a feeling she was making plans bigger than what they might dream for her.

"Ms. Rye, it's nice of you to show up today," Nicole said, her voice warm. She brushed her hair back from her face and bit into a sandwich with enthusiasm. "Have you tried these? The egg salad is insane. I think I've had three already."

"I know! Isn't this spread amazing?" Rye smiled.

"Leslie was telling me that her mom knows this amazing caterer who basically takes care of all of their parties. I guess Mr. Pond used to host a lot of people at their house, you know, when he was working."

"That must have been nice. I've heard such great things about his career. It seems like he meant a lot to the community."

"I hope people say that about me when I die," Nicole said breezily. Rye froze in the process of putting a cookie in her mouth, and Nicole laughed, a bell ringing out in the hushed room. "I just meant I hope I make an impression—that I do great things and people remember me." She patted Rye's arm. "Don't worry, Ms. Rye. I have a lot to do."

Zoe appeared behind Nicole, her hands on her shoulders. "Have some respect, girl! This is a funeral."

Nicole rolled her eyes good-naturedly. "Ma, I know."

"Well then act like it. Look at your friend. She's hurting right now, and she doesn't need you making a spectacle of yourself while she's mourning her father."

Leslie did look awful, her face pale, eyes unfocused. Rye's heart clenched. She remembered meeting death as a teenager and how difficult and important it felt to hold it together and prove her maturity. The girl was doing her best, but she was seventeen, and this was her father. It was asking a lot of herself to remain stoic for so many hours.

"I don't think Nicole was bothering anyone," Rye said. She knew it was her own deep-seated mother issues that made her speak up when it was none of her business, but to hear a teenager chastised for a laugh? It overwhelmed her sensible decision to remain invisible.

"I decide what's appropriate for my daughter," Zoe replied. The woman had almost a foot of height on her and a body that was all muscle and no nonsense. Rye felt sweaty and small. "You have no authority here, and you certainly have no right to tell me how to speak to my own child."

Rye held up her hands in surrender. "I was just pointing out that—"

"I didn't ask," Zoe said, and led Nicole away firmly by the arm.

Rye watched them go. Another successful parent-teacher conference in the books. She turned as Leslie came up to get a glass of punch. "Hey, Leslie," Rye said, ignoring her poor track record for the day.

"Oh, hi, Ms. Rye." Leslie cast her eyes down to the table and wavered over a few sandwiches before settling on a small bowl of fruit salad.

"I'm really sorry about your dad. What I learned about him during this service…well, it seemed like he was an amazing person."

Leslie didn't even glance up. "Yes, he was. Thanks."

"I know it's not really the same, but my mom left when I was ten. I haven't seen or heard from her since." Rye swallowed. She usually kept a hard line—more like an unscalable wall—between her personal and work lives, but there was something about Leslie that made her want to connect.

"It's not the same at all, is it, though?" Leslie said. "She chose to leave. Our father didn't."

Rye recoiled, biting back a nasty and completely inappropriate response just in time—that maybe Niels *had* chosen to leave his family. "You're right," she said, keeping her tone as even as possible. "I'm sorry." She realized that possibility had family ramifications that could break hearts. It was enough that Alzheimer's had taken pieces of him for years before his death.

"Our father didn't commit suicide," Wil said, startling Rye as he came up behind her.

"Of course not," she replied quickly. "I didn't mean to imply that."

"Are you sure?" Wil's gaze was penetrating. He looked older than twenty-three.

She wasn't sure. Rye took a deep breath. "We were talking about my mother." This family gave her whiplash. Cold and uncommunicative one minute, bubbling over the next.

Rye could see her boss across the room. Mendoza was in his element. The Dutch Ponds, Niels's friends, colleagues, admirers—he chatted with all of them. She did not want a scene with children who had just lost their father. On so many levels, she did not want it.

"He didn't." Leslie turned to Wil with a ferocious glare. "I don't care what you and Ro have been saying. He didn't. He wouldn't have done that."

"Les, he was healthy! What fifty-eight-year-old dies in his sleep?" Wil scoffed.

"It can happen," Leslie replied. "He'd never leave us by choice."

"He wasn't himself. He barely remembered who we were. I mean, Dad hasn't known my name in two years. I don't think it's a great stretch to think that in a moment of clarity, he might have wanted to end it."

Rye was shocked that Wil was voicing the concerns she and Wanda had. And she could tell from the face of the quickly approaching Bellona Pond that her private conversation with two grieving children was becoming public. She tried to ease back into her corner, but with Bellona bearing down on them it was going to be tough to play the part of innocent bystander.

"You need to lower your voices," Bellona said. Her gaze swept over Rye angrily. "What are you doing here?"

"Just paying my respects, Mrs. Pond," Rye said. "I'm so sorry for your loss. I really didn't think…"

"You didn't think. Exactly. You didn't know my husband. You don't belong here causing trouble."

"She didn't say anything," Wil said. "That was me. Saying what everyone else is thinking."

"Don't you dare use that tone with me," Bellona hissed. Rye wouldn't have been surprised to see icicles forming on her lips. "I expect you to behave appropriately, and if you can't do that, you can go."

"You're telling me to leave my father's funeral?" Wil's voice rose, and in a moment Ro was at his side, his hand gentle on his brother's shoulder. "I'm not leaving! You can't make me."

"Hey," Ro murmured. "Why don't we go take a walk?"

"Yeah," Leslie agreed.

Ro shook his head slightly at her. Rye watched Leslie's entire body cave. "We'll get a little fresh air and be right back, okay, Les?" He reached out to pat her shoulder, but she shrank away, wrapping her thin arms tightly around her chest.

"Sure. Whatever." She turned and made a beeline for the ladies' room.

"Wil?" Ro said, his voice soft. "Let's go."

"I don't know why you're hiding from the truth. You're a coward, and Dad would hate that." But Wil turned and let his brother lead him out.

Bellona wheeled on Rye, but before she could open her mouth, Lara was pulling her away, her mouth by her ear. Rye couldn't make out any words, but she took the opportunity to escape out the side door. She was almost to the car when Gerard Mendoza caught up to her.

"What in the h-e-double-hockey-sticks did you think you were doing in there?" he demanded.

Rye turned to him, her face a carefully composed mask of calm. "I offered my condolences to Leslie Pond. I didn't say or do anything wrong."

"She just about had a nervous breakdown!"

"Yes, she did," Rye said. "And I think we should both be more concerned about that than about what you think I did or didn't do just now. That girl's in a lot of pain. She's already run away once—and, yes, she came back—but still. She needs professional help."

"That's not your call to make," he replied.

"It's not? As your stand-in guidance counselor, I'd think you might take my professional opinion a little more seriously."

"You don't have a degree in psychology."

"I minored in it, as a matter of fact," Rye said. "But, what's more important, I've been working with teenagers for ten years, and I know a cry for help when I hear one. If you won't do something about it, I will."

"Don't go anywhere near that family," Mendoza warned. "I like you, Rye, and you've been a godsend this year, but Bellona Pond is on the warpath, and she will take you down."

"How is that more important than helping Leslie?"

He sighed and shook his head. "It's your job. Your career even. I can't stop you, but I want you to think about this—is it worth throwing all of that away?"

"Yes," Rye said without hesitation. "Otherwise, what's the point of having the job?"

By the time she put her car in reverse, Mendoza was gone.

24

COLE SWINDELL'S "AIN'T WORTH THE WHISKY" WAS pouring into the spring air when Wanda slammed her car door—and, yes, she could hear the music clear across the parking lot. It was that kind of place. "Take Your Time" by Sam Hunt began as she stood at the entrance, taking in the roadhouse.

What was that about, anyway? Every song not about cheating was about pickup trucks. She was in for a night of country, and, yep, this was perfect. She slipped onto a barstool and stared at the baseball game on the big screen. In a minute, she would figure out who was beating the Red Sox.

Popcorn appeared in front of her almost magically. "What's your pleasure?"

Country bar. For just the tiniest moment, Wanda was tempted to ask for a white Russian pudding shot. "Bud Light." She took a breath. "Shot of J&B."

"Oh, honey, you sure you want that stuff? This bar makes the best margaritas this side of Tijuana. Split a pitcher?"

Wanda thought that this woman who'd said this to her, who was not the bartender, and who looked vaguely familiar, probably had a few salty-lime beverages under her belt already, but she was friendly. "Sure." She turned back to the bartender, who was still hovering. "Skip the beer and booze. A pitcher of margaritas for us to share. This one's on me."

"Come and join me, Rev. I've got a booth."

Wanda followed her over. Twenty-five miles. She'd driven twenty-five miles to get away, and the first person she met called her "Rev." It was just not fair. Wanda had even snuck into the church thrift shop to "borrow" a sequined crimson and gold knit top to put with her blue jeans and complete her idea of a country look.

The pitcher arrived. They were, in fact, really good margaritas. Wanda leaned back and sighed.

"Rough day, huh?"

"You wouldn't believe."

"Wanna talk about it?"

"Nope, just numb it. Doesn't look much like the kind of place where a person can get a dancing partner, though."

"Well, now, there might be someone I could bring over, as long as you don't want to go home with him."

"I don't want to go home with anyone, but it might be nice to drink and dance and forget about work for a while." Let this woman, whoever she was, think Wanda was wrangling a hundred cantankerous deacons.

"The bartender is my brother-in-law, and he will twirl you around during his break, but my sister would cut your heart out if you put any serious moves on him. Besides, he would be real excited about dancing with a reverend."

"You're one up on me. I'm sure I've met you, but I can't place your face."

"Sharon Brinkley. No reason for you to know me. I live here. Got my own place after the divorce." Her voice had that soft-edged slur that was just this side of drunk. "I did think my loneliness was getting ready to pack up and head right out the door. But no! His daughter doesn't like me. Doesn't approve of me, Ms. High and Mighty Vice Principal."

Wanda looked up sharply. "You lost me." She hadn't, but Wanda wanted to see the dots connected.

"Here's the thing. I've been divorced for ten years. You ever been married?"

"Yes, two-time loser."

"Me, too. See, we have something in common. I saw you slide onto that stool, and I was sure we were sisters under the skin." Sharon took a drink. "Where was I? I'm divorced twice, and I was foolish enough to have kids with both of those deadbeats. A girl and a boy with my first ex, and another girl with my second. Elle and Justin are off on their own now, but Jaclyn is still at home. She's a junior at Lady of Loretto. You?"

"No kids."

"Oh, I'm so sorry." She paused. "Smart, though. Saved yourself a lot of fights. My second ex is still a pain in my you-know-what."

"I can imagine. I'm fine, though." She was, wasn't she? Not on Mother's Day, when it seemed like everyone in the world had kids, but at this exact moment she was not feeling terribly envious of Sharon. In fact, Sharon's conversation was the perfect antidote to a pity party.

The verbal tap shut off unexpectedly. Wanda turned around, following Sharon's gaze. That was one attractive man who'd just walked in. Too young for her, and trouble by the looks of him, but handsome. "Easy on the eyes." Wanda silently toasted the denim jacket over black T-shirt. The view wasn't bad from the back either, she noticed, as he grabbed a pool cue.

"That he is," Sharon agreed.

"So did you tell me that you're dating Hardy Rye now?"

"I am." Her eyes went a little unfocused, perhaps trying to remember when it was she had mentioned his name. "And he's the only nice guy I've ever been with. I have bad luck and bad taste, I guess. Anyway, Hardy is a real doll, and then he wants me to get to know his daughter. Do you know her?"

"Sure. We've met."

"Well, I have been hearing and hearing and *hearing* all these wonderful things about his amazing little Rye. So, Hardy set it up that I was coming over for Saturday breakfast. Now, Saturday breakfast is like this precious ritual they have. Seriously, we can't make any plans, because nothing can interrupt their bacon and Belgian waffles. Maybe he should have asked her, because she was not, I repeat, *not*, pleased to see me. "I try to make conversation. Red Sox? No. I mean, there's a bumper sticker on her car, and she doesn't even know how they're doing. I tried to talk about high school. I've got a junior, right? I bring up how there's all this pressure around visiting colleges. She says, 'College isn't for everyone.' Seriously—did she mean that a child of mine would not be college material? That's sure what it sounded like."

"Maybe she was distracted. She probably isn't used to meeting her dad's girlfriends, right? It's tough when kids that age come home."

"Has it good, she does. Free rent—little apartment out back all to herself. Justin wanted to come back and live with me, and I said no way. I am on the brink of getting my life back." She paused, and Wanda realized she was making a joke.

"Brink, Brinkley— That's you, Sharon. Ready to fly."

"You are so right. Mitch?!"

Wanda's margarita-infused brain came up with a conundrum—was the bartender bigger than he was bald, or was he balder than he was big? She was suddenly intensely sorry that she'd expressed an interest in dancing. Mitch, the brother-in-law, was the exact opposite of Mr. pecs-and-glutes pool player. Unlike the man in black, however, he had a big, friendly smile on his face, and Wanda decided that this was one dance partner who would make her look like a little wisp of a thing rather than a little plump of a thing.

Of course, she also would have to leave this fascinating verbal exchange—though she did agree that Rye, in the right mood, could probably nail ice queen. Maybe unconsciously, or even consciously, she did not want her dad dating.

Anyway, who could resist Brad Paisley's "American Saturday Night"—dance and laugh—and when that was over, on came Shania Twain's "Party for Two." Wanda was breathless when Mitch twirled her back to her seat. She thanked him profusely and wiped her face with a Kleenex and downed her…

…oh, no. That was not Mountain Dew. That was margarita number four. She would pay for that one. Wanda threw down a big tip and blew Sharon a kiss. In the hall outside the powder room, she called Tony.

"Tell me you are not doing anything and you want to take a ride."

Silence.

"Tony?"

"Wanda? Is that you? And by the way, 'Hi Tony, how are you?'"

"Listen, if you *are* not doing anything, could you come pick me up at Laredo's? I had a little accident with a pitcher of margaritas, and it ended up on the inside of me, and I am seriously impaired."

"You think?" There was an edge of laughter to his voice.

"Give me a hard time later, please."

"Oh, I will. With pleasure. And in fact you are extremely lucky, because I was dateless and actually looking over the Sunday service. You do realize it's Saturday night?"

"I'm not that impaired."

"You never go out on Saturday night, Cinderella."

"Lecture me later, please. Will you come and pick me up?"

"I'm on Route 27 already. Hands free! I promise."

"You are a savior."

"I know. So why did you go out and get yourself plowed? Oh. Never mind. I got it. I'll tell you all about this afternoon. Lock your car. We'll pick it up tomorrow. Meet me on the deck. Oh, and Wanda?"

"Yeah?"

"Go ahead and have another."

And just to prove that impaired meant "impaired," and because the dancing had made her thirsty, she put away a Sam Adams while she was waiting for him. It was while she was mixing her drinks on the deck, leaning out to see the road, that she saw Andy Soucek in the parking lot on the side of the building. He was arguing with Mr. Handsome. She could see his face in one of the floodlights, and it was twisted with emotion. He must not have gotten the answer he wanted, because suddenly he pulled back his arm and landed the taller man a right cross that put him flat. Andy drove off while she was still trying to shake the fog of alcohol away.

The man on the ground rolled over on one elbow, spat, and then sat up.

He was fine. It was a country bar. Just another Saturday night.

25

WANDA KNEW SHE HAD A HANGOVER WHEN WINK avoided her in the morning. He silently sat by the door. She pushed it open, looking away from the bright sun while nursing a coconut water. He was back at the screen door sitting patiently on the other side almost immediately—no yips at all.

Wanda gave him a perfunctory scratch behind the ears so he did not think that she had betrayed him completely. She then switched to tomato juice and scrambled two eggs. Back to the coconut water. She wanted coffee in the worst way, but she was pretty sure starting with caffeine would dry her out, and she was already very dehydrated. The shower was long and hot and then short and cold. Another coconut water, though she hated the stuff.

Finally, coffee. She eyeballed the sermon. It was perhaps the simplest one she had ever delivered. She had taken Tony's hymn of choice, "For the Beauty of the Earth," and talked about each verse with a story to illustrate it. Tony was helping by asking Nicole to sing each verse as a solo between.

For the beauty of the earth—creative, earth-based, early spring imagery. Then, "for the joy of every hour, of the day and of the night," something about holding time as precious, something that can never be retrieved once it is gone. "For the joy of human love—brother, sister, parent, child, friends on earth and friends above"—she would tell several tender stories. Finally, "for the joy of ear and eye, for the heart and mind's delight"—she would talk about the senses and give her own few paragraphs honoring Niels Pond and the gifts he'd brought to those who did not hear with their ears.

It was a plan. The whole congregation would be waiting. Everyone in town probably knew that she had been disinvited from officiating at the funeral and were curious how she would handle it—resentful or blithely ignoring or taking the whole weekend off, as if there were a reason for her absence on Saturday. This was her choice—briefly praising a good man for his very particular gifts, which she, as a woman with considerable hearing loss, had a right to affirm.

The last verse was about the church as a place of love. Bingo. It ought to be. She could feel the fragility of her job and still wanted very much to behave badly. Guess she got enough of that out of her system last night.

With the coffee inside her, she felt human, and Wink was circling six or seven times in preparation to making a nest on her black robe, so he'd decided she was not lethal. It was always good to get a second opinion. But not dog hair. She scooped him off, finished her makeup, and decided between more coffee or more coconut water for the drive. Coffee.

The pews were packed. Pretty suspicious, that. Announcements were projected on the wall, then Tony's flashy prelude, hymn, choir, lay reader with the scripture. Ah, the children's sermon—rug time with the rug rats. She felt at home again. When she sat for the choir singing "Precious Lord," one of her favorites, she was able to sway in her seat and look out without seeing vultures. She did her usual Sunday inventory for unfamiliar faces so she would know whether there were new folks in town or parishioner relatives she should greet after the benediction.

That was when Wanda saw the hottie. And Ro Pond. Hottie? Too much time with teenagers. The attractive blond man. He was sitting near the back facing Rocco, who was relaying the choir's words directly to him by silent recitation. "Hear my cry, hear my call, Hold my hand lest I fall…"

Lip-reading. Ah, sweet lip-reading. Lip-reading was Wanda's friend, especially in places with loud background music. She got up, shook out her robe, went into the pulpit, and the stranger in back turned to face her. The view from the front was just as nice as the profile. He appeared to be her age, early fifties. Wanda was pretty sure that she was looking at Niels Pond's younger brother, the one who had inspired his choice of career. Derek? Dieter? Pieter. It was Pieter Pond. Some parents should be ashamed.

He grinned at her, and her temperature rose.

Wanda smiled back. For just a moment, all the drama of the last couple weeks rolled off, and she was in a familiar place with a comforting message and a kernel of appreciation for this man's brother. He must be grieving. He turned to Ro for the translation. Wanda put aside all of her fears that something was criminal about Niels's death and nodded to Nicole to sing.

Nicole's beautiful voice lifted the hymn's first verse effortlessly above the congregation:

For the beauty of the earth, for the glory of the skies,
for the love which from our birth over and around
us lies.
God of all, to you we raise this, our hymn of grateful
praise.

After the worship service, Wanda stood in the narthex, tantalizingly close to the coffee and cookies. As though activated by a brain toggle switch, the punishing hangover returned, and she was aware that there also had been enough tension in her shoulders for the last hour that it was just bearable to reach out and shake hands and near misery to respond in kind to the parishioners who were huggers. She was pretty sure she was sweaty. She could probably blame her evening indiscretions for that! Never again. Feeling like this after alcohol was why Häagen-Dazs was usually her drown-your-sorrows of choice.

"Thank you for your kind words about my brother." There he was, in front of her with his hand extended. He was not quite as handsome as his brother had been, not quite as regular in his features. His nose bent to one side as if it had been broken, and one eyebrow was higher than the other. He used his face with the slightly exaggerated expression of people who sign often, but she suspected he also was trained in auditory oral methods. His voice was a high tenor and light. It was clear, with the slightly ironed-out affect, soft grunts, and fuzz on the final s that often accompanied the speech of those who didn't hear themselves. And were Dutch. "Ik ben doof."

She realized her face hurt. She was smiling too hard. Her Sunday smile. Wanda relaxed and kept her chin up. "Of course, your nephews and niece told me." She didn't make the mistake of saying she was sorry. Deafness was not something to pity. "I liked Niels, though I didn't know him well."

"Niels was not big churchgoer." His smile was wide. He was amused by his brother's nonexistent religious practice, or by her politeness, or possibly just by life. "You saw him at Christmas when the kids were little, in the panto."

"We call it a pageant in America. And, yes, Niels actually…" Wanda took a deep breath. The tiny detail she had forgotten until this minute brought tears to her eyes. "He always helped us set up the star wire. We make a device to control the passage of a large lit star over the heads of the congregation. It leads the shepherds and then the magi. Niels came up with the mechanics of it when Wil and Ro were little and loved all the pomp and excitement of being little kings from the East."

Wanda realized how hard it was to get rid of tears casually while being watched by a person who was lip-reading.

As if he read her mind as well as her lips, he said, "You don't have to keep your chin up so nicely. It's very courteous, but I read even if you bob and jerk."

She laughed and broke eye contact momentarily. It was like the temperature had dropped. That much personal warmth. A quick look around showed that people had given the two of them the little island of privacy that always appeared when she spoke with the bereaved in public places. It was as if everyone else was relieved that she, the professional, would say all the right things so they could relax. She did a surreptitious and quick wipe at her eyes, but when she looked back, she could see that he had not missed it.

"I have been accused of bouncing around a bit in the pulpit, but I've never heard it called 'bob and jerk.'"

"You are very clear. Even the deaf and Dutch understand you." He smiled again.

"You are Pieter Pond, yes?"

"I should have introduced myself. Yes, I am Pieter, Niels's baby brother. I came on Friday from Rotterdam."

"Welcome, Pieter. I am so very sorry about your loss." She took a deep breath. "And I am sorry about the illness. It took him from his family in many ways before his death." When had she taken Pieter's hand? Why was she still holding it?

Ro was suddenly at their side. His mouth was full of flaky pastry, and he quickly washed it down with coffee. He held a second cup and offered it to his uncle.

"Hey, Pastor Wanda. You met Uncle Pieter." None of the drama of his brother and sister.

"Hi, Ro. No thanks to you for the introduction. I see you're feeding your éclair habit." She remembered this boy, half the age he was now, caught by her with an entire plate of mini éclairs in the stairwell behind the sacristy. She'd sat down with him and polished off half herself, and they had been friends, until...

"Sorry. I figured—"

"Ik maak gemakkelijk vrienden. I make friends easily." Pieter took the coffee, which meant he dropped her hand, but even in acknowledging his nephew, he didn't take his eyes off Wanda's face. He smiled again. "Het helpt mij, want ik ben doof. I am not much of a churchgoer at home, but such a nice service as here, I might come more often."

He was teasing her. Wrong. He was flirting with her. Wanda thought quickly. The grieving brother of a man whose family kept her away from the funeral because she was too inquisitive was making a fifty-year-old's mild pass. She wouldn't believe it in a rom-com. And still—"ik ben doof," I am deaf—there was something very vulnerable about it.

"Thank you for coming this morning. I wanted to meet you if I had a chance," she said, and she was aware that it was true.

"I am sorry you did not lead Niels's service yesterday." No beating around the tulips and dikes.

Before she could guess what to say, Ro had his arm. "Uncle, Mom decided…"

Pieter didn't turn. Very effectively didn't hear him. "Reverend Macklin was very nice. Still, it should have been you. I came to see for myself."

Ro got around into Pieter's face, and he was signing fast, cutting Wanda out of the conversation, but she sympathized. Poor Ro. Pieter signed back, his face adding angry little accents. She so did not want to become a source of conflict in this family.

Wanda didn't know enough about the etiquette to know whether a speaker could interrupt sign. She usually experienced sign as interpretation of something already said aloud rather than its own conversation. This cut her out, but it didn't bother her the way the Pond kids' use of it among themselves had. Still, she wanted to say something, and this was a whole new dimension of getting a word in edgewise. Rather than speak, she put her hand up in a universal traffic cop gesture. This was probably rude, but they turned to her. She hoped her little bubble of privacy was holding or that people were lost in their own conversations.

"Excuse me, Ro, Meneer Pond. I visited Niels for several years during his illness and was able to say good-bye to him directly. Bellona Pond was more comfortable with Reverend Macklin officiating at the service. It's always best to make a funeral the most comforting experience possible. You are very kind to have come to meet me. Are other members of Niels's family from the Netherlands here?"

"My aunt Lotte is the oldest. We waited for her to get the okay from her doctor, forcing the whole family here to delay the services. She is the queen of the family. My sister and her husband and our oldest brother came as well."

"I hope you have a chance to stay awhile for a visit."

"The rest of the family returns next Thursday. A week here will give us a chance to get to know the kids better. Then I have two more weeks. I go to Boston and New York for a little fun before I head home. I'm a teacher, and this starts the summer season. My neighbor is taking care of…" He paused and signed briefly to Ro.

Ro added, "His spoiled, mischievous corgi, Bram, who otherwise completely rules his life." Pieter had probably signed "corgi."

"You should meet Wink!" No, he shouldn't. She needed to butt out of this family drama, not traipse through it with her dog. She covered for herself as quickly as possible. "That sounds lovely. Welcome, then. Brought here by sadness, I hope you enjoy your time in America."

"Dank je wel. I always have before. Perhaps I will see you again this week."

Wanda smiled her best professional smile. "That would be lovely. Please offer my greetings to Mevrouw Lotte and your family. And Ro, thank you so much for bringing Sonja. I was glad to meet her the other day."

Excellent completeness.

"I will pick you up tomorrow evening?"

What on earth? Her face betrayed her.

He was smooth. "*After* dinner. Perhaps we may go for a walk on the rail trails. En Vink?"

She was completely blank.
Ro helped. "Please bring Wink."

26

RYE CLOSED HER EMAIL AND LEANED BACK IN HER chair with a sigh. It squeaked in protest, and she sent up a silent prayer of thanks that her office was so small, there was no room for the chair to break and drop her onto the floor. The worst that could happen was that it would break, she would bonk her head on the wall, and then she'd have to reinflate her exercise ball to use as a chair for the rest of the school year. She didn't mind sitting on the ball; in fact, it was better for her back, but it was difficult to project an air of authority while gently bouncing behind her desk.

She could hear Gerard outside talking with Sherry, their office administrator, the queen of efficiency. The school would fall apart without that woman, and Rye knew the last thing she could count on from Sherry was a long story that might distract her boss from heading in to give her the chewing out she knew was coming. She knew it because he'd sent an email this morning saying he would stop by "sometime today" to have a talk with her, and since Mendoza was one of the more

Internet-illiterate fifty-year-olds she'd ever met, it had to be serious.

Her stomach had gone into high-anxiety mode, producing more acid than her roll of extra-strength Tums could counteract. A part of her really hadn't believed his blustering last week about the school board and Bellona Pond having enough power to get Rye fired, but after the debacle at the funeral, she was a lot less certain.

One parent could not take her down, but the Ponds had a sympathy cachet. No one was going to think twice about firing a woman who was practically a stranger at the behest of a grieving widow who'd spent years as president of the PTA, den mother for Cub Scouts, and coordinator of the statewide summer enhancement program for hearing-impaired students. Rye's only claims to fame were that she hadn't run screaming when she heard how little she would be paid for this job, and that her father had been sheriff.

That wouldn't be enough to save her if Bellona Pond really pushed. The best Rye could hope for in that scenario was that she could still find a job a thousand miles from here once the whole thing blew over. And maybe that wouldn't be the worst thing. Maybe coming back here had been exactly the huge mistake she'd been expecting, and now that her father was independent again it was time to move on.

Maybe you couldn't come home again—but it was unfair that she might be chased out of here with pitchforks and flaming torches. She really had just been trying to help Leslie. The girl seemed so fragile, and her place in her own family tenuous at best. Regardless of how Niels Pond had died, he'd left behind three kids who were struggling to deal with that loss. Rye could be a hard-ass about a lot of things, but at the end of the day she'd chosen this line of work because she knew how vulnerable teenagers could be. It meant something to her to be able to reach them, and, even if she only had about two and a half friends in this town, she didn't want to be forced out of here for doing what felt right.

The knock on the door startled her, and she did bang her head against the wall as she jostled herself up. "Come in?"

Mendoza slowly opened the door, shuffled in, then shut it firmly behind him. Rye couldn't remember the last time the man hadn't just barged in. Her stomach rebelled, and she placed a hand over it to will it to keep its peace.

"Rye."

"Have a seat," Rye gestured at the chair across from her.

He reluctantly settled himself into the narrow seat. "Rye, I thought I was clear last week."

"You were."

"So, you understood me when I said that aggravating Bellona Pond was the worst possible thing you could do, and that under no circumstances should you do it?"

Rye had expected yelling, or at least the barrel-chested boom that she often heard in the halls as Mendoza "encouraged" kids to their classes in a timely fashion. This serious, level tone was far, far worse. "Yes, sir. I understood that."

"And yet that's exactly what you've done."

"I didn't mean to. I wanted to go to the service to pay my respects to the family, and then I just sort of stumbled into some drama between Wil and Leslie. I didn't start it. I tried to rein things in, I swear."

Gerard stared at her for several long moments. "You've been a real help to me here, Rye. I like having you around, and, to be honest, I was planning to convince you to stay on for at least five years, see if we could make a townie out of you."

"Well, thank you…?" Rye said. She hadn't thought that far ahead, and it hadn't occurred to her that her boss, whom she thought of as, at best, flaky, might plan anything at all.

"You're welcome. You're a great teacher, and you've really come into your own this year as an administrator. I know it hasn't been easy taking on some guidance responsibilities while getting to know the ins and outs of our system, but you've been up to the challenge. More than up to it." He paused. "Some people doubted that you were the right person for this job, and I think if we'd had another candidate even half as qualified as you I might not have won. I probably would have ended up with someone who cared half as much as you do and needed twice as much help."

"I'm flattered. I had no idea you felt this way." Rye could feel the sweat pooling at the bottom of her back. No one was this honest and personal in evaluation if the axe wasn't about to drop.

"Maybe that's my fault. I'm not always good at giving positive feedback. Around here, I'm not used to things running so smoothly." He leaned forward and rested his arms on the desk. "Which is why it's breaking my heart to have to suspend you until the school board can meet and discuss the situation."

Rye felt the bile rise up in her throat. "A school board hearing? Don't you think that's…" She drifted off. Extreme? Uncalled for? Terrifying?

"Ridiculous? I do. Unfortunately, as you well know, schools have evolved. Parents have a much greater influence these days than I do, and even though I spent all morning fighting for you, I couldn't convince Glenn or Norah that there wasn't some truth in the complaints about the problems you're having with the Pond family."

"Are they ready to fire me over it?" Rye asked. "I feel like this whole situation has blown way out of proportion. I can't see how they could justify this with anything that I have I've actually done. What Bellona Pond thinks I've done— Well, that's fiction."

"I agree," Gerard said. "I also think you should get your union rep involved immediately, because I don't think the cause will justify termination, but it will be a blemish on your record. The whole smoke and fire thing." He steepled his fingers. "And I don't think you're going to want to face this group on your own."

Rye sank back in her chair. "When does my suspension start?"

He glanced at his watch. "About five minutes ago. I'm afraid you have to be off the premises in the next thirty minutes, or I'll be required to have security escort you."

"I understand," Rye said. It wasn't a complete lie. Her brain processed what he was saying, even though it felt like a tidal wave had swept her off her feet and was now pummeling her repeatedly into a rocky beach.

"I'll be in touch soon to let you know when the hearing will be scheduled and what you should expect."

"Thanks. I appreciate that." Rye stared numbly down at her desk. What did she need to pack up? How quickly could she reschedule all the students she was supposed to see? Not reschedule, unschedule.

"Sherry's going to coordinate with you about appointments," he said, reading her mind.

"Good, good," Rye mumbled. She wouldn't let herself cry right now. There was time for that later, but for the moment she needed to make the most of these last few minutes on campus. Her chest felt like it was going to explode, though. "Would you mind if I just excused myself to the ladies' room?" She pushed back her chair and hurried out of the room without waiting to hear his response.

27

Rye leaned against the concrete wall around the corner from her office. The halls were quiet, although behind closed doors she could hear a few teachers lecturing and, if she held her breath, the sound of pencils scratching across test booklets. With sophomore testing going on this week, many students were confined to their classrooms, at least until they'd finished the hour's exam. In this part of the school, no one was around to see her brush tears from her eyes.

She pushed herself up and walked a few steps to the teachers' restroom. Rye tried the door, but the lock was engaged. Greg Bernstein, a biology teacher who had been around since Rye herself was a student, bellowed something about it being occupied, and she made a quick retreat. If he came out now, he would see her red eyes and ask questions, and if he didn't come out soon, she certainly didn't want to wait around to experience the toxic environment left behind.

Instead, she ducked down the stairs to the ground-floor girls' room least likely to be occupied. It was hidden behind the gym and had only one window that often stuck shut, meaning that even after a thorough cleaning it maintained the most unpleasant of public facility smells. She was grateful she didn't run into any students on her way, because by the time she got there she was already crying, her nose too congested to even be bothered by the smell.

She leaned against the door, her eyes closed as tears streamed down her face. As much as she'd once hated this town and this school, a part of her felt better about coming back to face her demons. The students here, even the difficult cases, seemed to like her well enough, and with a few she even felt like she was making a difference. She couldn't do it if she lost her job. As much as she hoped her students would understand, she knew they would see her as one more adult who'd promised to help but left instead.

Rye shook herself. She wasn't fired yet, and she needed to pull herself together and come up with a plan to face the parents and the school board. She'd had a great reputation before this all began, and she hadn't gotten this far by giving up without a fight. She pushed herself away from the door and splashed some water on her face. She grabbed a few paper towels and ran them under the faucet so she could press them under her red eyes. It probably wasn't possible to erase all evidence, but still. Best foot forward.

As she turned to throw the papers away and grab a last one to pat herself dry, she caught a glimpse of a foot underneath the accessible stall door. It was wrong. Wrong for someone sitting. Someone was…

"Hello?" she called out. She hadn't even bothered to check that the room was empty, but she hadn't heard so much as a rustle.

She knocked on the door, pushed. It was locked. "Hello? Are you all right?" Rye threw herself down to peer under the door.

It still took a moment to register. "No!"

Leslie Pond was unconscious or worse. Rye was pulling herself under the door before the thought was fully formed, fumbling 911 with one hand, searching for a pulse with the other.

"Leslie? Leslie? Can you hear me?" Leslie's backpack was open, spilling a pharmacy's worth of pill bottles. Rye couldn't find a pulse, but she knew from training that even medics couldn't always find one.

"There's a female student in the ground-floor girls' restroom at Stoneridge High. Unconscious. Appears to have taken a lot of pills."

"Are you trained to perform CPR if necessary?"

"Yes, ma'am."

"I want you to stay on the line with me while I'm sending medical assistance to your location."

Rye paused to check Leslie's mouth for vomit. If only she knew where an AED was. A tiny, rational part of her mind knew the hospital was less than a mile from here.

By the time the emergency vehicles arrived and the techs bounded into the room, Mendoza on their tail, it felt like it had been hours since she first caught sight of the girl's pale face, though it was only minutes.

She could barely feel the hands pulling her up and away as they went to work. The bathroom was too small to accommodate all of them, and someone was gently walking her out into the hallway. She tried to tug away, but Mike's grip on her arms was too strong.

"It's okay," he murmured. "They need room to work in there. We're just going to come right over here." He led her across the hall so she could lean against the cool concrete block wall. "Just out of the way is all."

Rye stopped fighting him as she felt the adrenaline in her system crash hard. She began shaking, and he pulled off his blazer and wrapped it around her shoulders. "Leslie," she managed to say.

"I know," Mike said softly. "She's in good hands right now. You took good care of her." He looked around for another medic and waved one over as he came through the back door. "I think my friend is going into shock."

Rye tried to shake her head as the man gently led her out the side door to one of the ambulances. Her mouth formed the words "I'm fine," but Mike and the EMT ignored her.

Or maybe she had only spoken the lie loud enough for her own ears to hear it.

28

Wanda felt...well, happy. A Sunday afternoon nap and some weeding in her extremely small excuse for a garden was followed by a long walk with Wink. Supper was homemade chili that had cooked all afternoon in the Crock-Pot and grilled cheese. The good life. Finally, *Masterpiece Mystery*.

Three times, she considered calling Rye to ask about her perception of the funeral, and three times she resisted. The whole intrigue and investigation had been just a strange aberration in her life, and now she was going to get back to the real Reverend Wanda Duff. She wanted to be the person everyone liked and counted on. She went to bed early, and she must have been giving off very pleasant vibrations, because Wink was curled up behind her knees the minute the light was out.

She woke up in the same lightened spirit and arrived at the office by six thirty to outline the next week's worship bulletin. At eight, Lisa jumped when she came out of the inner office. The admin had clearly not been expecting to see her.

"Needed a head start on the week. Hope I didn't scare you."

"When did they take my reverend away and replace her with a pod person?"

Lisa then watched in awe as Wanda put on another pot of coffee for the two of them and pulled out a very special Harvey's bakery box. "Ta-da!"

The rest of the morning continued in happy, productive conviviality. She really did not want to admit to herself that her good mood had anything to do with Pieter Pond and the chance of taking a walk with him. She'd brought in her sneakers, though, and had them in the closet as well-being enhancers.

She looked up brightly when Lisa poked her head around the door and said "phone"…but then Lisa also said "hospital."

"Hello?"

"Reverend Duff?"

"Ro?"

"It's Leslie. She's here. At the hospital. Can you come over?"

Her cell phone was vibrating. She glanced at it. Tony. He could wait.

"Ro? What's happened?"

"They think she tried to kill herself."

"I'm coming. I'll be right there. Is…"

He was gone, and Wanda was glad that he hadn't given her time to ask whether Bellona wanted her to come. He'd called her. She would go. That would do for anyone who challenged her. She grabbed the cell as she took her purse. "Yes?"

Tony was uncharacteristically out of breath. "Leslie Pond attempted suicide. She's at the hospital. Vice Principal Rye found her. Rye's still here—all the teachers are. We have a stay-in-place as Mendoza goes around to talk with classes before they're dismissed. Rye said to call you."

"Ro called me, too. I'm already on my way."

Wanda's brain spun kaleidoscopes on the fifteen-minute drive to the hospital. The thin, quiet girl in the shadow of her brothers. A sheep in the pageant when they were kings. That big smile when she'd made her own s'mores at the church retreat. Absorbing and observing everything in the mosque, synagogue, and Buddhist temple on confirmation field trips. Drifting away from the church when Ro and Wil did. Sitting there crying at Fair Havens, stiff when Wanda hugged her. Her outburst of anger at her mother when Wanda was trying to plan the service.

What a mess. Wanda had never wanted to be drawn into this family's drama. And Leslie's mother would not want to see Wanda. She was sure of that.

It was Lara she saw first, though. She was pacing back and forth outside the intensive care waiting room. She looked like she was expecting Wanda and grabbed her arm.

"Reverend Duff, Leslie did not get the drugs from me. Not in any of the medicine cabinets, either. Nobody in the family takes any of those things."

"Of course not, Lara. Kids get drugs from each other. They have all sorts of sources."

"But...but..."

"Take a deep breath and tell me more. Lara, she's going to be okay, right?"

"Only because Ms. Rye was there. And, God, Belle practically threw her out of the funeral. You wouldn't believe—"

She would, actually. "It's okay. She was there today when Leslie needed her. That's all that matters."

"Belle was going to get her fired," the pharmacist gulped. "She saved our baby's life."

More for Wanda to file, but not right now. She grabbed Lara's arms and gently shook her. "Get a grip, Lara. The doctors are taking care of Leslie, and Rye is a grown woman. Right now, you need to take care of your family."

Lara blinked, surprised, but pulled herself together. "Come on in." She nodded at the waiting room.

Wanda could see why Lara had taken her anxiety out the door. There was another family huddled around a soap opera on TV the way they did to pass the time in the ICU, but even as she came in, the nurse opened the door and said to them, "Come on in, you can see Grandma. All the dressings are changed. Only ten minutes."

The four of them moved as one solid worry through the door. *How we brush against the troubles of others*, Wanda thought. The Pond family was a bigger group. Wil and Ro were on a sofa sitting together. Pieter and a man who must the older brother were looking uncomfortable with magazines on their laps. They were too big for the room. A shorter, dark, bearded man was lost in texting. She guessed the brother–in–law. Niels's sister must have stayed with Aunt Lotte. Bellona Pond was in the middle of them, arms wrapped around her knees, curled up, but she managed to appear completely separate. A mama, a gut-tightened, frightened mama.

Wanda went straight up to her, sat down on the coffee table, hoping it was sturdy, and threw her arms around the frozen woman. Damn the torpedoes. "Bellona, I came as soon as I heard."

Bellona got stiffer, then relaxed and leaned into Wanda's shoulder. Then she sat back, more composed. "Thank you so much for coming. She's going to be all right. They pumped her stomach. I don't understand…"

"She just lost her dad. You'll find a good therapist to talk with her, and with you. That's the best place to start."

"But what if that's not enough?" Bellona looked small and vulnerable. "I wouldn't have survived if she'd…"

"She's alive. Everyone gets another chance. You're going to help her cope. There are a lot of people who love her, and they'll help, too." Wanda wished she could promise more.

Wanda squeezed Bellona's hand and then drifted over to sit next to Ro just in case he wanted to speak with her. She wondered if he had called her on his own or had been asked.

"Thanks for coming," he said. That didn't leave her any the wiser.

Pieter smiled warmly and said, "Gedeelde smart is halve smart. Uh, company in distress makes sorrow less, is what…well, Dutch expression. Yes, thank you."

He looked about to say something more when the nurse came for them. She appeared a little daunted by the number of people. Wanda excused herself to go get a bite of lunch after telling Bellona she would stop in later to see Leslie. The nurse knew her and gave her a nod while the rest of the family filed in to see their youngest and most fragile member.

Wanda's stomach was indeed growling. She headed toward the coffee shop rather than the cafeteria. Big hot meals at noon in this summerlike weather didn't appeal to her, but frozen yogurt and a piece of fruit did.

She crossed the empty expanse of the hospital lobby. Why did they make these cavernous places when people sat in the cozier waiting areas on each floor? There was only one seat taken in the whole place, and it was in a corner. Sonja Mari. She looked up as Wanda approached. On her lap was an iPad mini with a solitaire game on it.

Wanda sat down next to her. "Hello, Ms. Mari."

"Sonja, please."

"Sonja. Are you here because…" And then HIPAA got her tongue, and she realized she couldn't really ask anything.

"I heard about Leslie, and I came over just in case Ro needed me."

"You heard about her?"

The younger woman shrugged. "My sister Jazmin runs the dispatch."

"So Ro didn't call you?"

"No. He doesn't know I'm here. But if he does call, I'm here."

She looked hesitant. Wanda thought that was one definition of a mother—being there in case one was needed. If she was never called, she would go away, and Ro would never know. Against all odds, Wanda found herself liking Sonja Mari.

29

Wanda and Sonja had lunch together in the coffee shop and talked about current events, fashion, even religion. There seemed to be a truce on the subjects they were really thinking about until Pieter Pond came into the coffee shop. Wanda waved at him. He gestured that he would join them in a minute.

"Have you met Pieter, Niels's brother from the Netherlands?" she asked Sonja. "He should be able to let us know how Leslie is doing."

"I saw him at the funeral, but I didn't meet him. I just sat in the back. But, Wanda, he's deaf."

"He's amazing at speech reading. I have never met someone so skilled in a foreign language. I'm sure he'll know what the doctors have said."

He came over and set his tray down.

"How is…I'm sorry. Pieter, do you know Sonja Mari? Pieter Pond." Wanda kept her face directed at Pieter and gestured with her hand.

"Pleased to meet you, Mr. Pond."

"Pieter, please. You are Ro's birth mother? I'm happy to meet you. I saw you at Niels's funeral, but you slipped away while we were still in the greeting line."

She cupped her hands up to her mouth in a nervous gesture. "Niels was an amazing father to Rocco. I wanted to be there, but then I thought it was important that I give the family space. I'm a…sensitive subject for them."

"Sonja," Wanda interrupted. "Your hands." She had realized that Pieter could not read what the other woman was saying.

"I'm sorry." The social worker pulled her hands away, looked straight at him, and exaggerated her speech just a little, slowing down. "Your brother was the most wonderful father that Rocco could have had. That a man like him raised Ro was something that has always made me very grateful. I went to the funeral to honor him, not to get in the way of his family."

"Dank u voor uw vriendelijkheid."

Hm, thought Wanda. Gracious, obviously. Dank was like "thank," she was pretty sure, but the whole phrase was something English speakers would not understand. Like hands in front of the mouth.

"How is Leslie?" she asked.

"She's awake, talking a little. Her throat is sore from having her stomach pumped. They are going to keep her tonight, and, I think, they want some psychiatric services in place before she goes home."

"Shall I go and see her now?"

He looked uncomfortable. "Bellona hoped you left. She does not want you to see Leslie."

"What? She was…she seemed…"

He smiled just a little. "My sister-in-law disappointed herself by showing vulnerability."

"Leslie should…I just want…"

He lifted his fingers and put them gently on her mouth, stilling it. "I will tell Leslie that you were with us. And I will see you after dinner tonight? Yes?"

"Yes?" Wanda felt odd. As he left with his heavily laden tray, she looked at Sonja. "Well, Bellona let me hug her and pray for them all just an hour ago. I told her I would come back."

Sonja gave her a professional glance. "People who are very reserved do not like to be reminded of times when they have shown emotion. Bellona doesn't have any other reason to distrust you, does she? She's just embarrassed, and now she is going to face all sorts of social workers and be offered therapist options and may be made to feel like she is responsible for her daughter's suicide attempt. Or, at least, guilty for not anticipating it. Hospital staff are not always as tactful as they should be. Because the immediate crisis has passed, she probably wants as few 'helping professionals' as possible."

"There speaks an experienced social worker!" They both laughed, and Wanda didn't feel the need to tell her that Bellona Pond had more reasons to distrust her. Or that Bellona had just done the thing most likely to get her investigating again. The woman's ability to flip the emotional switch on and off had just made up Wanda's mind. She needed to keep digging.

Wanda stood up with her tray and bid Sonja goodbye. As she headed to the dish return, she saw that Ro and Wil had come in to grab coffees. She gave them a restrained wave, though she couldn't help but linger when she saw the young men approach Sonja. Just within earshot.

Ro gave his biological mother a hug. "What are you doing here?" He seemed pleased and confused, but his warmth was contagious. Wanda could feel it from where she lurked as surreptitiously as possible by the trash, carefully sorting her compostables from recycling.

"Jaz called me. I hope it's okay?" she said.

"It's not," Wil said. "My sister is nothing to you."

Sonja looked at him, clearly surprised and hurt. "Leslie and I have been having lunch together for over a year—since Ro introduced us. I think your sister is an incredibly special person, and I feel honored that she was willing to get to know me. To reserve judgment."

"Unlike me, you mean," Wil spit out, his fair skin flushed.

"It's okay that you don't want anything to do with me," she said. "That's your choice, and I respect it."

"Well, I don't," Ro said. Wil looked at him, and even from ten feet away, Wanda could feel the man wilt.

"You don't understand—" Wil began.

"No, *you* don't understand!" Ro said angrily. "You've had a lifetime of blending in. Of being the son born to the right family at the right time. I've had to live with being the kid everyone raised their eyebrows at, the one they never would have adopted if they knew they were having you. So, if you think you have any idea, after a year of me exploring what it means to know another member of my family—of what I hoped might be your family too—then you're delusional." He took a breath. "Leslie loves me and wants me to be happy. I used to think you did too, but you've let this eat you up. Sonja hasn't taken me away from our family. You've taken yourself away from me. And I hate it."

Wil wiped his eyes. "I hate it, too."

"Then why are you holding onto this idea that our family has to look a certain way? Because of Mom? Do you think ten years ago she thought that Lara would be a part of our family? Do you think she imagined that we would lose Dad?" Ro balled up his fists. "I'm tired of pretending it's normal to have a father and a mother and two point five kids, Wil, because guess who's the point five?"

"Not you," Wil said softly. "I don't care what you believe. Our family never would have been right without you, just because it wasn't what Mom and Dad expected. It was meant to be."

"And so is this." Ro touched Sonja's shoulder gently. "For me, having another person who cares about me is meant to be. Do you get that?"

Wil sagged against the table. Wanda was glad she seemed to be invisible to them, because she couldn't have dragged herself away now if she wanted to.

"I just miss you," Wil said. "It used to feel like we were a team, and then college happened, and Dad was sick, and Sonja appeared. I guess I thought things would go back to how they used to be—"

"But we're not kids anymore, Wil," Ro said. "This is life. It's going to be messy and hard sometimes, but you're my brother. Nothing is going to change that."

"I used to think that," Wil said. "But Les is upstairs right now, and we were so close to losing her." The tears came again, and this time he didn't bother to wipe them away. He just leaned into his brother. Ro wrapped his arm around Wil. Sonja gave them a small smile and started to back away, tray in hand. Wil reached out, his hand hovering just above hers. "It's okay." His fingers rested lightly on her wrist. "You should stay."

Wanda took the opportunity to beat a silent and hasty retreat. Her own hands were shaking, and a lump had formed in her throat, but she was a consummate professional who at the very least would not be caught spying. Or crying.

30

SIMPLY TURNING HER CAR TOWARD FAIR HAVENS MADE her think about the threat she'd found in the back seat. She hadn't told anyone—not even Rye—about the threat. On a whim, she texted her. *Going to Fair Havens now. Lots to talk about. I'll call soon.*

Fair Havens at midafternoon was quiet. No blue Hyundai—or dark green beater, for that matter—was lurking in the parking lot. Wanda visited two parishioners. She advised one who did not want a ninetieth birthday party to let her family throw one. "They'll do it anyway, and, if you are engaged in the plans, you can control the guest list." That put a smile on Marion's face. It turned out she wanted to invite her ex, newly widowed from his second wife. It would shock everyone. She confided in Wanda that he was still pretty cute. People never hesitated to talk about the ins and outs of divorce with Wanda they like they did with some clergy. Wanda had ample personal experience and zero judgment.

Heading into the memory loss unit felt natural. Wanda was very patient. She started with Linda Tursi. She sat by her bed, held her hand, and read from the Psalms.

Zoe came in to check on Linda, and they both smiled as if the confrontation the previous week had never happened. Then on to Ben Cabot and Lou Martin, who were roommates. She watched the Red Sox on the TV in their room and pinned up a flier for the church Ham and Bean Supper so that Ben's son would know it was this week. Sometimes he brought the two men over, and they always had a wonderful time. Zoe stopped by their room to offer ginger ale and cookies.

She was keeping an eye on her.

Jenny or Joe? Jenny, sitting in her recliner with the late afternoon sun bright on her face. Wanda started to tiptoe away, but Jenny's eyes popped open.

"Don't you dare let me sleep."

"Are you sure? You looked peaceful."

"I have plenty of time to be peaceful. Limitless peaceful time. Don't you want to know what I discovered?"

Wanda hurried in. Did she dare shut the door? It would be suspicious, but anyone could stand just outside the door and hear what was going on. She pulled it against the magnetic opener and took a liturgical stole out of her bag and put it on. Maybe it would look like she was hearing confession to anyone who wondered about the privacy. Anyone, that is, who didn't realize that Congregationalists were not big on individual confessions.

"Wow, that's something," Jenny said, a little awed.

Wanda realized she would have to confess using her stole for deception. "Jenny," she said softly. "Someone doesn't want me nosing around, so all the blessings we can get are well worth it."

"Well, I didn't find out anything about Niels because I promised I would"—she held out her phone—"text you? That's a joke, you know. You'll never get a text from someone with Parkinson's. Most of the time the tremors are too bad to even get Siri to dial the damn thing."

"It's okay." Brief mental applause for the OT department. Siri, indeed.

"I did find out something about drugs going missing, though. They let me sit out on the patio sometimes without an attendant. There was a planter—you know, the round ceramic kind. It was in just the oddest place, so I rolled myself over and bent to move it, and there was a sheet of pills folded underneath."

Wanda lowered her voice. "What did you do?"

"I left it there. You think I'm nuts? I watched and watched to see who went out for the rest of the day. Andy, N. C., Mel Waters, and Zoe all went out. I didn't see anyone remove the pills, though, and I didn't check it again."

"What was it?"

"Oxy, I guess. That's always on the news, right? Wanda, I'm sorry I didn't check to see if it was there later. I was scared."

"Jenny, that was absolutely the right thing to do. Don't do anything else."

Wanda was truly concerned. She leaned close to Jenny to look her in the eye. She had never meant to put this woman in danger. She had certainly never meant to deal with this kind of issue.

Wanda took Jenny's hands and hoped that their closeness looked like prayer. The door swung open. Zoe Laferriere stood there. Jenny was really shaking. Wanda shut her eyes and started the Lord's Prayer. When she got to "amen," she opened her eyes. Zoe was gone, but the door was propped open.

Wanda lowered her voice. "Thanks, Jenny. I will follow up from here. Don't. Do. Anything. Else."

Jenny's smile was very small. "Don't really have that much courage. Sorry I couldn't find out more."

"You were great. And I've got a joke for you. Seems one of the ladies on the assisted side has been married even more times than I have. She says she was married first to a banker in her early twenties, and secondly to a circus ringmaster in her forties, then to a Baptist preacher in her sixties, and finally to a funeral director. One for the money, two for the show, three to get ready, and four to go!"

Jenny laughed, and there was laughter from the door. Andy Soucek was there with a big grin on his face. And a mark under his eye in purple. "That's bad, Reverend Duff. I'm no Stephen Colbert, but that was bad. Hey, Jenny, ready for supper?"

"I'd better go. I didn't know it was that late." Wanda couldn't look away from his face, where a huge bruise also had blossomed on his cheek. "Wow, Andy. Should I ask about the other guy?"

"The other 'guy' was a door. You're welcome to stay for grilled cheese and soup if you'd like."

Well, that was the first Fair Havens friendliness she had experienced in a while. Also the first lie she recognized without a shadow of a doubt. And from Andy, no less. "I'd better get going." Wanda kissed Jenny's cheek, gave her what she hoped was a meaningful stare, and headed out.

Joe was already at his table with Ben and Lou. She would have to come back. She was thinking about Pieter as she headed out to the parking lot. And then she was thinking about pills under flowerpots and notes left in her car. She checked the back seat before she got in.

This time, the rose was on the passenger seat, and the paper was wrapped around its thorny stem. *Stay away.*

31

"ANSWER YOUR DAMN CELL PHONE. COME ON." WANDA was shaking. That was what was wrong with the cell phone revolution—the expectation that people would answer it all the time. The rose in the front seat was scarier to her than the note in the back had been.

Her hands were shaking. She had heated up canned soup, and she was spilling it back into the bowl from her spoon. She crushed saltines to thicken it up and tried again.

"Come on, Rye, answer the damn phone." It went to voice mail. "Hello Rye, this is Wanda. I've been warned off again. I want to talk. Call me, please."

She couldn't eat anymore. She put the bowl and the plate it was on in the refrigerator. Maybe she could warm it up again later. She put on jeans, a light sweater, and fresh blush and lipstick. She glanced at Wink, who looked at her with canine superiority. "Yes, of course I am putting on Mocha Kiss just to take you for a walk. What did you think?" She was being snarky with the dog. To what levels would she descend?

She wondered about shoes. With Leslie in the hospital, she didn't really think that Pieter was going to come by, but she still wanted to have that magical and impossible combination—cool shoes that walked well. She found some rubber-soled flats with a cute pattern across the top that wouldn't hike miles but would support her feet for a half hour without sending her into plantar limpititis.

How long should she wait? She imagined that thought was going through Wink's mind, as well. Could she just walk around and around the house so she could see if anyone came to the door?

The doorbell rang and put her out of her misery. How quickly should she respond? Oh, never mind. She decided not to be coy. She flung open the door and asked the first thing on her mind.

"How is Leslie?" She signed it as well. Not fluently, but that much she could offer in his own tongue.

"Better. She is coming home tomorrow. Therapy appointments have been made, protocols have been followed. Belle looks old. Lara is being efficient. The boys are together. I think. Ro…Ro is not showing much emotion. So smooth, so helpful. He will fall apart all of a sudden."

"Do you think that I can help…with Ro or Leslie?"

There was a long pause. "Not right now."

"You would let me know?"

He nodded.

"Would you like to come in, or would you like to go for a walk?"

"Let's walk."

He made treat advances to Wink, who was never a dog to play very hard to get. It was a good thing the burglars of the world did not know about Wink's loose morals.

Of course, Wanda's Ben and Jerry's collection was the pinnacle of her purloinables, and that was replaceable. Pieter had come prepared for the most finicky of dogs with a peanut butter bone from the gourmet dog purveyors in town. Instant adoration.

They set out together side by side. No talking possible. It was that spring moment when the gold was greening and everything felt shady but also bright. The breeze was pleasant. Even though it was after seven, the sky was not yet pink. A perfect evening as long as they didn't want to talk.

Wanda's first hearing aid had arrived on the scene when she was thirty. That began the era of hairstyles that covered the ear. It was a decade without ponytails. She let her piercings close so earrings would not draw attention to her ears. It really hurt when she finally, in the wake of the second divorce, opened them up again.

There had been the times she would go without the hearing aid to some party or concert, assuming that the ambiance would be loud enough that she could mask any deafness in the general hubbub. Surely no one would notice that she was asking people to repeat themselves over and over and over and over again. There was always some incredible social gaffe when she totally misunderstood someone, and, since she would not own up to the hearing loss, people just thought her socially inept. She had been so young!

Hearing aids had become more subtle since then, and more expensive. Most of the advances in technology came with the need to buy new ones. Why was that? Oh, yeah. Profit. Anyway, she loved colored hearing aids. She started to strut them. Her current ones were purple.

If she needed glasses, she would wear glasses. If she needed help to hear, why was it different?

But it was lovely to walk in the evening with a man who was not trying to verbally communicate with her as wind and leaves rustling competed with the simplest conversation. How long had it been since her share of any outdoor conversation had not been punctuated with *I'm sorry… excuse me… I didn't quite catch that…*

Wink enjoyed being alpha in a very small pack, and he was not as pesty as usual about sniffing every little thing. They were in a comfortable rhythm. They turned toward a newly acquired piece of conservation land. As they entered the gate, it felt as though spring were being overtaken by summer warmth. It was beautiful. Wanda breathed it in and felt completely relaxed—so relaxed from the week of pent-up tension that she could have laid down right there and taken a nap.

Then her inner adult awoke. She should not be so isolated with someone she didn't know well. Certainly not when she was already being threatened and almost certainly stalked. Why had he invited her out anyway? She touched his arm lightly and gestured to the curve of the path that would take them back almost immediately to a residential street.

He smiled and complied. Wink did his very small donkey imitation. He wanted to stay where the scents were wildwood, not go where he would be removed from wilderness that could be so improved by his sprinkling. Pieter laughed. There was a low stone wall at the entrance to the conservation land.

"Do you want to sit down so we can face each other?"

She sat. They were close enough to houses and traffic. She put Wink on the land-grant side, blew her whistle twice, and unsnapped his leash. The terrier sprinted away in blissful romp mode, and she smiled after him. The signal training had taken a long time, but it was worth it. A long whistle blow would bring him back to her side as long as he had a minimum of about fifteen minutes to explore the damp grass and the small holes of creatures. Besides, he wasn't much protection anyway.

What made her think of that?

She turned and looked at Pieter. He had a quizzical expression on his face. She was even more uncomfortable—she was uncomfortable about his big hands, she was uncomfortable about his height advantage and about his closeness on this bench. And she was so uncomfortable about being uncomfortable. She felt like he was putting her in the wrong by not saying anything. Why couldn't he do small talk? Luke could do…

Whoa. Totally not in the same category, not in the same category at all.

"Look, Pieter. I'm going to be honest with you. I do not want to be alone with you in the woods. I've gotten some…warnings recently. I know you don't have anything to do with…"

Of course not. Why would he know anything about this?

She tried to make sense. "Look. I've been…"

He laughed then, and it was a more natural sound than his speech. "Reverend Wanda—"

"Just Wanda, please."

"Wanda, do not be embarrassed about being uncomfortable going into a lonely place with a man who could loom over you in an instant."

He demonstrated looming with exaggerated pantomime and it made her giggle, which was probably his point. At the same time, she couldn't shake her nerves. The little mini-date that she had been anticipating with such pleasure now felt like one unknown too many.

But this man could not have killed his brother. He was not the threatener. After all, he wasn't even in the country when Niels died.

Or was he? She could not know that for sure.

He was still looking at her bemusedly. She had to decide what to say. Thank you, Emily Dickinson. Tell the truth, but tell it slant.

"I'm sorry. The truth is that clergy can get into funny— not funny ha ha, but funny unnerving—situations. I seem to have upset somebody, or even more than one somebody."

He raised his eyebrows. "Belle?"

"Oh, well, yes, her, certainly." Wanda laughed. "That goes without saying. But no. It's something else. Maybe I know something about someone without actually knowing what I know. But the bottom line is that I have been receiving threatening notes." She took a deep breath and plunged on. "They were in my car after I had locked it, which means somebody broke in to put them there."

"You have called the police?"

"Well, no."

"You must call the police. This is a very bad thing."

"But I don't really know what it's about." That was just, just, just the edge of truth.

"Is it my brother's death?" All of a sudden, without having appeared to have moved at all, he was several feet away. She was not sure how he did that. "Is there something wrong about my brother's death?"

"Well…" She didn't know what to say. "I don't know. Would it be? Do you think there's something odd about it?"

"How would I know? I am the deaf little brother. Who would tell me anything?" He looked angry and turned away from her to look into the woods, where a brown-tipped white tail could be seen cruising the smells. Wink's head popped up as if the dog could feel the angry gaze.

He was shutting her out. When he turned away, he effectively refused to read her lips or the half-assed sign she was trying to use. Her hand on his arm was rougher than she intended as she tugged him back to pay attention to her.

She was immediately sorry. He was the one with the loss. It was Pieter's loss. Bellona's. Wil's and Ro and Leslie's. Even Lara's, but not hers.

"Well?" The arched eyebrows spoke volumes. He wasn't happy—not with her or the situation.

"If I knew what it meant to have a single red rose in the front seat of my locked car wrapped in a piece of paper that said 'keep away,' or to have somebody in a blue car taking photographs of me in the street—if I knew what that was about, I would go to the police. But I don't, and I can't"—God forgive her this lie—"imagine why it would connect to your brother's death. Do you have a reason to suspect it might be connected to Niels?"

She waited, but not long enough for a person—much less one who was working so hard to communicate with her—to respond. She rushed on with discourteous, un-clergy-like speed.

"Because from where I sit, I've been threatened, removed from my own pulpit, and banned from visiting a teenage girl in the hospital for no logical reason. If you can justify that or give me some reason why your family seems hell-bent on cutting me off at the knees, tell me. Please."

Wanda took a deep breath. Her mini-tantrum seemed to have brought his temper under control. Pieter's shoulders sagged, and he scrubbed his hands across his face. It was winsome, though she suspected it was a sign that he was tired of working so hard with her. For her. For this conversation that was not a date.

"I am sorry," he said.

"Me, too."

His hands began to fly in what was probably a mirror of the velocity of her rant except in sign—Dutch Sign, probably. She waited it out.

When he finished, she shrugged and laughed. "No idea. But I think I understand how you feel."

He switched to speaking. "I'm not sure I understood you. I think you said you do not know the connection between my brother's death and a rose?"

"The rose in the front seat of my car with a warning note around it." Wanda spoke slowly. "Or any of several other warnings."

"There's no connection, I promise you. Nothing to do with my brother's death." He looked at her carefully. "This is what Bellona wants me to say. Do not 'stay away' because you are too close. Stay away because you are far from the truth. I, Pieter, say to you again"—his speech slowed to a word at a time—"do not stay away because you are too close."

In the initial rush of hurt and embarrassment that he had sought her out under false pretenses—probably at the urging of Bellona, or more likely Lara—she decided to hold onto the message he was trying to give her. Obtuse? Yes. But there was something there. Do not stay away. You are too close.

Wanda blew the whistle once, quite loud and long. Wink was at her side immediately. He started to make nice to the kind gifter of the peanut butter bone before tuning his animal instinct to recognize that it was not, at the moment, a wise thing to do. "I will find my own way home," Wanda said.

He held her gaze, and for all her disappointment, she did not drop her eyes.

"I hear you, Wanda." Slower and deliberative. "I hope you hear me."

Just as she opened her mouth, they heard the gunshot.

32

SHE HEARD IT, AT LEAST. OBVIOUSLY, HE DID NOT. Could not. Wanda had never meant to be in his arms. She was just there. He held her for just a moment, puzzlement across his face, and then he sensed there was danger and pushed her down beside the bench.

"What?" Both hands and mouth.

"Gunshot." She knew her face was a mask of shock.

"Stay here."

"You can't go…"

"I can't hear, but I can go. Call the police."

She did, and they came admirably quickly. Pieter walked into the brush and looked. He was gone for ten minutes, which was enough time for her to have blurted out more, perhaps, than the police could take in. They were sure it must be a hunter, although the conservation land posted "No Hunting" signs all year long.

"People don't always abide by the law," the patrolman said. Wanda thought he looked about twelve years old. Officer Spagnolo. What did he know about breaking the law? His partner ranged down the path where Pieter had gone. She explained the dilemma of having a man who was quite willing to scout out the situation but who wouldn't hear either the shooter or the police.

"John! That guy can't hear anything. He's deaf." Officer Elementary School shouted as the older officer came up the path with Pieter.

"Yup. Got that," said his partner, whose name Wanda hadn't caught, but who at least looked old enough to have a driver's license. "Ma'am, we couldn't find anyone down that path. Did you have the sense that a bullet was coming this way, or was it in the distance?"

Pieter paused, sniffed, and went into the scrub that Wink had been investigating so thoroughly.

"I don't know," Wanda said. "I don't know much about guns in general, and it startled me. It seemed very loud. Very close."

"You sure it wasn't a car backfiring?"

"It was not a car. It could have been a hunter, I suppose, but I am sure it was a gun."

"Do you know of any reason why someone would be shooting at you?"

She stared at him like a rabbit on the edge of a cliff might stare at a hound. In either direction, there was danger.

"No…officer…I don't."

"No disagreements? No domestic disputes?"

"None." She was frosty. "Besides—"

"Yes?"

"Sorry. I was going to say that my dog wouldn't be so scared if it wasn't a gun. I know that isn't really anything."

In fact, both the men were country enough that they looked at the Jack Russell, who was still glued to her leg and shaking.

"Well, there is that."

"Here is this." Pieter had come up behind them. He had a shell casing in his hand.

The older officer took a bag out and let the casing fall into it. "You have mighty good eyesight to search that out when you didn't even hear the shot."

Pieter just shrugged. "Followed de hond. Also, it smells like shot."

"Want to show me where you found this?" At least the older patrolman knew enough to talk straight into Pieter's face without raising his voice. Pieter pointed, and they both went into the scrub and birches. Wanda was left with the younger man. "I'd like to go home, if that would be all right? Can I give you my contact information?"

"You don't want to wait for that gentleman?"

"I suppose so. I only met him yesterday."

She'd met him yesterday. His niece had attempted suicide today. His brother's funeral was two days ago. Wanda had the terrible feeling that time was constricting around her like a noose. She shook her head slightly. At least Pieter Pond had been with her when she heard the gun. Not that it meant he was above suspicion. Right now, everyone was suspicious except for Rye, who was simply incommunicado.

"I'll wait," she said. The officer would detain her if she wasn't careful. All of a sudden, she decided that careful was a thing she now wanted to be. "Mr. Pond is visiting from the Netherlands. I was just taking him for a walk and telling him about our town."

She wasn't sure that Officer Spagnolo understood the 'telling him' part, but at this point she didn't care about his diversity training.

Pieter and the other officer returned a few awkward minutes later, and everyone exchanged contact information. They turned down the offered ride back to the parsonage, and Pieter and Wanda walked back with Wink. The argument, the accusations, the sense of doom, and the authorities all weighed on the side of parting at the door and never, ever seeing each other again. On the other hand, there was that moment in his arms—how lovely and safe it had felt.

When they got to the door, she offered him coffee, and he declined.

"I have never known a Dutch person to turn down a cup of coffee."

He smiled at that but stood at the door. Wink wanted to go into the house, so she bent over and released his leash. He was gone, and she knew that he was instantly deep down in his favorite chair, the one that had once been off-limits. She smiled a little. "Pieter, I apologize for sounding so…" She drifted. Sorry for what? For everything—the disaster date and for still wishing he would come in despite the complications.

"We are both tired, frightened, confused." He reached over and hugged her, and she let herself be hugged, just letting it be. A kiss, maybe there would be a kiss. No, a kiss would be too much. A kiss would be lovely.

He didn't kiss her, but he waved from the car. She went reluctantly into the house. Her cell dinged. It was a text. Rye? No. It was Pieter from the driveway. *I will see you again before I leave.*

She laughed. Like teenagers, texting before they even got home. *I hope so.*

And then she tried Rye again.

33

IT WAS TWO IN THE MORNING WHEN HER LANDLINE rang. Most people in the church used the cell phone number. She shook her head to make the cobwebs disappear and answered.

"Hello?"

"Reverend Duff? This is the emergency department at the hospital. We are calling on behalf of Lisa Vaughan. She is here with her daughter and requested we be in touch with you."

"What's wrong?" A wave of panic rushed through Wanda. Lily. Nothing could be wrong with Lily. If Lisa could not even call herself, though—

"I'm sorry. HIPAA guidelines don't permit us to give you any details."

"Is she going to be okay? Let me talk to Lisa."

"I'm sorry, they're already in…" There was noise on the other end of the line. Wanda listened intently but couldn't understand what was being said.

"Can you come in, please, reverend?"

Wanda started to wake up. "Of course. I'll be there right away. Where should I go? What…?"

"Thank you so much. The family will appreciate it. Please hurry."

What family? Wanda wondered. As far as she knew, it was just Lisa and Lily, and Dottie. Lily's dad hadn't ever been in the picture, and Wanda had never heard about parents or siblings. Accident? Appendicitis?

She pulled on her slacks and a sweater and threw a cross around her neck. The hospital might have called her in, but it still didn't hurt to look official to get beyond the outer circle of confidentiality, not to speak of possibly Intensive Care. How unusual that the nurse had not identified himself by name, though. Surely they always did…it fact, in a rather priggish and precise and not very comforting manner. And at this time of night? She often wished someone would call her before it was too late to do more than help with grieving, but they rarely did, usually opting for six in the morning as the earliest respectable time to call nonfamily.

It must be bad. She brushed her teeth and threw things into her purse, and she was out the door. Under fifteen minutes from the first ring.

She slid into her car and felt adrenaline surge. Wait. She took a deep breath and put her hands at two and ten on the steering wheel. She prayed. For Lisa and Lily and for the doctors. For the surgeons, if there were any. She forced herself to calm down just a little. Speeding to the hospital wouldn't help anything. She backed out of her driveway and headed onto the two-lane curvy highway that would take her in 10.2 miles and…twelve minutes to the emergency room. Not technically speeding.

It was dark—not many streetlights out here, and trees grew close to the edge of the road. The shoulders were for turning into the small businesses like convenience stores and gas stations, an Agway and a farm stand.

Nothing was open this time of the night. Even homes were invisible from the road.

Wanda thought about Lily and her amazing smiles. She would put her hand up to be helped onto the big steps to the chancel for the children's sermon because she loved to sit right next to Wanda. Lisa would bring her into the office when she had to work late running a holiday bulletin or a funeral, and Lily would find little games to do with paper clips and pens and stack hymnbooks up like enormous Jenga towers. She would laugh when they tumbled down.

Wanda felt her foot get heavier, and she glanced in her rearview mirror. There was nothing like springing a Statie's speed trap for ruining all the false advantages of a lead foot. Although this was not a very likely place for lurking highway patrol. There would be a long time between cars at this time of night.

There was a car behind her though, pacing her. Her heart skipped a beat. Stop that. At least it was company. Someone else out on this lonely stretch of back road— the logical way from her house to the hospital, though certainly not the most direct way. Maybe this was someone who went to work really, really early. Someone who drove without lights.

Once she had forgotten hers en route too late at night until someone flashed a warning at her. Still sleepy. But she didn't think so. Wanda felt cold inside. Someone following her in the night fast on a road with no lights.

She would let them pass. Wanda slowed, and the car following slowed as well. She sped up, and her tail—her tail?—did as well. Wanda slowed down again, practically shutting her eyes against the expected impact. It didn't come. In fact, the car was gaining and was just going to pass her, and she would keep on going. It pulled out long and dark and was beside her just as she thought she should have noted the license number before it passed.

It was beside her and moving sideways, and then she was off the road and…rolling, so slowly, slowly and…

34

RYE WOKE UP TO THE SOUND OF HER FATHER BANGING
open her front door against the wall as he threw on the
light.

"What the hell?" She rolled off the couch and landed
on her feet. Not gracefully, but she made it, although
the blanket wrapped around her threatened to take her
down. "Dad?"

"Good, you're up," he said.

She stared at him, adrenaline pumping. Apparently,
the years of defensive training with Hardy's cadets had
honed her senses—just like riding a bike. An annoying
bike with no boundaries or concept of acceptable visiting
hours.

"I am now, yes." She pulled at the fleece trapping her
legs. She'd fallen asleep streaming an ancient season of
The Amazing Race. The screen still flashed behind Hardy.
Rye reached for the remote and turned the TV off.

"Great." He stared at her. "Because we need to have
a chat."

"You mean this isn't a social call?" Rye asked, flopping
back down and shoving her hair out of her face. "At"—

she checked the clock above her father's head—"two thirty in the morning?"

"Your friend Wanda is in the hospital."

She sat up. "What? What happened? How—"

"That's what I want to know, Prudence. What the hell are you two into, and why did the hospital call our home number? Why did Wanda tell the EMT on the scene to contact you and to tell you to be careful?" He stood glaring down at her, a coiled spring of procedural paternal intent.

"I don't know why they called you. I don't even know Wanda that well. Wwe only really started talking a few weeks ago after the father of one of my students died. She got in touch with me."

"Why?"

Hardy Rye had an excellent ability to detect omissions of truth, and he had the advantage. Rye had never been a night owl, and when she was wakened from a dead sleep, she might as well have been slipped a truth serum. "She thought there might be something suspicious about Niels Pond's death. She heard that his daughter was having trouble at school, and she wanted me to reach out to the family, see if I could find out anything."

"Why didn't she go to the police?"

"She didn't have anything. Just…a feeling."

"A feeling." Hardy didn't look amused. "A feeling that got her driven off the road in the middle of the night."

"Is she okay?" Rye's voice was soft.

He sighed, and his sheriff's mask slipped. "She will be."

"Neither of us thought this was much of anything. I would have told you."

"We haven't talked much lately," he said.

"No. You've been busy with Sharon."

"And you've apparently been playing detective while your job is in the balance."

Rye sighed. "I don't really care about the drugs, but I wanted to protect Leslie. She's just a kid."

The sheriff was back. "What drugs?"

"Wanda thought maybe Niels had been hoarding pills—that he might have committed suicide—and when she started asking questions, everyone involved started acting shady."

He raised an eyebrow. "Shady?"

"She got a couple of threatening notes in her car. I got some texts—"

"You what?"

"Leslie's mother started raising hell with the school board, that sort of thing. We thought it might mean we were onto something."

Hardy sat down on the chair across from Rye. "So then you called the police."

"Well, no." Rye shook her head. "We still didn't have any proof. Not really."

"Is a car accident enough proof for you?" Hardy asked. When she nodded, he sighed. "I still don't understand why you didn't come to me."

"Hereditary independence?"

He smiled. "Yeah, there's that. Also stubborn, pig-headed…"

"Also genetically likely."

"Don't be a smart-ass. And while I think you're probably a decent detective, you do remember me telling you that amateurs mixing into an investigation are…?"

"…a source of big trouble and occasional lucky breakthroughs. I believe I remember you saying that, oh, twenty or thirty times."

"But Pru, I don't think I need to tell you that drugs are a big business. If dealers think you're infringing or investigating, they will do anything to protect their territory."

"I know! We didn't plan this. I just wanted to help this girl, Dad, I swear." She twisted a strand of hair tightly around her finger. "I was actually planning to talk to you at breakfast on Saturday, but I forgot that Sharon was coming, and I just…I don't know. I didn't want to bring it up."

"You don't like her." It wasn't a question.

Rye shook her head. "I don't dislike her."

"Hmm. A rave review."

"We're not best friends, okay? But we don't have to be. If she makes you happy, I can deal."

He sagged back in his seat. "I guess I can live with that. She can be…a lot." He rubbed his eyes. "You want a lift to the hospital?"

Rye stood up and stretched before dropping a kiss on her father's head. "I don't think I want to drive alone tonight, so yeah. That would be great." She grabbed her clothes from where she'd dropped them the night before. "Any chance you have any of that blackberry crumble left from yesterday's breakfast?"

Hardy smiled. "I'll have coffee and a slice ready in the car in five."

After circling the garage twice, Hardy dropped Rye at the entrance to the hospital and went to park at a street meter. She waited for him to return so they could go in together, standing just outside the stadium-bright lighting of the doorway. She checked to be sure she had her phone. The texts had stopped after she changed her number, but she was still notifying her friends, and she couldn't remember the new number without referring to the note on her hand. Another part of her brain that technology had atrophied.

Rye's concentration was such that the hand on her arm resulted in a whip-around kick, her foot an inch from N. C. Harris's more sensitive bits when he stopped it with an iron grasp on her calf that kept her off-balance but held upright and nearly as terrified as she had been when he'd touched her the first time.

"Let go." Rye was impressed that her voice came out evenly when her heart had already galloped way past common sense. "Now."

After a long moment, he dropped her leg, and she backed away. "A little jumpy?" he asked, his face transformed from his professional sneer into a smug smile.

"What is your problem?" Rye asked.

"As a matter of fact, you are. You and that preacher friend of yours." He laughed mirthlessly. "Although it seems like she's out of commission for the time being. I'm going to have to thank whoever managed that."

"I'm calling the police," Rye said, ready to swipe her phone.

"I am the police," Harris said. "Well, essentially." He waved his hand dismissively. "Go ahead and call. I haven't done anything wrong." He thought for a minute. "Well, nothing I'm not approved for."

Rye stared at him. She wondered if her father had decided to go in through the emergency room door closer to the street. He should have been back by now, but maybe he'd expected to meet her upstairs. "I don't know what you're talking about, but you need to stay away from us."

"Can't stay away from one of my prime suspects." He smirked at her. "Let me tell you, it'd be real satisfying to take down your pretty-boy boyfriend and a woman of God in the same bust."

"You think Wanda is…what?" He'd lost her.

"I think she's involved in a drug ring running out of Fair Havens," Harris said. "Her and Soucek, that pansy boy piece of—"

"Watch yourself," Rye hissed. He might be twice her size, but she could do some damage trying to take him down. No way he could pummel her before somebody heard the commotion.

"You think this is the first time I've seen this? Drugs go missing at places like that all the time. Everyone's willing to look the other way until a resident dies because of diverted meds or refilled syringes. Then they call me to come clean up the mess. I'm a specialist in the diversion of controlled substances." Harris narrowed his eyes. "Of course, I've never had to pussyfoot around a couple of amateurs who can't detect their way out of a paper bag."

"You don't know anything about us."

"Don't I, though? I know your friend never locks her car. I also know she doesn't scare easy. I left her a few warnings—tried to convince her to keep her nose out of my investigation—but I guess somebody else was more effective." He looked thoughtful. "Not one of ours though. We're not allowed to, what's the word? Escalate." Harris stared at her. "Not professionally, at least."

Rye shivered. "I don't know what's going on at Fair Havens, and neither does Wanda. We were just trying to find out if someone had helped Niels Pond die, or if he'd helped himself."

"What you were doing was putting yourself in the middle of a dangerous investigation. Do you know what happens when a girl sticks her nose where it doesn't belong?" he sneered. "She gets hurt."

"I haven't been a 'girl' in a long time," Rye said. "I need to see your badge now." She held up her phone. "You think a cop raised me and I didn't learn to record when things start getting rough?"

He growled and lunged for her phone, but she jumped back toward the hospital doors, which slid open as a man wheeled his wife to the curb. They sensed the tension and hurried past, but Rye felt better with her feet on carpeted ground.

"Stay away from Fair Havens," he said, and he did flash identification at her. She thought it was DEA. She could see his photo, a seal, and yellow letters on blue. She didn't like him, but she knew from personal experience that law enforcement attracted a full range of personalities. "If I were you, I'd give your boyfriend a wide berth."

He pushed past her into the lobby and headed to the admissions desk. His bland countenance was once more in place. "Hi there"—he glanced at the woman's name tag—"Hannah. Could you direct me to Wanda Duff's room, please?"

Rye already knew the number. There was no way she was getting on an elevator with that man, but she also wasn't letting him anywhere near an incapacitated Wanda without supervision. Her father would just have to catch up. As soon as the doors slid closed, she dashed to the stairway and sent a silent thank-you to Mike and Camila for challenging her to that God-awful bleacher climb challenge last month. Legitimate investigator Harris may be, but he was also a legit creep and not to be trusted.

35

WANDA WOKE UP FEELING CROWDED. TOO MANY PEOPLE around her bed. Her bed. Why was she in bed?

When she woke up again, someone was reciting the twenty-third psalm: "Though I walk through the valley of the shadow of death, I shall fear no evil."

I'm…dead?

With a massive effort, she stayed conscious for another minute. "Thou preparest a table before me…" She was hungry, really hungry, and her throat was sore. Everything was sore. Her throat was the most sore. Ben and Jerry's…

Wanda woke up again, remembering…not much, remembering…oh, yes, Pete Allensby reading the twenty-third psalm to her. Peter Allensby was the conference minister. What was he doing in her bedroom? She'd never fancied him, and misconduct charges would be off the charts.

Her bedroom. If that's where she was, somebody had stolen her pillow-top mattress. She opened her eyes.

Rye. Rye? In my bedroom. Not, not my bedroom. Rye. And Luke. Luke was here. Oh my God, I'm in a Johnny. Or I'm dead. I'm dead! Someone thinks I'm dead. He's come to get the body. Her eyes flew wide open. Rye, Luke and…N. C. Harris.

"Stay with us, Wanda." It was Luke. He reached over and took her hand. When had she last washed her hair?

Wanda tried to lift her arm to make sure that the Johnny was closed. She was pretty sure that she was not appealing. Her arm, however, was an octopus with intravenous tubing. All the years of pastoral visitation finally helped out with something practical.

"I think I'm in the hospital."

"And who said you were not a bright woman?" Luke asked.

She bristled. "You have to be nice to me. I've…What's happened?"

Rye took over. "You were in an accident. You cracked two ribs. They'll mend by themselves, but you also broke your leg in several places, and the doctors needed to go in and do some surgery."

"Accident?" Memories started to crawl out of where they'd hidden. There were so many of them, though, and they kept coming before she could invite them in and set up appetizers and cocktails…No. Before she could entertain them—that was the word.

Wanda woke up again, and she was in a different room. It was pale blue. She could see Rye doing a crossword puzzle. "Was Luke here?"

"Hey, chicks before…Well, you know. Guess I'm an egg."

I guess I'm not going to die if she can be sarcastic, Wanda thought. *Good to know.*

"Luke was here a few hours ago, and our buddy from Fair Havens—the creep job."

"Can you fill me? I'm…I'm…Luke was here?"

"He was. Didn't seem mad at you anymore if that's any consolation."

"Mad. Yeah." She felt fuzzy. Morphine-dazed.

"How are you feeling?"

Wanda stared at her for what felt like an hour before she could decide how to answer that. "Okay?"

"The police are waiting to get in and ask you some questions about the accident. Do you remember anything?"

"Accident, yes. I do remember?…Maybe."

"What we know is this. You went off Route 113 at about two forty-five in the morning. Single-car accident. Maybe you went to sleep." Rye didn't sound convinced.

"I was run off the road by a car with no lights." A wave of half-buried terror washed over her.

"Are you sure?"

"Positive. A dark car. Dim headlights." Her throat burned. Wanda felt so vulnerable. She shook herself. *Aim for jaunty. Bury the rest.* "Rye, get to the good part. I did see Luke here when I woke up…where?…in the recovery room?"

"Yes. It seems that the emergency room folks associated you with him because you'd been there together, when—"

"When people have died, yes."

"Right. I mean, of course." She seemed awkward. "Well, when they failed to get any family, they called Luke. I guess they also knew he's the kind of person who's used to getting up in the middle of the night."

"Well, that's true."

"So, he came, and he called me. I gather you were very insistent that he do so. He was apologetic. I was already out the door because Hardy's cop telegraph is faster than anything else in all creation."

Wanda looked confused. She had no real idea what time it was, even now. "I'd been trying to reach you. All day."

"Luke stayed until you were out of surgery and doing well. He needed to get back to work—you know, since your body wasn't going anywhere."

"Is that a dead Wanda joke?"

"Yes. I regretted it immediately. He said he would stop back to check on you."

Unconsciously, Wanda put her hand to her head and encountered bandages. "Ow. How badly—" And then the memory struck. "Lily." Wanda tried to struggle up, but the movement brought such a wave of pain and nausea that she sank back. "I have to go. Lily Vaughan is here in the hospital. They called me. Lisa wanted me to come. It must have been something serious. That's why I was out. Coming here. I was coming here."

"You got a call?"

"Yes. The nurse. I didn't get a name. It was strange."

"You lie down, and I'll go find out what I can about Lily Vau…"

"VAUGHAN. She's three. Her mother, Lisa, is our admin at the church. The nurse who called me implied that Lily was in the emergency room, but they wouldn't tell me what was wrong and said I couldn't talk to Lisa. I bet Lily was in surgery. Go. Find out. Let Lisa know I'm here."

"Only if you promise to stay still and maybe rest a little."

"I'm not sure that I can do anything else. Go." Wanda shut her eyes.

The next time Wanda woke up, Rye was back with an older man. Wanda dragged his name out of her memory.

Hardy Rye. Well, a person couldn't always wake up to Luke Fairchild.

"Hey there," Rye said.

"You're still here? Don't you have to go to work?" Wanda could see that it was bright morning, or maybe it had become bright afternoon. She was not completely sure.

"How are you feeling?" Rye dodged the question.

Wanda did some self-assessment. "Better, I guess. I was really tired. I don't seem to be able to stay awake very long."

"They want you to rest. They do keep coming in and checking on you, and mostly you just grunt at them. I wish I could sleep like that." Her smile was forced. "Do you know my father, Hardy Rye?"

"Seems like I used to be at your place every New Year's Eve."

"It evens out. I'm at 'your place' every Christmas Eve."

Wanda grinned for the first time in what felt like a week.

"I brought my dad because pretty soon the police are coming in to ask you some questions, and we might want to share some of what we've been thinking about before they do."

Wanda tried to sit up and realized again why that was not a good idea—she was a slow study—and sank back down, but before she could say anything, Rye continued.

"Lily Vaughan was not in this hospital last night, and with the permission and assistance of the social work department, I called Lisa. Nothing is the matter with Lily. She's been fine, slept in her own bed and was having breakfast before heading to day care. Lisa was on her way in to work and was completely baffled by your story."

"But they called! I know they called."

"Maybe someone called, but it was not this hospital, and it wasn't any hospital authorized by Lisa. If it happened, then it certainly gave you a reason to be on that road in the middle of the night. It makes your story sound a lot more plausible."

"You didn't believe me?"

Hardy broke in. "People fall asleep, or they drink a little too much, and then they go off the road and into a tree. Apparently—I have not been to the scene—there were no skid marks, so you were not trying to brake."

"I was trying to let the car go past me. I slowed down, and it was coming so fast. There will be paint on my car, won't there?"

"Yes, I imagine there would be."

"Somebody lured me out onto that road. That phone call was not my imagination. The police can check, it was on my landline. I thought it was strange because nobody ever calls me on it anymore." Wanda wished she could pause and push a button to deliver her own morphine. "And somebody shot at me earlier today, too."

"What?" Rye's face was ashen.

"I was trying to reach you. I called and I called all day, and…"

"That's my fault. I changed my number because I was getting so many threatening texts. Then things happened at work." Rye paused. "Leslie overdosed. I…I just completely forgot to give anyone my new number." She shook her head. "I'm so sorry. There's been so much going on. I lost my job."

"You what?!" This was too much to absorb. "You…what?"

"She's been asked to take a leave because there have complaints about her questioning the Pond family,"

Hardy said. "I'm guessing this is not something she has been doing alone."

They swiveled to face him, united, at least temporarily, in silence.

"I see," he said.

"We need to talk," said Wanda, "and I need to get out of here."

"You're pretty banged up," Rye said gently. "It might be a while."

"I guess you don't know insurance companies like I do. They'll have me out of this bed in no time."

"Well, if you've been run off the road and shot at in the last twenty-four hours, you should be glad to be in a safe place," Hardy said sternly.

A reality check was not what Wanda wanted, not when it felt like so much work just to turn her head. "They'll send me to rehab. Where on earth is the hospitalist?"

"Maybe they're giving you privacy because you have guests," Rye suggested, shifting in the molded-plastic chair.

Wanda snorted—and it felt good. A whole career of trying to have a significant conversation or even pray with someone in the hospital, only to be repeatedly interrupted by medical staff, went through her mind. "I don't think so."

Hardy stood up. "I'll go take a look. Get someone to come in here and tell you what's happening. You two try to stay out of trouble until I get back?" The door swung shut softly behind him.

Wanda turned to Rye. "When I woke up the first…well, I don't know…when I woke up and you were here, and Luke was here, was I hallucinating that N. C. Harris was also here? Was that a really bad morphine dream?"

"No. He was here."

"Rye, I think he was the one who ran me off the road."

Rye shook her head. "I'm going to need to catch you up. It seems N. C. Harris is actually investigating the disappearance of medications from elder care facilities."

"What?!"

"He said he followed you, photographed you with Lara—he was checking up on you as a person of interest."

"For what? Drug trafficking?"

"I guess so. I still don't think that justifies what he did. He's the one who left the note in your car—"

"Notes, actually," Wanda said.

"Notes? Jesus. What a creep." Rye shook her head. "My dad is looking into him. His methods are definitely shady, but it looked like he was legit."

"So he was the one who shot at me yesterday? Or"— Wanda paused—"I don't know what day it is, but—"

"Nope. Not him. He didn't drive you off the road, either. He's not authorized to use that kind of force. He told me that like it was a real option. Like he was disappointed. He was trying to scare us off to keep us from blowing up his investigation at Fair Havens."

"So we were right?"

"We were right. At least partially." Rye sighed. "I still don't know what happened with Niels Pond, though, and he didn't volunteer any information about that." She looked pained. "He said I should stay away from Andy, though."

"Really?" Wanda was exhausted, but she even she could see that the implication that Andy might be involved in this was killing her friend. "I don't believe it, Rye."

"Me neither. At least, I don't want to, but I told Harris I would let him finish his investigation." She twisted the edge of Wanda's blanket between her fingers. "I know it's his job, and I guess technically he's—well, not a good guy, but I guess not *the* bad guy—"

"But he's a sleazy sleazeball."

"You have no idea."

"Andy's not, though," Wanda said as she closed her eyes. She wanted to keep talking, but she needed to do it without absorbing the pain in Rye's face on top of the pain in seemingly every part of her body.

"I know." Rye sighed. "And I know you're tired, Wanda. But I just want you to know I'll be here, okay? Anyone who has a beef with you is going to have to go through me first."

Wanda wanted to tell her thanks, and also that whoever had driven her off the road would probably do that to Rye without blinking an eye, but instead she let that thin comfort push her back into sleep.

36

IN THE EARLY DAYS OF HER MINISTRY, HOSPITAL DOORS were never shut. The rooms were never private! Wanda could remember evenings trying to pray with a parishioner whose roommate had a dozen relatives over, each with a radio. She even remembered four-bed wards at Mount Auburn hospital. Certainly, most covered-by-insurance rooms needed two beds, but now sometimes sharing a bathroom was enough for two singles to qualify.

She enjoyed the privacy when she was finally past the point of having constant interruptions—nursing staff, hospitalist, surgeon (did having pins in her legs make her a "pin-up" girl?), housekeeping, volunteers with magazines, and volunteers with small bouquets—one from "the church" and one from the funeral home. There were visitors. It was busy enough that she could block out the terror of the last few days.

Rye kept popping in, clearly concerned. Tony came and serenaded her. Lisa brought Lily over after day care with a hand-crayoned get well card. Lisa was particularly upset that Wanda had been lured out with a wild tale about her daughter.

"Don't worry," Wanda assured her. "Whoever it was had it right. If there's anything that will get me out of my well-deserved bed, it's worrying about our precious Lily." If Lisa's facial expression was anything to go by, this was not helpful.

"It feels creepy that they know about me and my little girl. I know that sounds so very selfish when something so bad happened to you, but it *has* made me…"

"Look in all your closets when you come home at night?"

"How did you know?"

"There have been a few things that happened to me in churches that made me do that for a while. I think it's an instinctual reaction. Look at it this way—changing your phone number or email is logical if you think someone knows too much about you. And if you think someone's watching your movements, always park under a light in the parking lot or buy a can of mace. But checking in the closets and—"

Lisa blushed to the roots as she filled in the blank. "Under the bed, too."

They both broke out in laughter and felt a lot better.

Lisa wiped her eyes. "Well, I'm not sorry to think that you would come to see us in the hospital, but I am really sorry that someone knows what a sweet, soft-hearted woman you are. Have the cops made any progress?"

"Not that they've shared with me."

"If it makes you feel any better, everything is going to hell in a handbasket with you gone. Ed is planning to do a valiant job of covering the next couple Sundays, but for all he's a preacher, I don't think he has ever planned his own worship service."

"Just wind Tony up, and he'll fill in all the blanks."

"Yes, he's being happily bossy. Basically, everything else is on hold until we find out how long you will be away. Committees are not going to meet. Church School Sunday won't have a theme. Every kid who can sing, play an instrument, et cetera is invited to perform in 'God's Kids Got Talent.' Then they will all sing together 'God Has the Whole World in God's Hands' in four-part harmony and four languages and receive certificates."

"If Billy Marsden is going to do his magic tricks, you better have a bucket of sand or water nearby."

They laughed again. Wanda thought that the pain in her broken ribs and leg was worth the sense that she was really alive again. It wasn't just the accident. For the last few weeks she had felt like she was being emotionally run over.

Lily was growing squirmy, and Wanda knew that Lisa really did need to get home and make supper. "Thanks so much for coming by. You know there's been so much drama that it was just really nice to see you." She could feel tears forming in her eyes. That was absolutely ridiculous.

Lisa gave her a hug. "Just get better soon. Even Dora in the women's group, queen of crabby, sends her love. She won't stay long in your fan club, so enjoy."

"I've only been in the hospital for three days. I've been out for the flu this long."

Lisa took her hand. "Wanda, you don't understand. You could have died. Everyone is feeling that—feeling how close that was. And somebody is out there who tried to hurt you, and that person hasn't been found. This wasn't the flu. We are all feeling what it would be to really lose you."

Wanda was embarrassed. She wanted to brush this sentiment away, but that would not be fair to her friend. "Thank you."

Lisa closed the door behind her. There was a vitals check and then another knock. Wanda was feeling profoundly tired from talking and wanted nothing more than to go to sleep—right after she found a way to look in the little closet and get somebody a lot nimbler than she was to check under the bed. Wanda thought it must be almost seven o'clock. How late did visits go?

"May I come in?" Lara Alesci was at the door. She didn't wait—she came in anyway. There were about a thousand thoughts and feelings running through Wanda's mind. Parishioner. Pharmacist. Murder suspect. Friendly helper. Threat. Lara started to shut the door behind herself.

"Please leave the door open." Wanda said this rather more loudly than necessary. She felt simultaneously very exposed and trapped with her leg. She had a quick vision of police procedurals in which victims were killed by someone adding something to the drip of an IV.

Idiot. Same thing as imagining monsters under the bed.

"Don't we want a little privacy?" Lara asked, hand still pushing the heavy fire door shut.

Wanda pushed her bell.

"No, we don't. I'm…I'm not supposed to be behind closed doors with a parishioner. It could be a misconduct issue." She wasn't lying. It was perfectly true—especially if she were the visitor and the person she was visiting was a man in a Johnny, or a lesbian. Which this one was. Boundary training was a good thing.

Lara pushed the door open again. "Goodness, that's intense. How are you, Wanda?"

"I'm improving. Thank you."

Lara tried again. "That's good. I heard some people say you were run off the road. That must have been the rumor mill going wild."

"Not rumor—completely true. I was run off the road by a car with its lights off. And that was after a completely fake call in the middle of the night trying to get me out onto that lonely back road between Brookside Drive and here. And I went…and somebody was waiting for me. It was the most frightening thing that has ever happened in my life."

Lara looked genuinely shocked. "I thought they were exaggerating. Lots of people go to sleep—I know—I sell as many over the counter wake-up pills as I do the go-to-sleep variety. But run off the road? Why you? What have you gotten yourself into?"

"Are you trying to say this was my fault? Because let me tell you that I don't know, or I would have stopped doing whatever it was."

"Of course you would. It's just so dramatic. You must know something about something."

How long did the nurses take to answer a bell, anyway? She had not rung it in the three days she'd been here because they seemed be around constantly, or at least every time she wanted to sleep. Maybe ringing the bell actually meant 'Do Not Disturb.'

Wanda sat up straighter, and it sent off explosions of pain. She fell back with a cry. Lara was immediately at her side. Wanda wanted to scramble off the bed, but she was attached in too many ways.

"Oh, I'm sorry. I didn't mean. No, please." Lara suddenly seemed to realize that Wanda was frightened, and she backed away abruptly to the visitor's chair. "I am sorry. This has gone all wrong. I didn't mean— I mean that I did want to say that I was afraid you thought…"

She took a big breath and dragged her fingers through her hair, which was a good thing. Wanda needed the time. The electrical currents of pain made her sympathetic for the very first time with the prototypical Adam for the loss of that rib.

"You don't think that Belle and I would do anything to you, do you? I didn't…I didn't know you were in such bad shape. Really, I didn't mean anything. I am sorry if I frightened you." She sat down on the visitor's chair, and Wanda fell her heartbeat coming under control. This woman wasn't N. C. Harris. No, she wasn't. She wasn't. Wanda took a deep breath. And it hurt. It really, really hurt. The nurse came in.

"Excuse me," he said. (*Your nurse is Daniel Yu*, said the white board. *Your aide is Melinda*.) "It's time for your pain medication."

"It is past time," Wanda said through clenched teeth.

He took in the twisted state of the sheets and her high color and pulled a blood pressure cuff like an offensive weapon. "You're supposed to be quiet and as calm as possible. I think maybe you've had enough visitors today."

"Of course." Lara stood up.

"Don't go," said Wanda. "We need to clear this up."

"I'm afraid that it would be much better for Wanda if you came back to visit tomorrow?" The way Daniel said this, it was less suggestion and more order.

"Yes, yes. I'm sorry for bothering you. Belle and the boys send their love and best wishes for a speedy recovery. Ro even made a little joke about clergy with lead feet. Maybe not so funny…" She drifted off. "You get better." It was actorish—either really embarrassed or insincere. Wanda did not know which one, and she was too tired and sore to care.

Lara backed out of the door. Wanda wasn't sure whether she'd overreacted. The woman had not been about to whip a syringe out of her purse and plunge poison in the IV bag or tube or whatever, but it had felt like a threat.

No, she was over-medicated. All in her mind. Daniel bustled around. Gave her another cup of pills and a drink with a straw. Melinda arrived and managed to straighten up the hospital sheets without seeming to move Wanda more than an inch or two. Really, the staff was far too present when a person was not afraid of dying at any moment. She should ask them about the use of the bell and whether hers was attached.

37

When Wanda woke again, Rye was back, and it was morning. She tried to fill her in about Lara's visit, but it didn't seem nearly so traumatizing in the light of day. In fact, Wanda hoped that Lara's professional understanding of pain medications might offer some excuse for the situation.

Rye, however, seemed to take her seriously. "I don't think you overreacted. Someone broke into your car twice, took photos of you, shot at you, and ran you off the road. I'd say we're well into freaking-out territory, even if we know that some of that was that creep Harris. I just can't understand what about Niels Pond's death could possibly produce such a reaction." She shook her head, her clean hair bouncing, taunting Wanda with its shine and volume. Day four of sponge baths was not cutting it.

"And honestly, Wanda, why are they targeting you? Both of us have been asking questions about the Ponds, but aside from some nasty texts and the situation with the school board, which seems a lot more Bellona Pond's speed, I've gotten off easy."

Wanda thought about that. It was true. Rye's career was taking a hit, and Wanda's was, too, both at the hands of the Pond matriarch. The scare tactics were something else entirely, though. It could be Wil and Ro, but Wanda couldn't imagine either of them terrorizing her—certainly not over a few questions about their dad. And although Lara had given her a bad feeling last night, Wanda had known her long enough that it was difficult to reconcile all the terrible things that had been happening with the woman who cooked for the church's soup kitchen once a month. So maybe she knew something else—something Rye didn't know.

It should have made her more nervous, but, in fact, Wanda felt better when she was told that it made sense to be frightened.

"Honestly," Rye went on, "you are particularly vulnerable right now because you can't just jump up and run away. We don't know if the car hitting you meant to kill you or just frighten you, but it certainly has made you a sitting duck."

Okay, now Wanda felt a little less comfortable. She hadn't even thought that far. Friends give and friends take away. And then she felt something kind of warm. Rye was a friend, wasn't she? An unexpected and younger friend, but yes. And that, just by itself, made her feel better. Better, not safer. The thought of police protection had not even crossed her mind. Maybe Rye took her seriously, but obviously the constabulary was less inclined to credit her reporting of the dark and mysterious car.

"Tell me if I am out of line, Rye, but do you think you could find out through your father whether the cops actually believe I was run off the road or whether they think I fell asleep at the wheel?"

"I can ask him, but he's out of the loop these days. You were hit, though. That much he knows. I haven't seen anything in the paper, so they are obviously keeping it quiet. The rear left fender of your car is crushed, proving a collision occurred. There was some dark green paint left on your car. That doesn't mean it was a car driving without lights or that it was anything other than, say, a drunken kid who ran from the scene. The physical evidence can't indicate one way or the other."

"I suppose it could have been a hit-and-run, except for the phone call. How do they explain the whole 'Lily at the hospital' story luring me out of the house?"

"I don't know. What was the police interview like?"

"Well, they asked me questions. I was pretty out of it. They brought the statement by the next day for me to sign. I was still out of it. This is my...fourth day?"

"Yes, counting the night you came in."

"Do you think I should call them and find out what's going on?"

"It couldn't hurt. If they had apprehended anyone, they would let you know. Still, they don't know you know that, so there's no harm in asking."

"I'm not so sure about that. Anyway, I'm going to be discharged today. No insurance company would let me stay any longer, and the church doesn't exactly have Cadillac coverage."

"What's next? You'll go home?"

"Rehab facility. I don't have a placement yet, but it will be two weeks of physical and occupational therapy."

"So where will you go?"

"Fair Havens is an authorized rehab facility—not the dementia wing, of course, but another end of the facility. Most younger patients—and that includes me, for this sort of thing—choose the more aggressive schedules of dedicated rehab hospitals rather than the gentler schedules of assisted living settings, which customarily offer rehab in shorter and less intense sessions. But if I am on site at Fair Havens…"

"You'll be vulnerable. Somebody ran you off the road, Wanda, and you want to be hobbling around, or not even—you don't hobble yet, do you? And sleeping in a place that just might house someone who was willing to risk vehicular homicide?"

"We need more information."

"I'll look into it. You go somewhere safe where they can get you back into the pulpit soon. Trust me, I've got the time, not to mention two working legs."

There was no avoiding it—Wanda needed to ask, even if it was awkward. "And what Harris said about Andy?"

"Harris is a creep."

"True. That doesn't preclude him discovering something, though."

There was a knock on the door.

Luke, Wanda thought instantly, and then wondered just exactly what she looked like at this moment. Not great. When was the last time she had used a toothbrush? And her hair!

Not Luke. Pieter. Pieter Pond was standing in the door with an exquisite bouquet. It had not come from downstairs in the hospital gift shop.

He let it be an entrance. Wanda pulled herself together.

"Rye, I would like you to meet Pieter Pond. He's here from the Netherlands for his brother's funeral."

It was obvious that Rye was impressed. Yes, Wanda thought—when flat on her back, sweaty, hurting, and lacking range of motion, she was luring attractive bachelors.

Rye signed a brief greeting to him while carefully enunciating. "It's nice to meet you. I am very sorry for your loss." Wanda hadn't known she could sign.

"Wanda." Rye turned around and eyed her meaningfully. "Enjoy your visit." She wiggled her eyebrows, and Wanda was thankful Pieter couldn't see the gesture. "Keep me posted about your placement."

She slipped out as Wanda's nurse came in to check on vitals and offered to get a vase. Pieter didn't seem to object to this visitor, but Wanda guessed that neither Rye nor the nurse suspected that this man could be a threat. She thought she was safe, but he was connected with this whole situation, too.

He had been with her when she heard the gunshot, though, and he could hardly have made a speaking phone call that was not easily recognized. Besides, he was lovely, and for the moment, the pills meant she was pain-free enough to enjoy the view. After everything she had been through, she deserved that much at least.

38

No, she didn't want the ambulance. Of course, she didn't need the ambulance. It cost money even with insurance, and church policies were notoriously *parson-monious*. Bill Fogerty, sixty-five-year-old marathon-running widower with a wandering eye—oh, and chair of the trustees—had a Land Rover, and she could be transferred from the hospital in that. Not a problem. Not a problem if he had any shocks. Or if he could be trusted to drive like one might think a trustee should. Or if he would stop talking long enough for her to concentrate on her pain. Not a problem—who was she kidding? She felt like she had been run over again. By the time Bill dropped her like a sack of greasy, unwashed potatoes in the wheelchair and spun her papa-wheelie-style into the Fair Havens rehab wing, she felt like she had tire tracks all over her.

Fair Havens had not gotten the majority vote for her ten days of rehab from her regular visitors. On the other hand, Wanda didn't think it needed to be a democratic decision. Rye would forgive her soon. Hardy might. Let's see…who else? Tony, Lisa—actually, no one thought she should be doing her rehab here. Even those who knew nothing about the "situation" thought that she should have headed to a much more aggressive facility that specialized in pushing younger people so they were back to their regular lives as quickly as possible.

"You're vintage, not geriatric!" Tony had insisted. Lisa knew more and dithered at the thought that this would be a place where Wanda might not be safe. Lisa was also still channeling a lot of guilt and a little anger about the original accident. Rye and Hardy just thought she was painting a target on herself, especially when it did not seem that there was much police activity pursuing the identity of her vehicular assailant.

Wanda just hoped that N. C. Harris never found out she was here. In fact, she fervently hoped that his cover as an investigator had been blown and he was gone from the memory care unit. Out of sight and all that.

A CNA put Wanda's clothes in the small closet on her side of the room, including the sweats Lisa had bought for her since Wanda didn't own any that were fit to be seen by the general public. The CNA also suggested that she might like to rest before supper. The dining room was down the hall, and she indicated that Wanda would be allowed to use the wheelchair to go there tonight and again tomorrow for breakfast. After that, she would be more independent. They were going to take the wheelchair away "for her own good." That seemed to Wanda like moving along quite fast enough. If they were more aggressive at other centers, she didn't think she would be able to handle them any better than her elderly parishioners. Her leg, at least, felt like it was a hundred and ten.

Luke brought her a plant. It was not as elegant as the flowers from Pieter Pond, but Pieter was gone, headed to New York. Before he'd left, he'd leaned over her bed in the hospital and kissed her long and thoughtfully, and her heart had raced, responding to, well, romance and terror. She was relieved and miserable.

Luke handed her a sweet little ivy with a card that said, "Get well soon." He looked around her room, smiled at the roommate who was deeply engaged in *Judge Judy*, and laughed. "Well, Wanda, this is a new perspective for you, isn't it?"

She grinned. "Yes, but I'm not planning to stay on this side of the bed for long, trust me."

"You didn't hear it from me, but you want to request Diane for physical therapy. Janine is very sweet, but she will automatically expect that you cannot do much each session, and so they will be short and lack challenge."

He saw her start to say something and held up his hand. "You were just transported over here, and, yes, I know you don't feel wonderful, but tomorrow morning you need to act like someone who wants to help herself get out of here."

"From whence do you draw this well of information?"

"I've got a titanium knee."

"Arthritis?"

"No, an old football injury and a really nasty ski slope fall turned me into a Nord."

"A what?"

"Cross-country skier. Anyway, I was all of forty-two and reasonably athletic, and I still had to prove to the staff that I was not geriatric and unwilling to move."

"Where were you?"

"Here. Price was right. Elderly folks are friendly and noncompetitive. And—"

"And?"

"Dad thought I would make client contacts."

Wanda had been drinking water, and the laugh forced it out her nose. Luke patted her on the back and then rolled her, in considerably better spirits, down to the dining room. He promised he would come back and see her soon.

39

RYE KNOCKED ON THE DOOR INSISTENTLY UNTIL
Rachel answered. She stared up at Rye, her dark hair
pulled back in a ponytail, a scowl fixed on her face.

"What do you want?"

Rye eyed the kid. She knew the type—bruised,
distrustful, vulnerable. This girl would protect Andy
with everything at her disposal. "I need to talk to Andy,
please."

"Why?"

"It's a private matter," Rye said, her tone neutral. "Is
he home?"

"No."

Rye cocked her head. Andy's car was in the driveway,
and she could hear bluegrass coming from the kitchen.
"Are you sure about that?" She locked eyes with the girl.
As a teacher, she had fine-tuned her stare. It accepted
nothing but the truth. Or silence, of course. The kid
chose the defiance of the latter. Rye had to respect her
for that, even if it was irritating at a time like this.

"Oi! Andy!" Rye yelled. Rachel flinched and slouched back into the living room to flop onto the couch with her homework.

"Rye?" Andy poked his head out of the kitchen, a dish towel over his shoulder. "What are you doing here?"

"I need to talk to you. It's important."

"I'm trying to make lunch. This isn't a great time."

Rye sighed and opened the screen door to let herself in. It took a certain jiggle to unlatch, but she remembered the trick like she'd used it yesterday. "I know things are weird right now, but my friend is in the hospital, and I've heard you might know something about it. We can either talk here or you can come outside with me. It's your choice, but I'm not leaving until I get some answers."

He was already halfway down the hall by the time she finished speaking. He grabbed her elbow and gently steered her back outside and down the porch steps. They were almost to the sidewalk when he stopped. Rachel had her nose pressed to the window, but Rye turned so that even if she was a child prodigy at reading lips, she wouldn't get a whiff of what was going on.

"Are you a drug dealer?" Rye asked point-blank.

"Of course not," Andy answered. His face was flushed. "Why would you even ask me that?

"I think you know why."

"I don't."

"Andy, you've never been a good liar. Don't start now. Someone tried to run Wanda Duff off the road, and I want to know what you had to do with that."

"Pastor Wanda? I would never do anything to hurt her! She's one of my favorite people. My patients are always happier after she's come by to visit."

Rye let out a breath she hadn't realized she'd been holding. "I believe you wouldn't hurt her intentionally."

"Of course not."

"The thing is, though, Harris—"

"Not this again. What is with you and that guy?"

"'That guy' is an investigator, and he admitted to leaving threatening notes in Wanda's car to try to warn her off of what's happening at Fair Havens." She clenched her fists. "He threatened me, Andy. If I hadn't been recording him, I'm not sure what might have happened."

"Are you kidding me?"

"No."

"That can't be legal."

"Absolutely not. And my dad has seen it, so you know that's not going to go well for Harris."

"What does that have to do with me?" Andy asked. "I mean, I'm sorry I didn't believe you when you said Harris was being a creep, but—"

"He said you were involved in the case he was investigating. He implied he was going to take you down."

"Rye, you know me. I would never do something like that." Andy shifted from one foot to the other. He glanced back at the window where a little face was still staring intently out at them.

"But you know something, don't you?" She looked around at the old tree house, the garden planted by three generations of his family. Andy's motivation wasn't the mystery. How long it had taken Rye to remember who he really was? Now there was a mystery. "Is it Rachel's dad?"

He sighed. "Eric is…He used to deal weed to kids, but lately he's into something bigger."

"Seriously?"

"He has some contacts outside the country, and one of my friends at work found out about it. She has family running a clinic in Haiti, and she wanted to send them some of our expired medicine or medicine from people who don't need it anymore."

"Deceased patients?"

"Sometimes. Sometimes it's just that their condition has changed. We're supposed to destroy the drugs—expensive meds that could make a real difference!"

"Andy—"

"I know. I shouldn't have set them up, but she told me all about the program these people were running and how they needed basic supplies. They have nothing, Rye. I don't know anything else about their deal. I didn't want to know."

But he had known. All this time, he'd known, and he hadn't trusted her. He'd pretended to be angry with her, tried to throw her off the scent. Made her feel like she was in the wrong. That betrayal cut deep. It stung of an anger he had been holding onto for a decade. Of abandonment and distrust. All things she had earned and had written off because he was, in his heart of hearts, a kind man. She was the sharp knife. She was also the wound.

"Wanda says she saw you get into a fight with someone a week ago. Outside a bar? Ring any bells?"

"Yeah. I guess my friend hasn't been making her payments on time, and now Eric wants to collect."

"This is really bad, Andy," Rye said. Her glance strayed back to the girl in the window.

"I know. I shouldn't have gotten involved, but Eric could exert some parental rights at any time, and Rachel can't go back to living with him. She's safe here. I want it to stay that way."

Rye stared at him, leaning against the posts on his grandmother's porch. If she caught a glance at this guy in a bar—tattoos, shaggy hair, soulful gaze—she would be head over heels for him in less time than it took to buy him a drink. Up close, though, she saw the dark circles, the stoop in his shoulders. He worked long hours, and then he came home and took care of two people who needed a steady hand. Still sexy, but the rush came with a hell of a lot more baggage.

It was an emotional battering that Andy took gracefully, and with every indication that it was his choice and even a pleasure. She admired that in him, and at the same time she could understand how exhausted he must be. How he could have made a mistake like this, thinking it was for the best without considering all the repercussions. Without considering that a man like Eric could steal his own daughter from a ninety-five-year-old woman any time he wanted when Andy was at work.

"We need to call the police."

"I don't want her to get in trouble."

"She's already in trouble. And we both know who 'she' is, right? If your cousin is in as deep as you think, you're in trouble, too. Rachel, your grandmother—there's no telling how far Eric could go in retribution. I doubt you personally have the money he wants?" Andy shook his head. "Harris is closing in, and you're his target. How long will you get to keep Rachel then? Eric is pissed. I don't think I need to tell you that this is getting bad fast." She wanted to reach out and grab his hand, but she couldn't bring herself to be that vulnerable.

"We can go to Fair Havens—at least try to talk to Zoe." He stopped. The "friend" had a name now. "Maybe she has the money. Maybe we can help her come up with it."

"That's not a good idea. We should just call the sheriff. The current sheriff."

"Please," Andy begged. "Can we try it my way first? I know I'm probably going to lose my job over this, but let's just talk to her."

"I really don't see how that can help," Rye said, but she was caving, and he knew it. He'd always been able to read her.

"Let's just try," he said again. "It couldn't hurt, right?"

"I very much doubt that." She sighed. "And for the record, who's going off half-cocked now?"

He raised an eyebrow. "You always were a bad influence on me."

"Oh, no! You don't get to pin this one on me." Rye shook her head. "What about that lunch you were fixing?"

"It's butternut squash lasagna, and I just put it in the oven. I'll set the timer and tell Grandma we're headed out for a while."

"That you're going somewhere with me? She'll love that."

"She really—"

"Likes me? No, she doesn't."

"You're right, but she hates Eric, and if I tell her he's causing trouble at work, she wouldn't care if I brought Satan himself along to fix it."

"Satan, really? I'm flattered."

40

FORTUNATELY, WANDA LIKED HER ROOMMATE, ELLEN, and they laughed together over a couple sitcoms in the evening. Wanda even took her hearing aids out and used the closed captioning. It was the simplest fun she'd had in a long time. She taught Ellen to say "Good night. Sleep tight" in American Sign. She slept with only a few medications.

Wanda also liked Diane, the therapist, whom she met the following morning, and she worked hard. By afternoon she felt proud of herself and also like she could not move one more muscle without a nap. Why was this physical activity making her so tired? Usually it was just when she wrote a sermon, dealt with a stressful marriage breakup, sat in an endless committee meeting, or visited people in distant Boston hospitals that she felt like she had to sleep in the afternoon. Physical activity was what she did to make herself feel better. But Diane took her measure and guessed she could do it (or maybe Luke had phoned her), and Wanda's therapy was conducted like a chain gang.

So, she did nap after lunch. At three o'clock she woke up with a start, feeling that someone was watching her. Adrenaline flooded her system, and she sat bolt upright to see Lily Vaughan giggling uncontrollably. Wanda dragged breath back into her lungs.

"I'm so sorry. Did we scare you?" Lisa was apologetic. "I told Lily not to get on the bed, but she was tired of waiting."

"How long have you been here?" Wanda dragged her fingers through her hair in a vague combing motion.

Lisa looked at her watch and laughed. "Oh, maybe four and a half minutes."

Wanda smiled. "Thanks for coming."

"Well, you've been such a faithful visitor to others all these years, the good karma should come around to you."

"Is work over already? Lily?" she opened her arms wide, and the little girl swooped over. *Thank you, pain meds.* "What did you do at school today?"

"No school today. It's Saturday!"

"Oh, my. It is Saturday. Of course. I guess I lost track."

"It's our day to come. One day is pretty much like another here. I'm not sure I exactly know how to visit someone who has all their mental capacities."

"Well, clearly I don't seem to have all of mine right now. Can you bring me the wheelchair? I'm not supposed to be using it much, but I want to visit the bathroom and have a quick face wash, and then maybe we can hobble somewhere for a change of scene."

"Where would you like to go?"

"Doh-dee!!" Lily shrieked. Wanda was glad her hearing aids were still out from her nap.

Lisa frowned, even as she rolled the chair over and helped Wanda make the transfer. "Grandma Dottie, in the memory care unit— I don't think you should go over there. Not till we figure out what happened to you."

"And who is trying to figure it out except me? This will let the staff over there know I'm here." Her voice drifted off. Lisa gave her a meaningful stare but kept quiet. "Okay, I see what's wrong with that, but I've got to start somewhere. I'll just be visiting with you, and I'll wave at Jenny. I promise I won't even speak to Joe." She shrugged. "I'll be with you and Lily. What could go wrong?"

41

"You're sure Zoe's working?" Rye asked as Andy waved to the nurse at the front desk.

"I make the schedule. She's definitely on, and she never misses a shift."

"What are you doing here, Andy? Don't you have the evening off?" the nurse called.

"I just couldn't get enough of you, Linda!" Andy strolled over to the desk to fist bump the older woman. "Actually, I'm looking for Zoe. Have you seen her?"

"She's helping Mr. Perkins with his bath right now," Linda replied. "She's been down there a while, though, so either he's giving her a really hard time or she's gotten sidetracked on her way back here."

Andy laughed. "Knowing Mr. P, it's probably the former. He's very private, you know, and Zoe can be a little intimidating."

"Don't I know it?" Linda turned and grabbed the ringing phone, winking at Andy as she did.

He guided Rye down the hall. "We can't interrupt her if she's with a patient."

"Of course not," Rye said. "Maybe she could take a quick break when she's done?"

"Hardly time for that around here," Andy replied, "but we'll give it a shot." He stopped in front of the second-to-last door on the right and knocked. "Zoe?"

"Andy?" She poked her head around the door. "Sweet boy, what are you doing here on your night off? You work too hard!" She saw Rye standing behind him, and the smile dropped off her face. "What's she doing here?"

"We just need to talk to you for a minute," Rye said.

Andy put a hand on her arm. "Zoe, can you give us five minutes when you're done here? For me?"

She looked cross but nodded reluctantly. "For you." Zoe turned and shoulder-bumped the door closed behind her as an old man's hand grabbed for her steadying arm.

Rye leaned against the wall and sighed. "This is ridiculous, isn't it?"

"What?"

"This. Us, here. Asking questions. We should just call the police anonymously and turn her in. Eric, too."

"She's not a bad person, Rye."

"I didn't say she was. But she's stealing drugs, and it's illegal."

Andy shrugged. "Maybe your world is that cut-and-dried, I don't know. We've seen each other, what? Four times since you've been back in town? You just breeze in and expect everyone else to see things your way."

"This isn't a me thing, Andy. It's a law thing, and I know you know that." She looked at him. "You're scared. I get it. But you also know it's wrong."

"And you're trying to do the right thing, but this is messy. Rachel, Eric, Zoe, me? We're messy."

"I get it."

"Do you? Do you know what it's like to try to protect a child from her drug-dealing father?"

Rye laughed bitterly. "What exactly do you think I do all day? Do you know how many students I keep tabs on?"

"It's not the same."

"You're right. It's not. Because at the end of the day, you can be with Rachel. You can make sure she eats and does her homework and goes to bed. You're fighting for her, Andy. Most of the kids I'm trying to help don't have anyone fighting for them."

"Except you."

Rye sighed. "Except me. But I'm just one person. And there are so many of them. Most days it's like watching a tsunami. It just builds and builds until one of them gets swept away. Then it's another. A dropout. A suicide. A drunk driving accident. And those are just the headlines. Every day on page six, buried under all the tragedies, are little stories of neglect and desperation. They just need so much."

"Like we did."

She looked up at him. "Exactly like that."

Andy leaned against the wall, side by side with her, his shoulder pressed against hers. "That sucks."

"It really does."

"But you like it? Your job?"

"I can't imagine doing anything else. If I don't get my job back...I don't know what I'll do."

"And yet you're still here. You're not dropping everything, which is what the condition for getting that job back is?"

"I didn't say everything I do makes sense."

He sighed. "I'm being selfish not calling the police."

"No."

"Yeah, I am." They watched Linda push a cart of laundry down the hall, an older man following closely behind her carrying a doll. Andy smiled at him.

"You're trying to protect yourself," she said.

"That's basically the definition of 'selfish.'"

Rye thought about it. "I guess I can't really argue with that. But I understand why. You've got a lot of balls in the air right now. If one gets knocked out—"

"The others are definitely coming down."

42

IT TOOK WANDA TEN MINUTES TO FEEL PRESENTABLE—clean teeth, brushed hair, just a hint of lipstick. Sweatpants! She felt like she was eighty in sweatpants, but she wasn't going to see many people who weren't eighty, and those would probably be in scrubs. She did feel a little hesitant, but she had every right to move around this facility. She was not going to let the anxieties of Rye and Hardy and Tony and even Lisa rule her life. She did decide to stay in the wheelchair rather than hobbling on the walker. It would be so easy to push her over.

The simplest route to the memory loss unit was going outside and around. There were no stairs to navigate, and they could breathe in the late spring warmth while Lily studied pansies winking their purple and yellow eyes at her. So Wanda arrived the way she always did, down the sidewalk, through the password-protected door. She just arrived much more slowly. She scanned the common room.

N. C. Harris was bent over between two patients near the large-screen television, obviously mediating a disagreement about channel choice, but, as if he could feel her presence, he straightened up and turned around the minute the three of them came in. The expression on his face was so hostile that Wanda suddenly had an intense desire to shift into reverse and roll right out the door. It was not his nurse's aide game face, although, to give his undercover skills credit, he transitioned to that face in seconds. If not welcoming, at least blandly displeased.

She didn't see any other familiar faces. The charge nurse behind the desk must be a weekend staffer. Neither Andy nor Zoe were in sight. There were two students in spotless white uniforms doing some kind of interning rotation. They were talking to each other awkwardly rather than to the residents. Lisa was scanning for her great-aunt. Lily spotted her first and ran across the room to where older woman was dozing.

Lisa locked Wanda's wheels. "Are you okay here? Or would you like to chat with Jenny? I will admit that Dottie is—" She paused, embarrassed for her grandma's losses. "She doesn't have speech anymore."

"I'm familiar with that." Something else seemed to be wrong. "Do new people make her cranky?" she asked, and Lisa immediately relaxed.

"I'm afraid so."

"Don't worry. I'll find my way to Jenny's room for a bit. I'll use my trusty walker. Let me know when you're ready to leave, and we'll roll on back to the other side. I promise I won't get in any trouble."

Lisa laughed. "FLW."

Wanda must have looked confused.

"Famous last words."

"Oh, you mean 'benediction'?"

Using a walker did not do much for Wanda's ego. She had asked Diane about using crutches instead. After all, football players bravely met their television interviewers on crutches.

Diane pointed to the wire mesh basket on the front of the walker. "As every self-respecting AARP member knows...?" She raised her eyebrows in question.

Wanda shook her head vigorously. She was not fifty-five. Not yet.

"Well, with a walker you can carry things—your purse, your crossword puzzle book, your car keys, and, with this handy insert, a cup of coffee."

Now that got Wanda where she lived. She could see the inconvenience of crutches. No place for coffee was serious.

She asked Lisa to unhook and unfold the walker from the back of the wheelchair, and then she attached the basket she'd brought along on her lap. She didn't have a crossword puzzle book, but she did have an adult coloring book and pencils to give to Jenny. Wanda admitted that she had been behind the times. She had not realized that this was the gift du jour for hospital visits, but she had received four of them with detachable pages just in case she wanted to hang up her finished intricate floral designs. The "adult" coloring page concept was disappointingly PG.

Although Wanda frequently took a small sketch pad on her walks with Wink and loved watercolor pencils, coloring in the lines just did not resonate with her personality.

She had tried a page. She really had.

Jenny might enjoy it, though, and, if so, she might enjoy three more. Wanda added one of her new sets of pencils and her keys, which made no sense, except that she never went anywhere without house, car, church, and two mystery keys from some past doors she no longer remembered, as well as plastic tags for Petco, the gym, Panera Bread, and the public library. She shrugged. It was a symbol of independence. It meant she could drive (well, eventually), and she was in a community where very few people had that privilege.

It was a lot slower heading to Jenny's room. Each step was a separate effort. All these meal tables and several cute little conversational settings were spread out in one very large room, probably for easy wheeling and great visibility for the limited staff. Hard on privacy. Harder on a walk-er using a walker. Wanda decided to stop at the desk and ask the charge nurse whether Jenny was in her room before heading down that endless corridor. Step, step, lean on the walker. Step, step, lean on the walker, grateful for strength training. She would never skip weights again. Her arms were feeling more than "burn."

Somebody went past her, moving quickly, but she barely looked up from the fascinating pattern on the carpet and her Sketchers.

Only halfway across the common room to the desk? What a terrible architectural design for people with limitations. How did anyone ever escape? She knew they did. That was why there were passcodes everywhere. She considered calling out to Lisa to bring the wheelchair and give her a lift, or rather a push. Dottie couldn't be that cranky. It would be embarrassing. She looked up, and there was a male butt she recognized.

She wouldn't have thought that was possible, but a great derriere was tough to forget. Laredo's. The guy in black at the pool table. The fight with Andy. Great—someone looking to cause trouble with Andy.

"Zoe. Where is she? I need to talk with her." His voice was low and threatening, and Wanda realized that she was in fact nearer than her original estimate based on the pain in her leg. She was the only one who could overhear them. There was a big faux leather recliner facing away from the desk, and she eased herself down into it, hoping it was the kind with the machinery to help her stand up again. Otherwise she was stranded.

"Look," the nurse said, irritated. "Personal visits are not—"

"I want to see Zoe Laferriere. Now, if you don't want any trouble."

Wanda shot mental tweets to the older woman, who clearly was more efficient than smart. *Say she isn't working today. Say she isn't here, for God's sake.*

"Zoe is busy. She's with a patient."

He just growled.

43

ZOE OPENED THE DOOR AND GLANCED DOWN THE hallway toward the common room. She turned back to Rye and Andy and stood with her shoulders braced. "This is about the texts, isn't it?"

"What texts?" Andy asked.

Rye straightened. "You've been sending me those messages? Those disgusting texts?"

"Zoe?" Andy's eyes were wide with realization. "Why would you do that?"

Zoe's face was pale. "You didn't know?"

"How did you even get my number?"

Andy shook his head slowly. "She knows my passcode. I let her borrow my phone to call her daughter."

"You took advantage of Andy to get my number and then got a burner phone and sent that filth? Why?" Rye demanded.

"You're making trouble," Zoe replied. "With Nicole. Here. You and that preacher. You need to mind your own business."

"Did you drive Pastor Wanda off the road?" Andy looked like he didn't want to know the answer.

Zoe shook her head. "No. No, I would not do that."

"But you know who did?" Rye asked, studying the older woman's face.

Zoe grabbed Andy's hand tightly. "He's a bad man, your cousin. Very bad. I shouldn't have gotten involved with him. He threatened me."

"Because you haven't been able to pay him?" Andy asked.

"He keeps asking for more and more money. I paid him the first time, and now he wants more. I don't have anything else. I told him I would get more, but I have to live. I have to buy food, pay rent. He doesn't care. He didn't even do what he said he would. He just took the medicine. Kept it as more payment." Zoe was on the verge of tears.

"You need to call the police," Rye said.

"I can't!" Zoe said. "What would I tell them?"

44

Three things happened at the same time. Lily was in front of Wanda with a smile as big as Alaska and a drawing to show. There was a weird painful squeak from the charge nurse. And N. C. Harris disappeared.

"You're hurting me."

Wanda turned in her chair. The young man had the nurse's arm in a tight grip, and she was pulling backward, a startled but not yet panicked expression on her face. "Let go of my arm."

"I am going to ask you once more. Where is Zoe Laferriere?"

The nurse's mouth opened and closed, a gaping fish. Nothing came out.

Wanda couldn't help herself. Stupid. Interfering. She stayed in the chair but tried to sound like a very old lady. "Hey, you? Mrs. Zoe will be back in a few minutes, and you can talk with her. No need to get so excited."

His attention shifted. He took in the room of mostly older people, but his focus went right to her—the only short fifty-something broken-legged woman. Everyone was watching him. Like most people, he had registered the residents and their dementia and dismissed them. But his eyes sharpened when he saw Wanda. He recognized her. He recognized her!

"If it isn't the nosy preacher." He dropped the nurse's arm. "Haven't you learned to mind your own business? I guess you need another lesson." He was over her chair in a minute, and when Wanda saw his eyes, she only had a moment to think, *He's insane, or he's high.*

He picked her up under her elbows like she weighed nothing, held her over the ground, and dropped her. When her leg hit the ground, she screamed. Everything went black. She was losing consciousness, and, oh, that would be so very much nicer, but she could see that he'd let her drop because he had a more portable hostage. She pushed the edges of blackness away by sheer force of will. Lily was under one of his arms. There was a gun in his other hand.

45

A WOMEN'S SCREAM CUT THE AIR. AND THEN, "WHERE is she?" a man's voice yelled again. "Where is she?"

Andy went gray. "Eric," he mouthed to Rye.

"What am I going to do?" Zoe whispered.

"Out the back door," Rye replied softly. "Just get out of here."

Zoe nodded and started to make her way to the emergency exit when a child's scream rang out.

LILY WAS KICKING HARDER. "MAMA!"

"Shut up, kid."

She started to cry. Or was that Lisa? Somewhere in the room, Wanda could hear Lisa crying. Her gaze came to rest on Harris. He was crouched behind a laundry cart, a gun in his hand. He shook his head slightly to encourage her not to betray his presence.

Wanda slowly reached into the basket of her walker, tipped on its side but near enough. She snagged her ring of keys, something to throw, distract.

Then there was another voice coming from the hallway where Jenny lived. Wanda could just see Andy, and behind him, Rye. "Eric, let the kid go." Andy waved at him. "You don't want to do this, man."

Eric's face went red, and he swung around. The gun went off wide, smashing a light sconce. Andy knocked Rye over and fell on her. And good Lily, smart Lily, brave Lily, Supergirl Lily, bit Eric's hand hard, and he dropped her. He swung back, but she was gone, hidden behind the nurse's station. The nurse wrapped her arms around Lily, God bless her.

Andy was back up on his knees. He toppled a table, and he and Rye rushed to crouch behind it. Residents were crying out, terrified. One woman was yelling, "Jesus, oh sweet Jesus, oh sweet Jesus."

Eric shook his head. *He is high,* Wanda thought. And then he remembered her. Not far from his feet. He pointed his gun at her.

"Too slow for a hostage," he said.

"No, no, no. You can take me. Wheelchair. I can cover you. No one will risk shooting me. That's a great idea. Can't kill a pastor, right?" She was babbling.

"Just shut up. Everyone needs to shut their mouths—"

And then he shut up as Harris reversed his gun and brought the butt of it down hard on the back of Eric's head. Andy's tackle hit him sideways a second later, and Wanda was deliriously glad none of them landed on her.

47

Wanda hated owing N.C. Harris. She was happier crediting Andy with her rescue, and extremely grateful that he was the one who volunteered to go with her back to the hospital. She was incredibly lucky that none of the surgical work on her leg had been damaged. She was also grateful for the pain meds. She did not remember much of the rest of the day.

Eric had a concussion but ended up in jail after brief observation. Wanda did not let herself drift away until after he had been removed from the emergency cubicle next to hers. Even with a police presence, it was hard to breathe normally with him near.

Diane the physical therapist didn't see any reason to cut Wanda any slack the next morning. The therapy session was fifty minutes but felt like two hundred, and Wanda didn't understand why she had all the manipulations and exercises while she could see other people enjoying ultrasound, heat packs, and massage. It was just wrong.

After Diane released her, the police arrived to take her statement. Wanda decided to be as honest as she could, mentioning that she had seen Eric before and had witnessed the fight at Laredo's. When she asked the officer whether Eric had run her off the road, the woman was evasive. Apparently the green paint matched Eric's car, but the investigation was still open. So no answers yet.

She was fading into a well-deserved afternoon nap when Rye arrived.

"I brought you something," the younger woman said as she flopped down in the visitor's chair.

"God help you if it's an adult coloring book."

"Nope. Food."

"Wings?"

"Ben and Jerry's."

"Florence Nightingale. There must be something that functions as a bowl around here."

"There's a pint for each of us. Your choice—Bourbon Brown Butter or Salted Caramel Core."

"What in the name of all that is holy is Bourbon Brown Butter?"

Rye read from the carton. "Bourbon brown butter ice cream with dark chocolate whiskey cordial cups and a bourbon brown butter swirl."

"Oh, yes, but oh, no. Probably not with the good drugs they're giving me. Salted Caramel it is."

"You don't have to eat the whole pint."

"I'm sorry. What did you say? My hearing aid must be turned off."

Rye laughed, and they settled down into some serious snacking. After a few minutes, Rye sighed happily. "My man on the inside told me that Eric is running some kind of drug enterprise by funneling off prescription medications from a number of senior facilities. Not a druglord by any means, but a tidy little living. Someone's on his payroll in each institution. He's spilling everything in hopes of a deal. He paid his suppliers, but not nearly what he was making. The problem here was that he let Zoe Laferriere believe the medications were going to a clinic in Haiti, and she became a big supplier, which risked his secrecy. Then he started charging her to 'ship' via mule to Haiti. Basically, he was getting her to steal drugs and then charging her for them. Pretty good deal until she got suspicious."

Wanda took it in. "I think he was using his product, and that impaired his judgment. When I was close to him, he looked high as a kite, and grabbing a kid—or shooting me in front of witnesses—how completely wild is that?"

"Agreed."

"But we caught him, so a toast?" Wanda and Rye bumped pints.

Rye eyed her. "Apparently, we came close to sabotaging the whole 'sting,' at least according to Harris. And get this—he works for Merck or AstraZeneca or Lilly or something. A cop? Not even close. Fake ID, or, according to him, 'not government, and not a forgery.' He's so full of it." She shoved her spoon into her pint violently.

"I sabotaged it? Eric was already harassing Linda when I arrived. I was just trying to deflect him."

"Mission accomplished."

"Did I say it wasn't dumb? Still. What about the accident? Have you heard anything?"

"Yes. Your paint was on Eric's car. His is on yours. He might have been running a drug op, but he's not the sharpest tool in the shed."

"I'm really glad. I don't want to think about someone else out there wishing me very bad things. Gunshots at Pieter and me?"

"Matched his gun. Not sure what else we're going to hear before this goes to trial."

Wanda licked her spoon. "Goes to trial—that sounds so official."

"And boring. The wheels of justice are crucial, and dull." Rye sighed. "We're back at square one with our actual investigation." She shook her head. "We thought this was related to Niels, but Zoe and Harris got anxious for completely unrelated reasons, and the minute Eric heard we were hanging around Fair Havens, it escalated. We should have known that the notes in your car, the nasty texts, a car bump in the night, and a job threat were the tactics of very different people."

"And Bellona is a stone-cold—"

"—grieving widow. But you know, Wanda, that's the piece that still has something to do with our original investigation. How did Niels Pond die? Everything else was about the drugs. We just stumbled on it." Rye paused. "Is Zoe still here?"

"She walked out the emergency door and was probably halfway to Logan before Eric was apprehended. I understand she's in Port-au-Prince now, and Fair Havens residents have been told that she went to care for a sick relative. Her husband and kids are staying in town until Nicole graduates. Win one for Tony's music program."

"I can't say I'm sorry she's gone. She did not like me." Rye sighed. "But we're not any closer to the answer we wanted."

Wanda nodded. "I think we should ask Joe. His identification of the drug problem was remarkably accurate. I'm pretty sure he has sundowners, but tomorrow morning I think the two of us should visit and see what he knows when we come at it directly.

Circumspect is not really a good strategy for Alzheimer's folks."

"What's sundowners?"

"Sundown syndrome is the confusion and agitation in people with dementia that usually strikes around sunset because of the lessening of the light. It's much better in the morning."

"Let's go now. It's June, for goodness' sake. Sunset doesn't come till eight thirty."

"Tomorrow is soon enough."

"That's avoidance behavior. You haven't been back there, have you?"

Wanda looked everywhere but at her friend's face. "I'm more cognitively agile in the morning myself."

"Tomorrow I am officially reinstated and back at school. I don't think Mendoza would love it if I took my first day back to investigate the case that got me in trouble in the first place." She held out a hand. "It's now or never."

48

RYE PUSHED THE WHEELCHAIR. WANDA WAS SURE that she never would have gone into the memory loss unit again if someone else weren't propelling her. There were multiple small explosions of fear at retracking these steps. The door. The big recliner she had cowered behind. Dottie dozing over by the television set. The wide central desk with the medication cart behind it. Each one set off a distinct terror.

She was obviously not successful in keeping the fear out of her face. Several of the residents already sitting at the preset dinner tables turned away from her as if she were disturbing them. A per diem nurse, who was probably taking the place of Linda, looked away as clearly as if saying, "Not a resident, not my problem." Andy Soucek came over to her and without even a glance at Rye squatted down to her level.

"Wanda, are you okay?"

"Coming over here is harder than I thought." She registered his concern. "How terrified do I look?"

"Hmm." He mock-considered, rubbing his chin. "Well, if we suddenly threw up the lights on an audience watching *Silent Night, Deadly Night*, you would not look out of place. If a bull elephant came running through the unit and you mistakenly had used female elephant pheromones instead of deodorant this morning, or if, say, the release mechanism on an MRI broke down and they told you that you would need to spend the next twenty-four hours locked in a steel tube…"

She was laughing. "I get it. That bad, huh?" But the tension was broken, and it was just an ordinary common room with ordinary folks living with and coping with dementia. This kind young man was used to breaking into their imaginary places of fright and returning them to safety. "Thanks, Andy."

He gave Rye a quick look. "Okay, ladies, no drama on my unit today, right?"

Rye snorted a little under her breath. "Drama, us? Never."

"Almost suppertime. Quick visit?"

"Going down to see Joe. Is that okay?"

"He's mobile and doesn't need toileting, so that's fine. We anticipate the supper carts in about twenty minutes, so if you want to visit and then walk him back here when you leave, it would be great. He doesn't have a roommate yet, but I think a new person is moving in tomorrow."

"That will be nice for him."

"It's going to wipe away most of his memories of his last roommate. That's probably a good thing. I am guessing you two want to talk with him about that, and while I'm not thrilled, I can't stop you." He leveled a long look at Rye.

Wanda took the lead. "Thanks, Andy. We aren't planning to upset Joe. If he gets agitated at all, we'll shut up. Promise."

"Thanks. I'll hold both of you to that. And Wanda?"

"Yes?"

"Next time I see you, I better *not* see this wheelchair action. I'll give you a pass because of the slam dunk you took yesterday, but I expect walker-on-the-way-to-cane, or I am going to report you to Diane."

"Threat is noted."

Joe had a small TV of his own, wall-mounted and too high to be pulled on. It was tuned in to PGA, and golf seemed to have a soporific effect. Rye knocked loudly on the already open door so Joe would not be startled to find people already in his room when he woke up.

"I'm not hungry," he growled without looking up.

"Good thing, because I'm not much of a cook," Wanda replied.

He opened his eyes and smiled. Then he took in the wheelchair. "What happened to you, Rev? Fall out of the pulpit?"

"I had a car accident, Joe, and broke my leg. Mostly I'm up on a walker." She nodded at his. "This is my friend Rye."

He looked at Rye. "Take after your mother in looks. Good thing, because old Hardy is plain as the back of a barn."

Rye was startled. Small town. Of course he knew her father. She wasn't going to think about the fact that he knew her mother. "I've been told I have my father's cranky disposition."

"Heart of gold underneath. Way, way underneath."

They laughed. Wanda asked, "What's new with you, Joe?"

"Shoot-out. Like Dodge City in here yesterday."

"You see it? Anybody hurt?"

"I missed it. Dozing with my man Tiger Woods—now there's a comeback kid. Gives an old man hope.

They arrested the bad man, you know. I'm glad. I hated it when he came to our room. I pretended to sleep. But they arrested him. I'm glad. Oh, and old Slinky Shoes is gone, too. Good riddance."

Wanda was trying to compute Zoe and the nickname 'Slinky Shoes' when the penny dropped. "Nurse Harris. Slinky Shoes. That's a good one."

He looked proud. "Always popping up with no warning."

Wanda's and Rye's eyes met. Joe was very lucid today. One false move, though. Mentally, Wanda lobbed the ball to Rye, who sat down in the visitor's chair.

"Joe, I'm the vice principal at the high school." She waited, but he didn't say anything.

"Niels Pond's daughter is one of my students."

Without a moment's notice, big tears welled up in his eyes. "I'm so sorry," he said. "I am so very sorry." His soft old face dissolved into creases, and they were all wet. Wanda couldn't budge the locked wheelchair, but her whole body strained forward. Rye moved right over and sat on the bed next to his chair and took his hands in hers.

"It's okay, Joe. You don't need to be sorry."

"I shouldn't…I did something. I shouldn't. But…"

"What is it?"

He looked up. "I don't know. I don't…I should have just…not…"

"Joe," Wanda took over. "Niels Pond. He died. He's at rest. His kids are sad, but they are going to be all right."

"He shouldn't have done it. Not to his little girl. She came even when the others didn't bother."

"Joe," Rye asked. "What did Niels do?"

"He found all those pills. A bag in his shoes, his fancy ones. In his drawer. I put them there because he hates those shoes. Never wears them. Never." He stared down at his hands. "Shouldn't have hid them. Should have left it alone."

"Joe," Wanda asked, "where did the bag come from?"

"I took it." His hands clenched. "She left it here one night, in a hurry. Left it right there." Joe pointed a shaking finger at his own dresser. "Left it there, and I took it. Hid it in a shoe."

"Nurse Zoe?"

He nodded. "She was so mad. Couldn't find it, though. She was mad. And the bad man, too. Plugged the wall good." Joe paused. "Old Slinky-Shoes is gone, you know. And Tiger."

"Joe, did Niels take the pills?"

"No. No. Didn't see that. No. They were so mad. Yelling. Then Niels was yelling, and he threw his shoe. Bag fell right out," Joe said, wiping his eyes. "Thought they'd be happy then, but no. Gave him his meds. You know. He was mad. Niels could get mad. Not at me, though. No."

Rye and Wanda stared at each other. Not suicide, then. No evidence, of course. Nothing but an old man with dementia to prove their suspicions.

"What did you do to yourself, Rev?" Joe asked. "Only way you could get shorter than you already were is sitting down." Joe laughed at his own joke.

Rye stood up. "I think it's suppertime. Let me get you a damp washcloth to wipe your face. You want to look nice for supper."

He accepted the cloth and got rid of any evidence of tears. Wanda wondered whether Rye was being so solicitous for the sake of Joe's appearance or to avoid Andy's displeasure. They went with him down the hall and waved good-bye when he sat down with three ladies who seemed particularly appreciative of his male presence. He didn't seem to notice Rye and Wanda leave.

They were on the sidewalk outside when Rye locked the wheels and sat down on a bench. "They killed him, Wanda."

"We don't know that. Not for certain."

Rye stared at her, incredulous. "You don't think Zoe and Eric force-fed Niels Pond drugs?"

"I think we only have the word of a man with dementia. I doubt Eric will admit to it, whether it was accidental or not. Zoe's gone." She sighed. "Any evidence is long gone, too."

"So they'll get away with it."

"Zoe's left her entire family behind. She can never come back to the life she built. Eric will go to jail. I don't consider that getting away with it, do you?" Wanda asked.

Rye bit her lip. "I guess not. It just seems…"

"Unfair?"

"Very." They looked at the flowers planted along the bath, heard the sparrows chirping to each other. The parking lot was quiet. No screeching tires today, or threatening notes. "What do we tell the Ponds?"

Wanda let out a half-hearted laugh. "Nothing." She looked at Rye. "They don't want to know this. They don't want to know us."

"So, we just let it rest, then?" Rye asked.

"No," Wanda said. "We let him rest."

49

RYE SAT STARING UP AT THE BIG HOUSE. SHE KNEW SHE should get out of the car, but her legs were ignoring her. At the end of this song, though, definitely. Unfortunately, the front door opened, and Lara Alesci waved at Rye, inviting her in. She sighed and grabbed her bag off the front seat.

Stepping onto the walk, she gave Lara a reserved smile. "Good morning."

"Ms. Rye. Please come in." She ushered her into the empty living room. "Bellona will be in from the garden in just a minute. I'm putting on tea."

She disappeared down the hallway, and Rye sat gingerly on the edge of one of the expensively upholstered couches. She looked up at the sound of someone coming down the staircase. Leslie paused in the doorway. The girl was dressed in leggings and a sweatshirt that seemed to engulf her. Still, she looked better than the last time Rye had seen her, and for that, Rye was grateful.

"Hey," Rye said.

"Hey."

"I didn't know you were on the swim team." Rye nodded to the logo across Leslie's chest.

"Not anymore. Didn't like getting up at four a.m. for practice."

"I don't blame you." Rye shuddered. "I had a friend who did it when I went to Stoneridge. She was eighth in our class and managed to be in the pool about ten hours a day. I still don't know how she did it."

"Maybe she had a time turner," Leslie offered.

Rye smiled. "She was definitely the kind of person who deserved to try one of those out."

"Does she still swim a lot?"

"I don't know. We don't really keep in touch anymore." Rye shrugged. "I'm not great at keeping up with a lot of people, you know?"

Leslie came in and sprawled at the far end of the sofa. "Yeah."

The silence stretched out between them. Rye could hear Lara in the kitchen, cupboards opening and closing, dishes clattering. Leslie seemed to be waiting for something.

Rye cleared her throat. "Can I ask you a question?" Leslie just stared at her, alert. Her body was still relaxed, though, so Rye pushed on. "Do you know what happened to your dad?"

Leslie pulled her phone out of the pocket of her hoodie and fiddled around with it. She was quiet for so long that Rye had an eternity to regret asking. Finally, Leslie handed the phone to Rye. Leslie had pulled up a picture of herself with Niels and his roommate, Joe. They were smiling, wearing children's pointy party hats. Leslie and Joe were both holding up plates with slices of cake.

"I liked going to see my dad. More than anyone else, I think. I didn't really mind that he was…different. Before he got sick…" Leslie paused. "Before, he was too busy for me. He was always flying to conferences and getting asked to lecture. I know he was doing important stuff, but it felt like we never saw him. I know you probably think this thing with my mom and Lara is weird, but Lara's always been around. She's always been part of the family, I guess, even when my dad was here." She took back her phone and looked down at the photo. "My dad was a lot more fun, sometimes, after he got sick."

"You got to spend time with him."

Leslie nodded. "He and Joe were friends. When Joe was doing well, I think Dad was too. When Joe got pneumonia last winter, my father got angry a lot more. He didn't really recover from that, though, even after Joe got better."

"I'm sorry."

"I should have realized how bad it had gotten, but my friend Nicole and I were really busy in choir. We got to go to Spain last month to sing, and I just didn't know."

"There's no way for you to have known. Alzheimer's is a complex disease. It's unpredictable. Good days and bad, there's really no way you could have known—"

"But I saw it."

"Saw what?"

Leslie glanced toward the kitchen, but neither Lara nor Bellona had made an appearance. She lowered her voice. "This baggie of pills in his bottom drawer. A couple of weeks ago, I was putting away one of his winter sweaters, and I saw it."

"What do you think they were?"

"I don't know," Leslie said, "but he had a lot of them. I should have said something. It's my fault." Rye looked up at her to see that she was crying. She stayed very still, as though she were coaxing a wild hare out of the brush. She didn't say anything, just let Leslie cry. When she glanced at the doorway, she realized that Bellona and Lara had come in together. Bellona had tears running down her cheeks. She walked over and knelt in front of her daughter and took Leslie's hands.

"I'm so sorry," she whispered.

Leslie looked up, her eyes wet and red. "It was my fault."

"It wasn't," Rye said. She hated to interrupt this moment, but she had to share at least a sliver of truth with this girl. "There was an incident at Fair Havens the other day. I don't know if you heard."

Leslie nodded hesitantly. "Nicole's mom—" Her eyes overflowed. "She was…involved?"

"There were drugs being smuggled from the facility. I think Nicole's mom was trying to help people in Haiti. She thought she was helping them, at least. The man she got involved with, though—he was dangerous. Joe and your father—" She looked at Leslie. How much to say? "They were in the wrong place at the wrong time." There was no way she was going to tell Leslie that her best friend's mother, now a fugitive, might also be a murderer.

Bellona glanced at Rye. She knew, and she was protecting Leslie, too. Rye had talked to Hardy and let him decide who needed to know what. She was glad Bellona had been told, regardless of what Wanda said. She was also glad it hadn't come from them. "After that, the staff conducted a thorough search of the facility, and they found other bags like it in other rooms."

Leslie shook her head. "I still should have said something. Wil and Ro—"

"We'll sit down and talk about it together. They need to know, too," her mother said.

Leslie looked like she was going to cry again. Rye instinctively reached out and grabbed her hand. "Look, I'm going to say something that maybe your mom and Lara wish I wouldn't, but it's the truth, and I feel like you're old enough to be told the truth." Leslie straightened up and wiped her eyes. "You *should* have said something."

Bellona narrowed her eyes, bristling, then nodded in consent.

Rye pushed on. "In the future, I hope if you see something that scares you, you'll be brave enough to say something about it to somebody you trust." She squeezed Leslie's hand. "It's not an easy thing to do. The right thing is almost never easy." She looked at Bellona. "And the thing is, your mom is right, too. This wasn't your fault. Not at all."

"It feels like it is," Leslie said softly. "It feels like he would still be here if I hadn't messed up."

"And that's why you swallowed pills, too?" Rye asked bluntly.

"Yes," Leslie said.

"You were trying to punish yourself by doing the same thing you thought your dad did?" Rye continued.

Leslie just nodded. "It felt…right."

"Oh, sweetheart," Lara said, stroking Leslie's knee. "What can we do?"

Leslie stared down at her own hands. "I don't know. I don't want to feel this way anymore, but I don't know how to make it go away."

"If you feel like you're ready to talk about it," Rye said, "I know some really great therapists. I'm happy to make introductions if you want to try it."

"I think I need that."

Bellona cleared her throat. "I think I might, too."

"Leslie, I was talking to Joe yesterday, and he feels the same way you do—that on some level he knew, and he didn't say anything, and that he is responsible."

"Oh, no, Joe couldn't—"

"I know, and you couldn't either, and yet you both feel really bad. When you've had some time with a therapist, maybe you can visit Joe and help him feel better."

"She doesn't need to—" Bellona interrupted.

"I'd like to, Mom. It's something I could do to help someone."

Leslie stood up and wrapped her long arms around her mother. "I told Nicole I would come over. Is it okay if I take your car?"

Bellona looked momentarily stunned by the adolescent conversational shift, but she blinked and nodded. "Of course. Invite her over for dinner, would you? We haven't seen her in far too long, and I think she's probably having a pretty tough time right now."

"Okay," Leslie said, squeezing Lara in a quick hug as she grabbed a set of keys from the hook by the table. She turned back to Rye. "I'll come by on Monday for those names, okay, Ms. Rye?"

Rye glanced at Bellona, who shrugged and nodded slightly. "Sounds like a plan."

50

WANDA OCCASIONALLY CONSIDERED WRITING A BOOK about the emotionally healing power of time, but she knew that no one would buy it. Time was too slow (except when it wasn't), too passive, too boring, too uncontrollable, and too cheap. It was amazing what people were willing to spend to fix their hearts.

Allowing its passage was the most effective way to process and deal with just about anything. Nobody wanted to hear that, though. They wanted a fix. So the advice she gave parishioners offered them one. It was always twofold—time and therapy; time and prayers; time and a massage, pedicure, and new shoes; time and exercise in the fresh air; time and a new job; time and a profile on a dating site; time and chocolate. She guessed that time all by itself would be just as helpful without any of the additives, but people wanted to help themselves in an active way to get out of whatever swamp of sadness or self-pity they were stuck in. Americans—and chief among them, she suspected, New Englanders particularly—hated to wait.

Wanda also loved—personally, passionately, and unashamedly—avoidance behavior. It had such an unfortunate reputation. Contrary to folk wisdom, many things really did give up and go away when you didn't feed them, pet them, coddle them, or brood over them. Just letting time pass had the tangential benefit of rendering unnecessary the undoing of too-hasty responses to situations—selling a house after a death, disastrous rebound dating, accepting the first job offer, moving to Hawaii. Well, maybe moving to Hawaii was never a bad choice.

How much time? people would ask. They did not want to hear, *You'll know.* It was, however, true. True did not necessarily sell. She wasn't ready to write the book yet.

So Wanda had either intentionally given it time, or she had practiced avoidance with Lisa's low-grade anger about Lily's endangerment. Wanda was not completely sure which it had been. Probably some of both. She apologized once for putting the little girl in such a scary situation, and then she just let it go. No excuses. No defensiveness. She held her breath. Lisa did not quit her job. Wanda knew that she had looked at a number of online want ads, because she had left them open on the office computer. Wanda refused to guess whether having her boss discover them there was the purpose or whether she was in a genuine job search. Wanda envisioned an imaginary headline: "Seeking Job Less Hazardous Than Church Administrator."

And then it was over. The storm of emotions had blown out to sea, and the friendship was still intact. Wanda was hugely relieved when her admin stuck her head around the door instead of buzzing though and announced, "Hottie on line two."

"Which one?"

"Funeral Hottie. Your fave."

"I refuse to accept that talking to the funeral home is in any sense my favorite."

"Last rites can't go wrong."

"You didn't say that!"

The blond head disappeared.

"Hello, Luke."

"Hi Wanda, how are you?"

"I'm walking with a cane, and I have put off my zip line and samba lessons until autumn."

"I was thinking of a sport with a little less impact. How about dinner on Friday?"

"Sure, and who died?"

He cleared his throat. "This is Luke Fairchild, and I would like to ask Wanda Duff out to dinner…with her cane."

"Which I will definitely need, because it is extremely hard to walk with one's foot in one's mouth. No one died. You're just being nice. I'm so sorry."

"Gosh, that sounds nice. Can you repeat that last part again?"

"I am a complete—"

"Okay, stop! It was wonderful. I live for moments like that, but in fact…"

"You do have a death. You malicious mortician! You made me feel so—"

"So predictable, my delightful Wanda. So easy to tease. So good-natured. So rarely, but occasionally, humble. So excellent a pastor to the unchurched. Hmm?

"But, yes, Irene Perkins, not a member of any church, but a good soul anyway, says everyone who knows her, died at the advanced age of one hundred and two at the county home. There's not much in the way of family. Her children and their spouses all predeceased Irene, and there is one grandson, Brandon, who is coming from Michigan. I suggested that we have a service in the Community Room at the home. Mrs. Perkins was very popular with the other residents, and a Miss Elizabeth Murray will play the piano as long as you pick four of the five hymns she knows."

"I'll bite. Why only four?"

"Because number five is 'Silent Night.' Not a big June favorite."

"Whom should I contact?"

"I'll give you Brandon's number, and also Elisa Farley, activities director."

"I know Elisa. Sending me the obit?"

"It's in your inbox."

"You don't have to take me out to dinner, you know."

"I knew you would go there." He was laughing. "We've just been on the wrong…uh, foot for the last few weeks since Niels Pond died."

And Pieter Pond came to town, Wanda thought to herself. She didn't let herself go there. The visit in the hospital was lovely, the kiss even better, though she worried that maybe the memory of that was a painkiller-induced dream and not reality. The only follow-up was a text that he was heading to New York and would depart from there to Rotterdam, and best wishes for her recuperation. Casual. Light. She matched the tone with a text back and good wishes to the corgi Bram.

No good sighing over plucked Dutch tulips when there was a Tuscany poppy within reach. "Is this dinner at a certain place where the saxophone gets going later at night, and you change from Luke Fairchild to Luca Fraticelli, and I change from respectable clergy colleague to fervent groupie?"

"Great wing appetizers."

"I've gone 'cold chicken'—no wings. But I think I remember some amazing potato skins with cheese and jalapenos."

"Wanda without wings? All the angels in heaven are drooping in despair. Shall I pick you up at six?"

And that would mean he would have to drive her home. This was a world of difference from 'meet you there.'

"That would be great."

"We'll have a good time."

Time. The best part of healing. Another chapter in the bestseller of her future: "Having a good time."

51

RYE SHIELDED HER EYES FROM THE SUN. ON THE FIELD below, she could hear Mike's good-natured bellowing as his team ran sprints. Camila was doing laps on the track around the football field, her long legs effortlessly covering distance, killing time until practice was over. At five on the dot, Mike would release his team, and the three of them would get a much-needed dinner at the only sushi restaurant in a forty-mile radius. Ana seemed to be enjoying the company of someone special these days, though as Ana was the "careful twin," it would be weeks before he'd be introduced—if at all—for the inevitable grilling.

Rye preferred to do her waiting up here, where she had a view of her school, with conversation a pleasantly muted backdrop. And it was hers again, thanks to a phone call from Bellona Pond, probably prompted by her better half, though Rye had no desire to investigate further and risk drawing any more attention to herself. It felt like ages since she had been able to relax with her friends without worrying about nasty texts or grieving widows. She was ready to kick back in a sports bar where they could yell at as many different televisions as they wanted while stuffing themselves with half-price happy hour snacks.

Of course, she'd only been back to work for a week, and already she was dreaming about summer vacation a month down the pike. How quickly she was able to forget the anxiety of an uncertain future in exchange for the run-of-the-mill challenges of high school drama. It was a remarkable ability of the human brain, that protective shield that allowed forward progress.

Rye looked up as she heard the clang of steps reverberating on the bleachers. Andy, still dressed in purple scrubs, made his way up to her. She moved her bag over to make space for him.

"Hey!" he said, dropping down onto the bench beside her.

"What are you doing here?"

Andy smiled. "I can't imagine how it is you rubbed the Ponds the wrong way, putting that kind of gracious foot forward."

She rolled her eyes. "You know what I mean. I thought we were meeting at eight?"

"We are. I stopped by the office, and Sherry suggested I check here."

"You stopped by the office? Why?"

"I wanted to give you this." Andy dug around in his backpack and pulled out a package. He handed it to her. "I found this a couple of years ago when I was doing my spring cleaning, and yesterday I came across the box in the garage. I thought you might like it."

Rye carefully unwrapped the paper. On top, there was a T-shirt, dark green, which she recognized instantly. "These are the shirts they gave us senior year!" She held it up. Sure enough, it read "Stoneridge High School" in yellow lettering. Underneath, in sharpie, someone had scrawled "sucks." Definitely hers. "This is amazing! I can't believe you still have this!"

"You left it in my car," he said. "I'm pretty sure it was the night we went skinny dipping."

Rye blushed. "I forgot about that."

"Really? I would have thought it was burned into your brain forever. I can't believe we thought it was a good idea to do it in Lindsey Chase's pool. Her dad found us, remember?"

"Oh, God," Rye said. "I think I'd repressed that. What were we thinking?"

"That it was hot, and that if we didn't, we might do something even more…stupid," he replied, staring down at the field.

Rye glanced over at him. It had been maybe a week before graduation and already over eighty degrees. Sometime during those last few months of school, something had changed between them, and they had done everything in their power to ignore it. She'd wanted to get out of that town without any strings attached, and she had.

She looked down at the second part of his gift. It was a framed picture of the two of them from the night of graduation. They both looked sweaty, cheeks flushed and hair sticking up all over from where their caps had been pressing on their heads. If she'd seen it that day, at eighteen, she would have hated it. It felt strange to look at those faces now and be so bowled over at how beautiful they were.

"Where did you get this?"

"My grandmother took it. She ordered doubles. I got it framed, I guess thinking you might come back, and it's been sitting on my dresser ever since."

"Really?"

"Yup."

"You've been looking at these goofy grins for that long? Never thought to rotate it out for a picture where I don't look like a bird nested in my hair?"

"Never did," Andy said.

"Wow." She tried to hand it back to him. "I love it, but if you've been holding onto it all this time—"

"Oh, no, this isn't my copy. She made one for you. I found the spare in that same box. I thought you might like to have it."

Rye leaned in to try to hug him and banged her nose against his chin. She pulled away laughing. "I love it, Andy. Thank you. I'm not sure I can pull this shirt off at work, but the picture is definitely going on my desk."

"Maybe you can wear it underneath a sweater or something. No one has to know," he said.

"If it still fits." Rye held it up.

"I'm sure it does."

Rye glanced around. "Think anyone will notice if I take my blouse off to try it?"

"Definitely," Andy said, his eyes meeting hers.

She smiled. "A whole soccer team?"

"At the very least."

Rye shrugged. "You've convinced me. I guess I'll have to wait until tonight."

"Shame."

"Bet you didn't know I could do grown-up this well," she said with a grin.

"You mean restrain yourself from stripping down on the school property where you were very recently reinstalled as vice principal? You're right. I'm shocked."

Rye stuck her tongue out. Andy reached over and tickled her in the exact spot under her arm that reduced her to giggles. "Stop! Stop! Uncle!"

"You deserved that," Andy said, pulling his hand away.

"You broke the tickle pact!" Rye replied, rubbing her arm.

"It was void when you left town. We'll have to reestablish terms. If you're planning to stay, that is?"

Rye leaned back, balling the T-shirt up and putting it under her head to cushion the bleacher. She closed her eyes as she heard him settle back on his elbows next to her. "Well, we'll just have to see how these negotiations go."

AUTHORS' ACKNOWLEDGMENTS

WE ARE SO GRATEFUL TO BEN MILLER-CALLIHAN FOR pulling *Death at Fair Havens* out of the stack and recognizing kindred spirits on the page and in us.

Thanks to Courtney Miller-Callihan and the Handspun community of writers for their support over the past few years. We are delighted that Brain Mill Press decided—on the brink of a life-changing pandemic—to offer Rye and Wanda a path to the wider world.

There have been many gifts we've received:

Thanks so much to our beta readers, Nancy Hardy and Adi Rule, and to the amazing circle that is Portsmouth Writers' Night Out, led by Jeff Deck.

Thanks to Trish Harris of Aotearoa New Zealand, who writes profoundly about disability issues, the wonderful work of sensitivity readers Rachel Noble and Jackie Overall around hearing concerns, Titia Bozuwa's help with Dutch language and culture, and the technical assistance of David Mankin and Jennifer Gray.

There are four amazing memory care facilities that have been a part of our lives over the last twenty years. The staff left us in awe of their commitment and patience, and the residents with their laughter and trust in the ultimate vulnerability. We were blessed to care for Russell, Clyde, Elizabeth, Josephine, and Kimball through the changes of years living with dementia.

Finally, we offer love and gratitude to our family for supporting us through the events that have shaped us and this book since we first filled a notebook with ideas for Rye and Wanda on a road trip in the White Mountains. To Donald, to Matt and Julia, to David and the boys—you make everything better. Thank you.

ABOUT THE AUTHORS

MAREN C. TIRABASSI'S FORTY YEARS' EXPERIENCE IN mainline ministry shape Wanda Duff's professional life (but not her personality). Tirabassi is a former Poet Laureate of the city of Portsmouth, New Hampshire, and has published twenty-two nonfiction titles, as well as poetry and short stories in fifteen anthologies.

After teaching and working in early education for a decade, Maria Mankin has published six books with Pilgrim Press and has contributed to several anthologies. She is also a coauthor of *Circ*, a mystery set in Skegness, England, published by Pigeon Park Press, and *Pitching Our Tents: Poetry of Hospitality*. She is a regular contributor to Living Psalms, a collection in which the Psalms are reinterpreted in poetry and art as a reflection of God's work of justice and compassion.

CPSIA information can be obtained
at www.ICGtesting.com
Printed in the USA
LVHW092341170422
716461LV00019B/911

9 781948 559652